JOSH

LIGHTHOUSE SECURITY INVESTIGATIONS

MARYANN JORDAN

Josh (Lighthouse Security Investigations) Copyright 2022

Cover: Graphics by Stacy

ISBN ebook:978-1-956588-01-9

ISBN print: 978-1-956588-02-6

❀ Created with Vellum

1

The shrill alarm jerked Josh from his sleep. Waking from a dream, he bolted upright in bed, taking a few seconds to try to ascertain what the hell was going on. Throwing the covers back with one hand, he swiped the other over his face, blinking. *Alarm. Outside. Fuck.* The same damn alarm had gone off earlier in the afternoon when he was at work, but finding no threat, he'd reset the system.

The rain outside still pelted against his windows, squashing any desire to go out in the inclement weather to check on his house. Stalking to the corner of his room, he stared at the computer monitor that beamed with multiple shots from his various security cameras. He blinked the sleep from his eyes as he gazed at each one.

Front of the house. *Nothing.* Back door. *All clear.* Driveway. *Just the rain pouring down.* With a few taps of his finger on the keyboard, he checked the cameras pinned near the structure in his backyard. Still seeing nothing, he stretched his arms over his head, yawning. *Must be just the movement from the trees or the heavy rain that caused the alarm to go off.*

Resetting his system, he took a last glance at the monitors before walking back to his bed. Uncertain if he'd be able to sleep after a jarring wake, he crawled under the covers. While the rain continued to pound outside, his head had barely hit the pillow and he only flopped a time or two before falling back into a deep sleep.

The shrill alarm sounded once again, and he jumped. With a sense of déjà vu, he tossed back the covers and stomped across the room. *Jesus, if this keeps up, I'll have to shut the system down until the storm passes.* His house was far back from the road, and he wasn't sure he'd ever had anyone find him that he hadn't invited, but with all the expensive computer equipment, he wasn't about to take a chance.

Yawning widely, he bent over the table to stare at the monitors. Front of the house. *Nothing. Again.* Back door. *All clear. Again.* Driveway. *The wind and rain hitting the trees.*

Movement near the structure in his backyard caught his attention. Leaning closer, he could see a dark, unmoving lump at the edge of the camera view. *What the fuck is that?*

Irritation flooded him as he hurriedly jerked on a pair of jeans and headed downstairs. At the back door near the kitchen, he grabbed a rain slicker and shoved his feet into boots. Opening the pantry, he pulled out an LED flashlight with a high beam. Jerking his hood up, he opened the door and continued cursing as he stalked down his back steps. It only took a moment to come upon the dark lump he'd seen on the screen. Still uncertain what was lying on the concrete slab, he bent closer.

Pulling back the edge of material covering the object, he jumped. "Fuckin' hell!" he shouted as a pair of clear, dark blue eyes peered up at him for a few seconds before closing once again.

Earlier that morning

Josh stood in his empty dining room, one hand on his hip, the other wrapped around a strong cup of coffee, and he stared out the window as the early morning dawn broke through the night. Dark blue sky. Gray clouds. Ocean waves crashing on the rocks below. And if he looked into the distance, he could see darker clouds beginning to roll. Rain was predicted to hit the coast near the end of the day. "Shit, I need to call my parents soon," he muttered to himself. Storms always reminded him fondly of his parents

"For every problem, there is a solution." His father's oft-said words quoting William Alger came to mind, but it was his mother's words that always followed, along with the scowl sent toward Josh's dad that hit him now. *"You know that's not the whole quote! It's, 'After every storm*

the sun will shine, for every problem there is a solution, and the soul's indefeasible duty is to be of good cheer.'"

His dad would laugh and wink toward Josh whenever that would happen. He sometimes wondered if his father didn't leave off part of the quote just so his mother would jump in to correct him. It certainly fit their personalities. His mother always looked for the sun to shine. His father, who loved to tinker with cars and fix engines, was always looking for solutions.

Taking another sip, he continued to stare at the view out his window and remembered exactly why he'd bought this house. Dropping his chin to his chest, he shook his head. *Okay, the view isn't the only reason I bought this house.*

Sure, the eccentric house had captured his attention. Who would have expected to find a huge Victorian house on the coast of Maine? When he'd seen it advertised, he hadn't waited for the real estate agent, instead choosing to look at it immediately. And as he drove down the drive through the trees, he was stunned at what sat in front of him. The house nestled amongst the tall pines near the rocky coast was pale blue, resembling a dollhouse. A wraparound porch was on one side and a three-story turret on the other. The attic had a large circular window, and three incongruent, staggered rectangular windows moved up the side. Climbing from his vehicle, he walked toward the porch and chuckled at the heavy, ornate wooden double doors, resembling old church doors that had been purloined and fitted into the space by the previous owners.

The landscaping was overgrown, giving the house a

neglected feel. He wasn't surprised it had been sitting on the market for a while. But there was something about the house that intrigued him. And then, he'd walked around to the side, and he knew he'd found more than just a house—he was home.

Draining the last of what would be the first of many cups of coffee that day, he walked back into the large kitchen and rinsed out his mug. He had a dishwasher, but considering it was just him, he rarely used it. Now that he thought about it, the last time he'd turned it on was when he'd hosted his coworkers and their significant others after they'd insisted on checking out his house.

Glancing at the clock on the stove, he headed out the door but not for work. Nor for a run through the woods on his property. Nor for a kayak outing. Nor for a workout. The thought that most of his coworkers would be spending their early mornings in bed wrapped around their women made him snort. Hell, he'd like to do the same if he ever met someone that could hold his interest for more than a few hours.

He walked through the tall grass, heavy with the early morning dew, reminded that he needed to mow. Coming to the concrete stairs at the back of the property, he remembered one of his coworkers had commented that it resembled a small, outdoor amphitheater. True, but with the sprigs of grass that had gone to seed and rose from cracks in the concrete and the overgrown shrubs and vines that crept along the top, he couldn't imagine anyone thinking it was a place to spend time other than him.

Bounding down the final steps and around to the side, he came to a reinforced steel door, painted and dented to retain the appearance of the rest of the area. Flipping open a keypad, he tapped in a code and entered the lit concrete hall.

The door slammed shut behind him, and just like he had every time he'd walked into the space since purchasing the property five months ago, he grinned. The World War II military bunker had been a dream find for Josh. The inside consisted of an entryway that led to a hall ending in a thirty by twenty-foot room. There were several smaller rooms off to the sides of the hall: a functioning bathroom, a small kitchenette, and a bunk room.

He'd placed a spare bed in the bunk room along with a change of clothes. While cleaning and working to set up his computers, he'd spent the night in the bunker in the early days. Now, he mostly lived in the large home but kept the bunker ready for those late nights when time slipped away from him.

Pouring his second cup of coffee from the kitchenette, he moved into the large room, settling into his chair in front of a large bank of computer screens and monitors. While most of his work was done at the Lighthouse Security Investigations compound, his boss had permitted him to set up secure equipment in his bunker. It made sense to have a backup system in place. Plus, his boss, Mace Hanover, knew that Josh continued working missions around the clock when necessary. If he could do them from the convenience of his own home while maintaining security, it would be suitable for all of them.

Sipping the hot brew, he cast his gaze about the room as his feet pushed the swivel chair around. *Not bad for a computer nerd!* Preferring to work by himself, he'd been surprised when he'd found a group of coworkers that he not only liked but considered to be friends. And while he spent most of his work time at the LSI compound, he enjoyed the quiet time in the mornings and late evenings when he could continue working on a mission or improving LSI's computer systems.

For the next hour, with nothing pressing to work on, he tweaked several of his security programs to allow LSI to more efficiently collect information when they were on an active mission and needed to do so quickly and without a trace.

His phone alarm sounded, something he'd learned early on to set if he wanted to get to the compound on time. He was always up but lost track of time now that he had the secure bunker and needed the reminder it was time to leave.

The LSI compound was not far, and he was soon parking near the lighthouse, pulling his SUV in amongst the others that were already there. He jogged through the door leading to the kitchen, and his stomach rumbled.

The gray-haired woman standing behind the counter lifted an eyebrow. "It's a good thing I fixed breakfast this morning!"

Marge Tiddle, a combination drill sergeant and grandmother, had met Mace when she worked as a CIA operative. Now retired from government work, she considered it her mission to help the LSI employees. Her husband, Horace, a former SEAL, took care of the grounds and compound. They were as much a part of the LSI institution as any others, and Josh never took them for granted. But, considering his stomach grumbled again, he reached for one of her breakfast sandwiches, not waiting before he sank his teeth into the burrito, egg, sausage, peppers, and cheese goodness.

"You better get downstairs and fix a cup of your coffee before you choke!" Marge had coffee in the kitchen, but everyone was aware that Josh fixed the coffee in the main compound room, not being the only Keeper who liked it strong.

With a wave, he walked out of the room and into a back hall. He glanced up toward the lighthouse tower instead of ahead at the hidden door of the elevator leading to the caverns below. When he used to arrive at work early, he'd often climb up and watch the sunrise from the top of the lighthouse. Deciding to put that on his list of things to do this week, he hurried into the elevator after moving through the security measures he and Mace had put in place.

Once at the bottom, he stepped into the cavernous main room of the compound, glad to see there were only a few already there. Hustling over to the counter, he fixed coffee in the industrial pot, taking another bite of Marge's burrito while waiting for the brew.

"You've got to have a cast-iron stomach," Drew said, plopping down his sugar-and-cream-filled mug of coffee onto the counter. "Man, I like it sweet."

"That's why you got me, Flyboy!" Babs, one of the Keepers who also helped with administrative duties, walked over and hip bumped the much larger Drew.

Drew threw his arm around his wife and pulled her close. "Sweet as sugar, baby!"

Rolling his eyes at their antics, Josh called out greetings as others made their way into the room. The sound of a voice he didn't recognize caught his attention, and he looked over his shoulder as Mace and his wife, Sylvie, LSI's office manager, walked into the room accompanied by another man. The gathering quieted; not surprising considering Mace never brought visitors into the compound.

When Mace had left Special Forces and CIA special operations, he'd spent five years creating Lighthouse Security Investigations. Having bought an abandoned lighthouse near where he grew up, Mace had the caverns created into their large workspace and numerous smaller rooms holding equipment, a gym, locker rooms, weapons rooms, and anything else they would need. LSI took on security missions and joint investigations with law enforcement and the government. Mace had spent a fortune, but in the years they'd been operating, they'd made a helluva lot more. He employed former military special operators, referring to his employees as 'Keepers' based on the old lighthouse keepers tasked with providing light and safety to those caught in the storms.

Mace's deep voice cut through the silence. "Everyone, if you'll take a seat, I'll introduce a good friend of mine."

"It has to be a good friend for Mace to bring him down here," Walker said under his breath as he reached into Marge's basket to grab another burrito.

Silently agreeing, Josh took his seat in front of the bank of computers while most others filled in the chairs around the large conference table. The newcomer was about two inches shorter than Mace while still being over six feet tall. Thick muscles, short hair, and piercing light brown eyes that didn't seem to miss much. Curious, Josh, like the other Keepers, turned his attention toward his boss.

"Everyone, I'd like you to meet Carson Dyer. We served in the Special Forces simultaneously although always on different teams, then we had a chance to work together on several CIA special operations. When we got out, Carson headed back to California. He started his own security business, obtaining bodyguard contracts, which is a lucrative business out west. But he took that money and began building up an investigative business, as well. He and I've been in contact for the past couple of years, both as friends and possible business partners."

Shocked that Mace was considering being a business partner with someone else and hadn't mentioned it, Josh sat up straighter, his attention captured.

Mace chuckled as though he knew he'd just dropped a surprise bomb. "Don't worry, LSI here won't change at all." After an audible collective sigh of relief was heard, Mace continued.

"Carson's business is now renamed Lighthouse Security Investigations West Coast and is based on the coast of California. He has a few of his former employees that have made the transition given their military background. They've started the business, and Carson has already had private visits and tours of this facility with me. Still, since I officially have a partnership in the expansion, he wanted to come out and meet everyone." Mace cast his gaze around everyone, his expression serious. "It's important for you to know he is not here to recruit. But, if anyone wants to move to California, we're open to discussion and negotiation."

Josh found the idea of any one of their team moving to California disconcerting. Granted, employees at many firms moved around all the time, but since starting with LSI, Mace had kept the same original group of Keepers, only adding a few new ones as they'd gone along.

"And this afternoon, if the rain holds off, we'll have a picnic on the grounds," Sylvie said, her smile bright as she stood next to Mace.

"Okay, let's talk missions now," Mace said. "This is one of the few times that everyone is here, and we know that won't last. Walker, do you want to report on the Honduras situation? After that, Tate and Cobb, you can bring us up to speed on the Conselli case. The FBI director has been in contact, and I've got Levi as acting liaison."

As the others began their reports, Josh's attention turned back to his computer screens. It wasn't that he was dismissing the meeting, but his mind worked best if he could pull up the information on the screens as the others reported.

He'd heard about Mace when in the Special Forces, but they hadn't worked together until he'd run missions from a tent in Afghanistan, his computer programs often what saved some of the teams as they relied on his intel. It had sure as hell beat trying to carry what he needed on him as his team made their way over the rough terrain. But looking around at what he had at his fingertips now, he grinned. *Fuck of a lot better here.*

By the time the meeting was completed, Josh was working fast and furiously to provide the other Keepers with the computer backup they needed. He worked in the field at times, but his skills were often best utilized in the compound where he could run multiple programs for multiple missions simultaneously. So focused on work, he didn't realize when Mace and Carson approached until Mace's hand landed on his shoulder, and he jumped.

"Fuck!" Glancing around, he felt the tips of his ears burn. "Sorry, boss."

"Never apologize for concentrating on your job. Carson, I'd like you to meet Josh Appleton. He was one of the first people I hired when I started the business. I knew I needed the best in cybersecurity and computer programming. I know you've got someone already working for you in California, and if you ever need them to consult with Josh, I'm sure he'll be amenable."

"Nice to meet you, Josh," Carson greeted. "And I do have someone, but one of the things I've talked to Mace about is having more open communication between LSI here and LSI West Coast."

Holding the other man's gaze, Josh nodded. "That

sounds good. Especially if there's the possibility of any shared missions, it would be a waste of time and resources if too much was duplicated unnecessarily."

Brows lifted, Carson nodded. "You're absolutely right."

As the morning continued, Mace and Carson walked around and talked to the others, spending time with Sylvie and Babs to get the administrative viewpoint. Josh tuned them out as he continued to work, surprised when Sylvie called out, "Wind it up, everybody. We're in luck because the rain is still out to sea and hasn't hit our coast yet. So, let's head on up and have a good afternoon."

Josh stood and stretched, the last one to leave, as usual. He enjoyed their downtime and camaraderie building but found it difficult to pull away from the computers when information was coming in. He sometimes felt like one of his programs and found it hard to turn off the internal computer. Once outside, he breathed deeply, the impending rain making the coast-line air even fresher.

2

Tables were set up near the house at the base of the lighthouse. Josh greeted the women affectionately. Most of the Keepers were now involved with wives or fiancées who'd all settled in Maine, and he couldn't imagine them wanting to leave. And, while still single, he had no desire to move to the other side of the country.

He stifled a rueful snort. *Still single, and considering I haven't met anyone I wanted to date long-term, it looks like I'll stay single.* He'd often felt ill at ease when on a date. An only child, there'd been no girls in his house growing up. High school had proven to be a dating desert for a computer nerd. His teen years were the antithesis of every high school clique. The jocks... not him. The cheerleaders... no, he didn't date one. The artsy crowd... not his thing. And yeah, even the math nerds.

Engineering college paid for by ROTC had left little time to improve his love life other than a few dates that left him feeling as though occasional sex might be the only thing he could expect. But, it was a place where being smart was cool, and he had friends that were girls but few girlfriends. By then, he'd grown into his body and built muscles by working out at the gym, and he had little time for anything other than ROTC, math, science, and computers.

And in the past few years, he'd discovered that while he had a body women would approach in a bar or social setting, he found that difficulty in knowing what to talk about kept him from finding something more than short-term relationships—some *very* short-term.

So far, all the other Keepers had met their mates on missions. Mace had stepped in when Sylvie and her young son needed protection after David witnessed a murder. Rank had to keep Helena out of danger when she stumbled into a mob's money laundering scheme. Cobb did the same with Josie. Walker and Blake met their wives overseas while on rescue missions. Drew and Babs had finally stopped dancing around each other when she needed assistance in the Caribbean. Levi met Claire on his way across the country to become a Keeper. Tate married his high school sweetheart only after rescuing her in Wyoming after they'd been apart for many years. John met his teacher wife through letters sent from her class to him, and when he returned and they began a relationship, he'd had to step in when she became the target of Canadian drug runners. And Bray was sent on what should have been an easy security mission only to end up saving Marie in the middle of the Canadian Rockies.

Now, Rank's brother, Rick, and Drew's brother, Knox, were the only single Keepers along with Josh and a new hire, Cole. And the way they serial dated, he wasn't sure any of them were ready for anything more permanent.

Marge's hands were filled with Mace and Sylvie's baby boy, but Rank walked around with his baby daughter, not willing to give her to anyone else to hold.

"You know, there will come a day when the last thing she's going to want is her daddy hovering around all the time," Helena quipped, her lips curving as she stared at her husband.

As the others laughed, Rank scowled. "Won't matter if she doesn't want me hovering or not. She'll have to put up with me!"

Rick, not cowed by his brother, walked over with his hands out. "Come on, bro. Let me at least hold my niece for a few minutes."

Rank hesitated, then, with an expression of great consternation, handed her over. Rick walked away, cooing at his niece with Rank hovering right behind. "Don't drop her. Watch your language. Don't—"

Rick glared as the others laughed. "What do you think I'm going to do, bro? Take her clubbing at the age of four months? Geez, give me some credit!"

While the brothers quarreled, the others got in line for the food. "Carson seems to fit in well with Mace, doesn't he?"

Josh glanced behind him and nodded his agreement with Blake's comment. Blake's wife, Sara, leaned in close and whispered, "He's not trying to recruit any of us to go to California, is he?"

"No, but I did see Rick and Carson having a private conversation earlier." Blake shrugged, adding, "I know Rank and Helena just had a baby, but I could see Rick wanting to strike out on his own."

He turned as Walker and Julie came over, a beautiful, dark-haired woman at their side. Abbie, Walker's sister, was in town and had joined the gathering. "Hey, Abbie," Josh greeted, kissing her cheek. "Good to see you again. How's the land of the pharaohs?"

She laughed and shook her head. "Wish it was just the ancient pharaohs I was dealing with. Cairo is a hotbed these days of too many factions to keep up with."

Abbie had only been in the Army for three years when she was recruited by the CIA and had spent the last two years in Cairo. He wasn't sure of her position, but then, he was well acquainted with the CIA's secrecy. Not a lot different from their special ops. As he watched her walk away, he noticed she managed to stand next to Rick once he'd given up his niece. The two of them wandered to the side of the gathering, and he blinked in surprise as Rick tucked a wispy tendril of hair behind her ear. She laughed at something he said, and Josh wondered how Walker would feel about Rick hooking up with his sister. He liked Rick but didn't get the feeling he was looking for anything more serious. But then, Abbie probably wasn't, either.

Swinging his head toward Walker, he found Julie leading her husband back toward the food tables in the opposite direction. *Yeah... she knows something's up.* Chuckling, he followed.

Once the picnic was over, an impromptu soccer game started on the flat, grassy field to the side of the house. All the Keepers and a few of the women joined in. Mace's stepson, David, arrived from his summer camp and was soon out in the fray, as well.

Josh loved the game days Mace planned, reminding him of the stress-relief games from his days in Afghanistan. Considering all the Keepers had been with Special Forces, their competitive side came out with the team-building.

The wind was beginning to whip stronger, and a glance toward the ocean showed the dark clouds rolling closer.

Laughter abounded as the game resulted in disregarded rules, lots of illegal kicks and maneuvers, and more than a few pileups not usually found in soccer. David had christened the game Keeper Soccer, a combination of European football, rugby, and rules that were ever-changing. Josh bent to steal the ball from Carson, ran a few steps, then kicked it over to a teammate before they crashed into a tangle of arms and legs.

Carson sat on the ground, shock and confusion warring for dominance on his face. "What the hell was that maneuver?"

With a wide grin, he extended his hand out toward Carson, pulling the other man to his feet. "Crazy-ass no rules, man. You'll get the hang of it. It makes you think on your feet!"

Carson stared for a few seconds, then burst into

laughter. With a warrior yell, he ran toward the ball. Overtaking him, Josh raced past the others and kicked the ball into the makeshift net, earning cheers from the sidelines.

"How the hell does a nerd play so fiercely?" Carson asked, his smile wide.

"ROTC at MIT, my friend," Josh shouted back, racing to the other side of the field. He didn't play athletics in high school, but being a math geek meant he'd had to learn how to fight to keep the bullies at bay before he grew into his tall frame. Once he'd packed on the pounds while attending MIT on an ROTC scholarship, he'd earned his athletic stripes with the physical training that was required.

His phone vibrated, and he stepped to the side to see that his house security alarm had sent a signal. Calling out to the others, he jogged off the field. Bray was talking to his fiancée, Marie, and Josh clapped him on the shoulder. "My bunker alarms went off so I gotta get home. See you tomorrow!"

By the time he jumped into his SUV, fat drops of rain were starting to fall, and he watched as the others rushed to get inside or to their vehicles. Getting home as soon as he could, he ran through the rain to the back but couldn't see anything that would have triggered the alarms. Already soaked to the skin, he ran to his back door, letting himself in as quickly as he could.

Grabbing a towel from the laundry room, he rubbed his face and hair, shucked off his shoes, and hustled upstairs to his bedroom. Double-checking the security monitors, he determined the wind must have set off the alarms. *They must be oversensitive. After this storm, I need to reset them.*

With a final look toward the screens, he turned and headed into his bathroom. Flipping on the water in the large shower, he stripped, then stepped over into the warm spray. As he washed off, he thought of Carson's words. He was never bothered by the assumptions of others. He'd been a surprise to a lot of people during his life.

When he'd excelled at math in school, teachers assumed his parents were college graduates and barely hid their surprise when meeting them. When he'd grown into his height, coaches expected him to go out for sports, surprised when he preferred to spend time tinkering in his dad's garage with the other members of the robotics team. The math club sponsor was surprised that he ran in a few local marathons. Even his parents had been surprised when he chose to attend an engineering school, covering most of the cost with an ROTC scholarship after having never expressed an interest in the military.

Toweling off, he pulled on a pair of sweatpants before going downstairs to the kitchen. His stomach let him know it was time to eat. He hadn't found a need for a table so far, standing at his counter to eat, as usual. Munching on a massive sandwich with a bag of chips opened next to his plate, he thought back to his favorite high school teacher, Mr. O'Dell, and calculus. *"You're a Renaissance man, Josh,"* Mr. O'Dell had said. He didn't know what that meant at the time but had looked it up at the first opportunity, discovering it meant he was good at a lot of different things.

Josh was never sure how good he was, but he sure as hell had a variety of interests, something Mace and the other Keepers seemed to understand.

Washing off his dishes, he listened to the rain pelt against the windows as he walked around the house making sure everything was secure for the night. Once in his room, he flipped on the light next to the comfy chair and ottoman setting beside a bookcase he'd built. The library downstairs contained many more books, but he tended to keep the dizzying array of ones he was currently reading in his bedroom. Philosophy. Mathematics. Computer science. Poetry. A modern mystery sat next to historical nonfiction.

He'd started the mystery last night, finding himself pulled into the story. Reading until his eyes grew heavy, he'd laid the book to the side, flipped off the lamp, and crawled into bed. Awakened by his alarm after midnight, he'd gone to sleep once again when the alarm had him bolt out of bed at nearly two a.m.

Now, ten minutes later, he was leaning over the dark lump lying on the concrete pad outside his bunker door. Pulling back the material that covered the top, he jumped. "Fuckin' hell!" he shouted as a pair of clear, dark blue eyes peered up at him for a few seconds, pulling him in like a siren's call that would have left sailors crashed on the shore in their wake. Then, just as quickly as they penetrated his surprised fog, they closed, shuttering the lure but leaving him desperate to see them again.

"Shit!" Josh shook his head as he dropped down to one knee, squatting to pull the cover back a little more, exposing a soaked young woman. Dressed in dark pants and a white blouse, she resembled more of a drowned rat than a siren with her hair plastered against her head. Uncertain if he should move her, having no idea what injuries she might have sustained during whatever brought her to his property during a driving rainstorm, he didn't want to keep her lying on the cold concrete. He looked around as though the answer to where she came from might suddenly appear, but the dark night and falling rain were all that responded.

Taking her into his bunker would be the quickest way to get her out of the rain, but without knowing anything about her, he was afraid to risk bringing her into the work area with access to LSI's security.

Making a hasty decision, he scooped her into his arms and carried her quickly back to his house, trying not to slip on the wet grass. Once inside, he stalked to the large family room and held her with one arm while he snagged a thick blanket from the back of the sofa with the other and managed to wrap her in it as he laid her on the soft cushions.

She hadn't regained consciousness throughout the short trip despite being jostled as he'd hurried to get her inside. Grabbing his phone, he placed a quick call to Tate. As soon as he answered, Josh jumped straight in. "Sorry to call in the middle of the night, but I need Nora here as soon as you can get her to my place. My alarms went off again, and I found an unconscious woman near my bunker. I've got her into the house, but I have no idea what to do. Since Nora's a nurse, I figured she was my best bet."

He could hear Nora in the background as Tate relayed the information. "Okay, Josh, Nora is up and getting dressed. We'll get to your place ASAP."

Disconnecting, he stared down at the swaddled woman lying on his sofa. Her face was pale, with a light smattering of freckles across her nose. For the few seconds her eyes had opened, he could tell they were blue but wasn't sure she'd focused on him. Her hair was wet, and while dark, it appeared to be more red than brown.

He hated to leave her in wet clothes but didn't want her to awaken while he was trying to get her into something dry. *I'll let Nora handle that.* He had no idea how old she was, and he battled the urge to check her pockets to see if any identification was on her. *I'll let Nora check that, too.* He winced at the idea of handing over too much to Nora. Unwrapping the blanket slightly, he reached in and took her wrist, finding her pulse steady. Her skin was cold but not blue. Her breathing was also steady.

There was something about her dark pants and white blouse that seemed familiar, and it dawned on him that she was dressed like so many upscale restaurant servers. *But why the fuck would she be out in the middle of the storm? With no shoes?*

3

Before Josh had a chance to ponder those questions any further, headlights flashed across the front window and he raced to throw open the door, welcoming Tate and Nora inside. Leading them to the sofa, he said, "I haven't done anything other than try to keep her warm. Breathing and heartbeat are steady. I'm sorry, but I had no idea what to do. Considering she was near the bunker, I didn't want to call an ambulance unless absolutely necessary. I didn't see any obvious signs of injuries other than scrapes on her arms."

Nora whipped out a blood pressure cuff, quiet while she took the woman's blood pressure and pulse. Nodding slowly, she then pressed the diaphragm of the stethoscope against the woman's chest and then, with Josh's assistance, against her back. Draping the stethoscope around her neck, she said, "Blood pressure is slightly low but within normal bounds. Pulse good, breathing good." With an infrared forehead thermometer, she noted, "Temperature is low, but not dangerously."

She gently felt around the woman's head. "I'm not seeing any lesions or feeling any bumps."

Movement captured their attention, and Josh leaned closer as the woman's eyes fluttered open once again. She furrowed her brow, slowly lifting her shaking hand toward her head, then gasped, sitting up quickly.

Nora leaned into her line of vision and smiled. "You're safe. My name is Nora, and I'm a nurse. You were found by a friend, and I just want to make sure you're okay."

The woman blinked several more times, and the lines in her brow deepened. "Wh… what…"

Nora continued, "I'm not sure where you came from, but you were found outside and we brought you in. You're near Rockland, Maine."

She shifted, her eyes darting between the others. "Rockland?" A breath escaped her lips.

From the ease in her shoulders, Josh thought the woman's sigh appeared to be more from relief than just being in this part of Maine. *At least she recognizes the location.*

Nora looked over her shoulder toward Josh and Tate. "I need to get her undressed so I can ascertain if there are other injuries, and I'd like to get her into a warm bath or shower."

"The main bathroom upstairs has a soaking tub as well as a large shower. I'll carry her up, and you and Tate can start the water in whichever one you think is best." Gaining Nora's nod of agreement, he stepped closer, hating the way the woman eyed him with undisguised suspicion.

"Please let me help you. I promise Nora will stay right with you the whole time."

She said nothing, but her gaze moved between Nora, Tate, and Josh before she finally nodded.

He bent and carefully scooped the woman back into his arms and carried her easily up the stairs and into the main bathroom, murmuring the entire time. "This is my house, but I called my friends over since Nora is a nurse. I wasn't sure if you needed to be taken to the hospital, so I—"

"No!" the woman croaked, her voice hoarse, blue eyes now wide, staring intently into his.

He kept his grip firm so they wouldn't fall down the stairs but wanted to offer reassurance. "No one's going to hurt you. I'm only taking you upstairs so we can get you warm. But as soon as we get up there, I'll call for an ambulance—"

She struggled but was so weak she was unable to do much more than flail her arms. "No... no ambulance..." Heavily sighing as though speaking drained her energy, she stopped fighting. "No hospital."

He stalked into the large bathroom, glancing up to see Nora had started the water in the shower. Uncertain what to do, he waited.

Nora stepped closer, a friendly smile gracing her beautiful face. "I know you're scared, but let's get you into the shower and warm. All your clothes will stay on since they're wet anyway. Once you're warm, Josh can bring you some dry clothes, and I'll help you get dressed and check you out while the men wait outside. Okay?"

He gently set the woman's bare feet on the floor, making sure she was on the mat and not the cold tile. The top of her head would easily fit underneath his chin, probably even if she wore heels. Her fingers clung to his arms, digging in almost painfully, and her gaze lifted to his. No words were spoken, but the air between them thickened as though her eyes begged him not to let go.

Uncertain of the reason but without questioning, he gently shifted both of them into the large shower, letting the water hit his back to offer her shelter until the steam had a chance to warm her skin first. Glancing toward Nora, he offered the only explanation that he was able to give, "I'm already soaked."

He slowly turned so that the water now sluiced over her back, and she closed her eyes as a sigh drifted from her lips.

"She must have come from the beach."

At Tate's softly spoken words, Josh jerked his gaze toward his friend and then down to the tile at the bottom of the shower, seeing sand from her clothing wash down the drain. Certainly, there was a strip of beach at the back of his property, but his house was set on the edge of a steep slope, making it difficult for anyone to come by water. Her eyes had popped open again, only this time, he clearly read fear.

"You're fine, you're safe," he assured, not knowing if assurance was what she needed. It simply seemed like the right thing to say. While the fear did not completely leave her gaze, she nodded ever so slightly.

"That should be good enough," Nora said. "If you want to help her out of the shower, I'll stay with her while you go dry off, get dressed, and bring her anything dry she can put on."

He assisted her onto the plush bathmat and bent until his face was directly in front of hers. "Stay with Nora and let her check you out. I'm going to another room, and I'll hand some clothes to her. Then we can find out what happened to you and how we can help." Her fingers tightened on his arms for a few seconds, then slowly loosened. Taking that gesture as her acquiescence, he nodded toward Nora before he grabbed a few extra towels, and he and Tate left the bathroom.

The desire to not leave her alone was strong, but he needed to give Nora a chance to ascertain whatever injuries the woman may have sustained. Stalking into his large walk-in closet, he stripped out of his wet clothes and toweled off before pulling on boxers and sweatpants. Adding thick socks and a long-sleeved T-shirt, he dumped wet clothes into a pile to take down to the laundry later with hers. Grabbing another T-shirt, he found a soft ROTC sweatshirt and sweatpants from days gone by. They'd still be much too large, but they were the best fitting items he'd have for her to put on.

Walking back into the bedroom, he saw Tate standing with his arms crossed over his chest, hovering near the bathroom door. Keeping his voice down, Josh asked, "You worried about Nora being in there alone with someone we don't know?"

Tate sighed, saying, "I know I'm overreacting, but I want to stay close. We haven't told anyone yet, but Nora's pregnant."

Josh grinned widely, then suddenly startled. "Oh, fuck, man. I'm sorry! If I'd known, I wouldn't have called you guys."

Tate waved his hand dismissively. "Hell, that doesn't matter. Nora works full-time and would be pissed as hell if you hadn't called her." Inclining his head toward the closed bathroom door, he added, "I just want to stay close since we don't know anything about her."

"She sure as hell didn't want an ambulance to take her to the hospital, did she?"

Tate shook his head. "You think she's running away? Maybe wanted?"

Josh hated the idea that the eyes that stared up at him with trust might not be trustworthy. "I don't know. Maybe just scared." He stepped around Tate and tapped lightly on the bathroom door. Nora opened it a few inches and accepted the clothes he handed her. She met his eyes and must have understood his unasked question, giving a quick nod.

With the door shut once again, he and Tate stepped back so they wouldn't overwhelm the woman when Nora brought her out. Low voices came from the bathroom, but he was unable to discern what was being said. When the door opened, he startled, his gaze jumping to the woman following Nora. The sweatshirt and sweatpants were huge, but she'd managed to roll up the sleeves and legs.

It struck him that no woman had ever worn his

clothes before. Not in college. Not as a girlfriend. Not as a one-nighter who was looking to claim a piece of clothing. There was nothing overtly sexy about the way she looked, and yet the barest hint of a smile slipped over his face seeing her in his shirt as though she belonged there with him.

Her hair had been combed away from her face, still wet but at least toweled dry. Her complexion was pale, with dark circles underneath her eyes.

Nora kept her hand on the woman's back, gently rubbing. Looking toward Josh and Tate, she said, "I'm pleased to let you know that other than bruises and scratches, physically, Eve is doing okay." Turning toward Eve, she added, "This is my husband, Tate, and this is the man who owns this property and your rescuer, Josh."

He wondered what Nora wasn't saying but remained quiet, glad to know the woman had given her name.

"She's dehydrated, and I've given her sips of water. I think she should eat and drink more before trying to rest." Nora's gaze darted up toward Tate.

"I don't want to put anyone out," Eve said, her voice hoarse and soft as her gaze shot toward Josh before dropping back to her clasped hands. "I'm not sure what to do. I don't have my purse with me… or my phone."

"It's no problem," he said quickly, wanting to allay her concerns. "I have a guest room, so you'd have your privacy. At least, until you have a chance to eat and rest, and then I can take you wherever you need to go."

"Of course, we can stay, too, if that would make you feel more comfortable," Nora said.

Josh hesitated for only a second, wondering how to make arrangements that would satisfy everyone. "Absolutely. I just need to put clean sheets on my bed and you and Tate stay here." He shrugged as he added, "I only have one guest room with a bed, but I can sleep on the sofa downstairs."

"I can't have you do that," Eve said. Her hands twisted tighter, and she looked as though she would pass out.

For a few seconds, Josh, Tate, and Nora stood in indecision, their gazes locking. Eve was finally the one who broke the silence.

She turned toward Nora. "You've done so much. You don't need to stay. As you say, Josh rescued me, so I feel safe enough to at least sleep for a few hours before leaving."

Nora and Eve followed him to the bedroom next to his. "I'm gonna walk my friends out and then fix scrambled eggs and toast so you can have some protein and get something in your stomach."

If he thought Eve was going to argue, she didn't. She stumbled toward the bed. Her body slumped with exhaustion, and she pulled up the covers after saying goodbye to Nora. Her eyes closed almost as soon as her head hit the pillow.

Once downstairs, Nora offered a hug before she and Tate said goodbye to Josh. "I put her wet clothes in your laundry room."

Tate leaned in and whispered, "I'm calling this into Mace first thing in the morning. If she has trouble or is in trouble, then we'll step in to help."

With a nod, he watched his friends leave and then hustled into the kitchen. It only took a few minutes to pop the bread in the toaster, pour a glass of orange juice, and scramble a couple of eggs. Carrying the plate and glass upstairs, he realized the guest room door was still open. Walking quietly into the room, he stared, the desire to let her sleep and the desire to have her eat warring inside. Knowing she could always sleep after she ate, he set the plate down and gently shook her shoulder.

Her eyes darted open, fear roaring through them as she bolted upright, her head barely missing his chin. Her eyes were wide, and once again, he was struck with their beauty. Crystal, clear blue. Like the water he could see from his property on a sunny, cloudless day.

"Whoa, there, you're okay. You fell asleep as soon as you laid down, and I really hated to wake you, but I think you should try to eat something and get more liquid in you."

He felt sure she was going to object until she glanced toward the plate and her stomach rumbled. Grinning, he set it on her lap and then backed up to give her space. There was a rocking chair in the room and he settled into it.

She nibbled on the bread, sipped the juice, then began eating the scrambled eggs. Moaning, she licked her lips. Looking up, she blushed. "I'm sorry. I'm much hungrier than I thought I was."

Still smiling, he nodded. "I know you need to rest, but you'll feel a whole lot better once you've eaten. So, you're Eve?"

"Yes. Um… Eve Phillips." She dropped her gaze as she drained her glass and cleaned her plate. Twisting to set them back onto the nightstand, her eyes warily followed as he picked up the dishes and stepped back.

There were so many questions he wanted to ask her, but she blinked several times, and it was evident she was barely awake. Plus, the dark circles underneath her eyes made him want to ease whatever had caused her to land on his shore. "Well, I'll leave you for now and hope you get some rest. There's a bathroom right down the hall. And for what it's worth, I know you're right to be cautious and my assurances don't mean much since you don't know me, but you really are safe here."

He made it to the door, and just as it was about to close behind him, he heard her soft voice call out. "Thank you, Josh."

The tone was still hoarse and yet it pulled him in. His mind raced with possibilities of how she'd ended up on his property—and why. *Could she be wanted, running away from the police?* He wanted to dismiss that thought but knew that just because she seemed more innocent than criminal, he'd be foolish to discount any possibility at this time. *Maybe she's running away from an abusive relationship?* But Nora had found no evidence of older wounds other than a few scrapes and new bruises, most likely from her being deposited on his shore.

He set the dishes into the sink and went to the laundry room. Nora had draped Eve's wet clothes over the top of the washing machine. He walked closer, staring at them as though they were going to give him answers, but they were simply basic black slacks and a white button-up blouse. He felt certain Nora would have done this, but he checked the pockets, finding nothing. He placed her clothing into the washing machine and added detergent before starting the cycle.

As he walked back upstairs, he pondered what little he knew about her. She gave no information but her name. Not why she was out in the storm. Not why she wasn't wearing any shoes. Not where she came from. Not where she lived. But she gave her name. He jerked, the thoughts slamming into him. *Someone with that many secrets isn't going to tell the truth with the most vital piece of information about them.* Intuition told him that Eve Phillips wasn't her name, and as a Keeper, he always listened to his intuition.

Moving into his office, he quickly searched and discovered no women with her name and matching photograph in the database for a driver's license in any state.

Dashing downstairs, Josh donned gloves before taking her juice glass out of the sink. Walking into his utility room, he grabbed a specially designed fingerprint kit that he used when he was in the field or analyzing what other Keepers sent back to him. Moving into the kitchen again, he placed the glass into a box, then flipped on the infrared light located inside. His design was replicated from his days in the CIA, used for their LSI missions. Pictures were taken of all angles of the glass, and once finished, he went back upstairs as his program removed his fingerprints and captured the woman's. Running them through the databases that he had access to or tapped into, he knew he would have a wait.

Out of habit, he scanned the outside monitors, finding the rain had stopped and all was quiet.

A low moaning came from the room where she was sleeping. He moved to the hall as the moaning intensified, and he quietly opened her door enough to peer inside. The lamp by the bed was still on, and he could easily see that her dry hair was indeed red. She thrashed in the throes of a nightmare. He walked over, stopping when he was five feet from the bed, not wanting to get too close to scare her. "Eve? Eve? Can you wake up?"

She rolled to her side and curled up, still moaning. Moving closer, he reached out and placed his hand softly on her shoulder. "Miss?"

Her eyes blinked open, and she bolted upright as she had done earlier, one hand straight out as though to ward off an unknown enemy while the other brushed the tangle of red hair back from her pale face. It only took a few seconds for recognition to hit as her gaze landed on his face. "Oh... I'm sorry."

"Don't be sorry," he assured, once more mesmerized by the blue of her eyes. "You had a bad dream, and I thought it was better to wake you than to let you continue being disturbed." He reached for the glass of water on her nightstand and held it out to her. "Can you sip a little more water?"

She nodded and reached out, their fingers touching as she took the glass from him. They had been so cold earlier that the warmth of her touch now surprised him. She drank deeply, thanked him, then slid back under the covers. He was surprised at how quickly her body relaxed, and in only a few minutes, her breathing deepened as she slept once again.

He backed out of the room and had almost closed the door when an idea struck. Uncertainty moved through him, the idea that he would continue to invade the privacy of the young woman giving him pause. But, right or wrong, the desire to help her overrode any hesitancy. *I've got the skills. I've got the ability. If I consider her a mission, I'll do whatever it takes to keep her safe.*

Before he had a chance to act, his phone vibrated and he grinned, seeing the caller. "Mace, I take it Tate has already called you."

A deep chuckle sounded. "I sure as fuck wouldn't be calling in the middle of the night if I didn't think it was necessary," Mace replied. "What can you tell me?"

"Not much, boss. She gave us the name of Eve Phillips, but she was very evasive, and to be honest, my gut tells me that's not her real name." He squeezed the back of his neck, admitting, "I've got her fingerprints and am running them through the databases. That might be extreme, but—"

"Not at all," Mace cut in. "You've opened up your home as a refuge to a woman who, quite literally, washed up in the middle of the storm. Considering you've got the backup LSI computers and programming in your bunker, it would be neglectful of you not to find out everything you can. If she's truly in trouble, she might need our help. If not, we need to know that, as well."

"What about facial recognition?" He winced as the

question left his lips. While they'd certainly used that tool on many missions, he wasn't sure what his boss would think about using it to help identify the woman sleeping in the room across the hall.

"Absolutely." Mace's definitive answer cut through Josh's uncertainty.

"Okay, I'll work on that now."

"Stay at your place until you have an idea of what you're dealing with. If you need any of us, let us know. Otherwise, report in as soon as you have more information."

With that, they disconnected. Slipping back into the room, he pulled out his phone and snapped a picture of her face. He knew he would have a better chance of accuracy if her eyes were open, but he'd take his chances that something would turn up.

Retracing his steps again, he closed her door and hustled back into his room. The sun would be coming up in a few hours, but he wanted to get started on confirming her identity. Downloading her picture into his laptop tied into the programs in his bunker, he went back downstairs to toss her now-clean clothes into the dryer. Glad he was in shape as he climbed the steps once again, he finally climbed into bed after setting his alarm, wanting to check the identification process early.

After a few hours of sleep, he tossed back the covers as soon as his alarm sounded, anxious to see what his programs could tell him about the woman. Plopping down into his chair, he quickly scrolled through the information that had been coming in. Her fingerprints did not show up in his databases. *So, no arrests. Hasn't been in the military. Not in any of the government databases for public employment.*

Turning to another set of data, he pulled up what his facial recognition software had discovered. *Bingo.* Eve Phillips was actually Philippa Everly. *Damn, even her driver's license photograph is beautiful.*

Fingers poised over his keyboard to search for more information now that he knew her name, he only had a few minutes to search before hearing stirrings from down the hall.

4

Philippa woke with a start, uncertain for a few seconds where she was until the memory of the previous night slammed into her, causing her to suck in a quick breath as her hand flew to her chest. *The dark water. The pounding rain. A light in the distance. Josh.* So many things were hazy, but not him. Dark hair, longer on top but trimmed close on the sides. A thick, dark beard and mustache, neatly trimmed. Tall. Muscles that bunched under her fingers. Tattoos that ran down his right arm. And pale green eyes with a ring of dark blue. Mesmerizing, and yet she remembered breathing easier when he smiled at her. A smile that managed to convey concern while making her wish they'd met somewhere conducive to conversation and the possibility of hot sex. *God, I must be losing my mind! Who's got time to think about hot sex right now?*

Trying to pull up more memories, she had a vague recollection of a pretty woman named Nora. *His wife?*

Girlfriend? She rolled her eyes. *Of course, a man as handsome and nice as he would have someone special in his life.*

Looking around the room, she discovered she was in a large bedroom with spartan furnishings. The queen-size bed was comfortable, with a thick blue bedspread covering the soft sheets. Sunlight was peeking through the slats of the blinds, and she winced, now lifting her hand to touch her forehead.

The need to use the bathroom took precedence, and she tossed back the covers. Glancing down, she took note of the large but incredibly soft sweatpants and sweatshirt she was wearing. Holding the pants up with her hand, she opened the bedroom door and peeked out, glad to see an open door to a bathroom at the end of the hall. Taking care of her urgent business, she wondered where her clothes were while washing her hands.

Standing at the sink, she stared at her reflection. An oversized sweatshirt with the faded letters ROTC emblazoned on the front. Her red hair that was normally tamed into soft waves was a riot of unruly curls. Her pale complexion that, along with a smattering of freckles, now showcased dark circles under her eyes. Sighing, her mind raced. *Jesus, how am I going to get out of this? What am I going to do?* The room remained quiet, no solutions to her current situation appearing.

Determined to focus on the most pressing problem, she needed to find her clothes, find Josh and thank him, and then beg him for a ride to her apartment. *But what if they're there? What if they're looking for me?*

Nibbling on her bottom lip, she jumped at the sound

of a soft knock on the door. Opening the door slowly, she peeked out to find Josh standing in the hall. She remembered little of the previous evening except for him. He'd carried her inside. He'd woken her to offer her food. He'd provided shelter and safety for the night. He looked beautiful, and she looked a mess. Licking her dry lips, she held his gaze, gathering her courage. "Thank you… for everything…"

His lips curved softly into what seemed like a shy smile. And yet, he'd taken charge and helped her, an act incongruent with a shy person. She blinked, trying to think of something to say, glad when he spoke instead.

"You're welcome. How are you feeling today?"

His voice was appealing, curling around her like a soft hug. She nodded, some of her tension easing. "Much better. You're very generous to offer your guest room to a complete stranger."

"I could hardly leave you out in the rain, now, could I?"

"No, I don't think *you* could have." *But I've seen what others can do.* His eyes sharpened intensely on her, and while she had not spoken her last thought aloud, her emotions must have shown on her face. Opting to fake a bright smile, she said, "I'm at a bit of a disadvantage. Do you know where my clothes are?"

"Absolutely, yes. I'm sorry. I should've already brought them up. Nora put them in the laundry room, and I washed them overnight. Let me run down and get them."

He turned and disappeared down the stairs, leaving her uncertain what she should do. Deciding to return to the guest room, she'd barely entered when he appeared at the doorway with her clothes folded neatly. Realizing her panties and bra were on top, she blushed, but he simply laid them on top of the chest of drawers without seeming to notice. "Once you're dressed, come downstairs and we'll have breakfast, Eve."

Her eyes widened slightly at the use of the name Eve, remembering that's what she'd told Nora. Before she had a chance to think of anything else to say, he turned and walked out, closing the door behind him. The air rushed from her lungs, both glad to be alone and already missing his calm, steady presence. Looking at her black pants and white blouse, her gut clenched at the thought of putting those clothes on again, the reminder of the previous day turning her stomach.

Deciding not to overthink her options, she dropped the sweatpants and pulled off the sweatshirt, donning her panties and bra. Then, pulling the sweatpants and sweatshirt back on, she tightened the drawstring at the waist. Not waiting to give herself a chance to change her mind, she threw open the door and, with his thick socks still on her feet, went downstairs.

The house was large, but she squashed her curiosity and didn't look around. She followed the scent of bacon and had no problem finding the kitchen. He looked over his shoulder and his gaze swept over her from the top of her head down to her toes and back again, his smile wide.

Feeling the need to explain, she rushed, "I know I should've put on my own clothes instead of the ones you gave me, but… well, these were so comfortable and warm. I promise I'll change into my own clothes—"

"I want you to be comfortable," he said. "I haven't been able to wear those in a while, so it's nice to see them get used."

Her hands twisted at the bottom of the shirt, and she looked around. "Um… is Nora here?"

"Nora? No, she went back home."

"Oh, I thought maybe she was your wife."

He pulled the bacon out of the frying pan and placed it onto paper towels to drain. "She's married to my friend, Tate. I guess you don't remember much about last night, do you?"

She hid her smile, wondering why that tidbit made her feel lighter. Scrunching her brow as the memory of another man slowly came to her mind, she nodded. "Oh, that's right. There was someone else here last night."

"I called Tate because Nora is a nurse. You were adamant that you didn't want to go to the hospital, but I wanted someone to check to make sure you were okay. I had you in the shower, fully clothed, to get warm, then Nora assisted you into those clothes. You were completely safe, I assure you."

"I know. I trust you."

He grabbed the toast from the toaster and plated the eggs. Turning, he leaned his hip against the counter. "Trust? You don't know me."

She swallowed deeply. "I know, that's true. But… I just feel like you're… trustworthy."

He nodded slowly, his gaze never wavering from hers. "And you? Are you trustworthy?"

Her breath shallowed, and she reached out to hold on to the edge of the counter. She felt her emotions stripped bare in front of his gaze, wanting to unburden and yet terrified. She replied, her words barely a whisper. "I want to be."

Time seemed to stand still as his intense gaze almost penetrated the wall she'd thrown up around her. Just when she thought she couldn't hold it in anymore and was ready to confess all, he pushed away from the counter and said, "Let's eat."

She nodded in jerks, both glad for the diversion and yet wishing she could reach out and clutch the strength he exuded. He pushed the plate to the other side of the counter, and she settled onto one of the barstools while he stood on the opposite side, his plate in his hand.

"I should have fixed something different considering you just had scrambled eggs a few hours ago," he said, his expression having lost some of its confidence.

"Oh, no, this is perfect. I love breakfast food," she assured.

He stared at her for a few long seconds before nodding, and she felt sure he was constantly evaluating her. With another nod, he moved to the refrigerator and pulled out several jars, placing them on the counter. "I've got strawberry jam, grape jelly, and orange marmalade."

"Thank you," she mumbled between bites, surprised at how hungry she was. They remained quiet for the next few minutes, and her mind began to wander. *What do I do after breakfast? How will I get back to my apartment? What if I get back and someone's looking for me? I don't even have my phone, keys, or wallet.* A sense of vulnerability crashed over her, and she closed her eyes, wincing at the realization she had no idea where to go or what to do.

"You're thinking really hard about which flavor of jelly you want to put on your toast."

Her eyes jerked open, seeing Josh's smile aimed at her. She couldn't help but grin in return, shaking her head slightly. "Maybe I'll have all three," she said, mesmerized as his smile widened.

They finished eating, and he waved away her assistance as he rinsed off the dishes and poured coffee into two large mugs. "I make really strong coffee," he said. "How do you like yours?"

She normally flooded her coffee with sweetener and flavored creamer but, not knowing what he had on hand, hesitated. "Um… sugar and milk?"

His eyes crinkled as he smiled again. "You seem unsure. You do remember how you take your coffee, don't you?"

A small chuckle slipped out, and she nodded. "Yes, I remember. I normally throw in flavored creamer and sweetener, but a little milk and sugar are fine."

He pushed the sugar jar toward her and reached inside the fridge to pull out a carton of cream. "Not the preferred way you like it, but hopefully, it'll be okay."

"It's perfect," she rushed, doctoring her coffee. Taking a sip, she blinked. "You weren't lying when you said you like it strong." The tension inside was easing in spite of the shitstorm swirling through her mind. *It must be him… his warm comfort.*

"Let's go sit down. We need to talk."

Josh's words dumped icy water on her mood, and the strong coffee in her stomach curled. "Oh… okay." Unable to think of an escape plan, she followed him into the family room, feeling as though she was walking toward the guillotine.

He took a seat in one of the comfortable chairs, and after she set her mug on the coffee table, she curled up on one end of the sofa, her legs bent and tucked tightly, her arms wrapped around her legs. His gaze dropped to her defensive posture, but with her heart pounding an erratic beat, she couldn't bring herself to relax. And there was no way she was going to start the conversation. Whatever Josh wanted to know, he was going to have to ask. And she prayed she'd have enough time to come up with an acceptable answer.

The silence stretched between them, and it was all she could do to hold back from blurting out everything. His interrogation, which so far involved not speaking at all, had her nerves frayed. Just when she thought she couldn't hold out any longer, he sighed heavily.

"I'm glad you weren't injured worse than you were when you were caught out in the rain and very glad that you set off my alarm so I was alerted to your presence. If not, you might have stayed out all night."

It hadn't dawned on her how he'd found her in his yard in the middle of the night during the storm. She remembered a light in the distance that she'd tried to focus on, but by the time she'd arrived, she'd collapsed. Pressing her lips together to stop the quivering, she finally managed to whisper, "I'm glad, too. Thank you, Josh. I owe you so much—"

He waved her gratitude away, shaking his head. "You don't owe me anything… except, perhaps, the truth."

Her eyes widened, but he continued.

"While my property isn't far from the nearest town, I'm not exactly close. Your clothes had sand on them, and so did the abrasions on your arms, giving evidence that you hadn't come by the road but up from the beach. Where did you come from? And what were you doing on the beach, in the middle of the night, in the middle of the storm?"

She had the strangest sense that she was in the presence of Superman. Josh had the ability to appear so unassuming, almost quiet and shy. But there was a strength in his body and intensity in his gaze that made her feel as though he could see right through her. She wanted to lay all her fears out to him but that was a chance she couldn't take. The problem was, though, with him staring straight at her, she couldn't come up with a plausible story. Finally, opening her mouth, she mumbled, "I… I… um…"

He leaned forward, his forearms resting on his thighs and his hands clasped together. "Before you start talking, how about let's begin with the truth? Okay, Philippa Everly?"

Eyes wide, she gasped.

5

When Josh had discovered her name early that morning from his facial recognition program, he'd gained hits from her driver's license, her college ID, and social media. Philippa Everly. Twenty-nine years old. In her senior year at The University of Maine. Part-time employee at The Maine Event Catering Company. She was older than the typical college senior, but it took almost no effort to find out that her education had been interrupted. She lived in a small apartment about thirty minutes away from campus.

Her social media held little information other than a few older photos of some friends and family. No arrests, not even a parking ticket. On the surface, an ordinary life. But something drove her out in the middle of the storm, landing her on his doorstep where she offered a false name and equally false bravado.

There was something about her that drew him in. Fear was in her eyes, and he wanted to erase it as much as he wanted answers.

Her wide eyes and gasp let him know the fear was real. *Shit, now she's afraid of me!*

"How do you know my name?" Her body tensed, wired for flight.

Lifting his hands up, he shook his head. "Please, don't be afraid of me. I just want to help." He scrubbed his hand over his face and sighed. "When you gave your name, it just didn't feel right. You were so reticent to give any information, and to give your name so readily made me suspect it wasn't your real name. You were in my home, and yes, I wanted to make sure you were who you said you were, but I got the feeling you needed help. Please, Philippa, let me help you."

She remained quiet for a long moment, and he wondered if she was going to speak. Her arms had tightened around her legs, tension radiating from her body. Her tongue darted out to moisten her bottom lip. "You didn't answer my question," she accused softly. "How did you find out?"

"It's what I do."

She blinked, her head tilting slightly to the side as she kept her gaze on him. "I don't understand. What is *what* you do?"

"I'm an investigator," he replied, hoping his simple answer would satisfy.

"But how did you investigate me? I don't have any ID on me."

"I have certain methods at my disposal." He stood and said, "I'll be right back." He jogged upstairs, grabbed the wallet he'd tucked into his nightstand drawer, then hustled back down, finding her still sitting in the same position. Opening his wallet, he pulled out IDs and handed them to her. "My driver's license, my professional license, and my employee ID."

Her hand shook as she reached out, taking the cards from him. She looked them over carefully, her eyes darting between the IDs and his face. He remained silent as she swallowed audibly, finally handing the cards back to him, her fingers still shaking.

"Okay, I believe that you're Josh Appleton. I believe that you're an investigator and you work for a security firm." A small snort slipped out, and she shook her head. "You can't blame me for being reticent. A woman, alone, ending up in the house of a man she doesn't know. Only I'd have the dumb luck to land at the feet of an investigator."

Tossing his IDs onto the coffee table between them, he sat in his chair, settling into his earlier position with his body leaning forward and his arms propped on his knees. "Philippa, what you're not getting is how lucky you really are." Seeing her startle, he continued. "You could have landed where you weren't found. You could have been found by someone with no honor, having no problem taking advantage of you." Her eyes widened in fear, but he pressed forward. "You could have been found by somebody that would have called the police or an ambulance, and you'd be interrogated, and possibly, the secrets you're trying to hide would be known by many."

She closed her eyes slowly, and her nose reddened, giving evidence she was battling tears.

He continued, wanting her to realize how precarious

her situation had been. "I feel responsible for you and want to help. But the reality is that I had a stranger in my house with no ID so I used whatever means I had at my disposal to find out who you were." He lifted his hands to the side palms up and added, "You're not a prisoner here. You can call for a taxi, walk out the door, ask me to take you somewhere. But my gut tells me that something happened yesterday that's scared the shit outta you, and what you'd really like to do is take me up on my offer of help."

She opened her eyes during his little speech and slowly nodded. "I... um... don't feel like I can tell you everything. But you deserve to know how I ended up needing your help. I was out with friends yesterday. On a boat. Um... I didn't feel comfortable when the weather turned bad, but the others had been drinking. It got dark, and I felt certain we were lost out on the water. I could see some lights not too far away, and while I was comforted that we might be close to the shore, it was also scary not being able to have any control."

The idea that she had been in danger with a bunch of idiot friends on a boat had his fists clenched on his legs. "Did the boat capsize? Was there a wreck? Did they drop anchor?" He knew he was firing questions off at her, but the urge to find these so-called friends and put the same fear in their eyes that was in hers was strong.

"I... um, fell, sort of. I guess I just freaked and wanted to get to safety. Anyway, I'm a strong swimmer, and thank God, it wasn't far to the shore. There weren't a lot of waves, just the rain. I remember crawling toward the lights of this house, but that was all." She dropped her chin, staring at her hands fiddling in her lap.

Her story screamed with inconsistencies. *Out with friends and yet wasn't wearing clothing that would fit the situation. She'd made no attempt to let them know she was safe. She fell overboard when the boat rocked and yet said there weren't a lot of waves. She had difficulty holding his gaze. And gave a false name to begin with.* "So, what's your plan now? Your friends must be really worried."

"I don't have a phone," she reminded in a rush.

"Here, you can use mine." He slid his phone out of his pocket. "Call whoever you need to let them know you're fine. I'll go freshen up our cups of coffee to give you some privacy."

He walked into the kitchen, careful to stay out of her line of vision, staying busy making fresh cups of coffee. He could hear her voice murmuring, catching a few words: *"Yeah, I'm fine." "You can tell the others I'll be home as soon as I can." "It's all good."*

He reached for the two mugs when he heard her approach and smiled when she entered the kitchen. "Everything okay?"

Her eyes widened a little too much, and she answered with a voice that was a little too bright. "Yes! They were glad to hear from me. I feel so stupid that I hadn't thought of that myself." She set his phone onto the counter, her fingers still shaking before she jerked her hand back. She only held his gaze for a few seconds, then looked away, her eyes darting around the room until finally coming back to him.

Staring at her, it was hard not to shake his head. *She*

can't lie for shit. She's still afraid. That much is for sure. "So, if you'd like, I can drive you back to where you live."

"Oh, um… sure. But I don't want to put you out. I can call for a driver and pay them when I get to my place."

Her words were breathy as though speaking sucked all the energy from her. He hated to put her on the spot, but he wanted the truth from her. Something was terrifying her, and he felt certain whatever had happened yesterday had nothing to do with her being on a boat with friends. But whatever had occurred to have her in the water and washed up on his beach, scratched and bruised, scared out of her mind, she was going to have to trust him before he could help.

"Look, Philippa, it's obvious you're nervous."

"I had an argument with someone on the boat," she confessed, her fingers once again fiddling with the bottom of the sweatshirt she was wearing.

Dipping his chin, he held her gaze. "Argument?"

Her head jerked as it nodded. "Yes. A… um… a boyfriend. Well, an ex-boyfriend. And I'm afraid. Well, not really afraid. Um… I don't want to go to my apartment right now until I know he won't be there. So… um…"

She was still lying, and he fought the urge to shake some sense into her. But whatever she was hiding, she wasn't ready to let him know what it was, obviously feeling the need to make up stories instead. "I don't want you to go anywhere unsafe, so why don't you stay here for a little bit? I've got to go to work to check on some of my cases. You're more than welcome to rest, take a nap, read, whatever you feel like doing, Philippa. Just remember, you're not trapped here. If you want to leave, that's up to you."

"Thank you," she whispered, her pale face even more white, including her lips. "I am feeling tired. Perhaps I should lay down while you're gone."

She left her mug on the counter and walked to the bottom of the stairs. Once he heard her bedroom door click shut, he snagged his phone. It only took a few seconds to discern that she hadn't placed a phone call, only pretended, further cementing his opinion that she was a shit liar. *But she's desperate and scared of something or someone.*

Checking the security of his office and house and bunker, he left her to rest and jogged out to his SUV. He had no idea if she'd still be there when he got back. He couldn't force his help on someone who didn't want it but hoped she'd eventually trust him enough to let him in. Driving down the road, he grinned. What she didn't know was that he'd slipped a tiny tracer into the back pocket of her pants when they came out of the dryer. Tapping his hand on the wheel, he turned through the gates leading to the LSI property.

As he waved toward Marge and Horace on his way through the kitchen, she snagged his attention when she called out, "When you head back home, I've got some food for you to take for your houseguest."

Grinning, he offered a chin lift before heading down to the compound. Once there, he discovered the others were curious about what information he had to share. Sitting down at his station, he swiveled around in his chair. "Okay, I found out she gave a fake name, not a very good one, and she can't lie for shit." Shaking his head, he continued. "Her name is not Eve Phillips but Philippa Everly."

"Well, hell, I think that's a pretty good play on flipping her name around!" Babs laughed. "And I know I'm usually the suspicious one, but you can't blame a lone woman for giving a fake name when she ends up in a strange man's house."

He nodded slowly, agreeing. "I get that, but I'm telling you she's fuckin' afraid of something. And she is definitely not itching to get back to whatever life she came from."

"What story did she give you for how she ended up there?" Walker asked.

"Said she was on a boat with friends when the storm came up. She was scared, not happy with them, and when the boat rocked, she went overboard. She'd already seen lights in the distance and swam to shore."

"And you said she wasn't in a hurry to get back to her place?" Bray asked. "Seems like that would be the first thing she'd want to do."

"She said her ex-boyfriend was on the boat and they'd had an argument. She didn't want to be around him anymore, so she didn't even try to get back on the boat. When I gave her my phone and some privacy this morning, I heard her talking to someone, but when I checked my phone, she hadn't actually made a call."

Brows lifted on some of the Keepers sitting around the table, chuckles coming from most.

Tate leaned back in his chair, shaking his head. "And she didn't think that you'd check something so simple?"

"I'm telling you, she's not used to lying. Whatever happened yesterday, whatever scared her, it's got her scrambling to come up with a plausible reason for being at my place, not wanting to leave, and offering lies that don't make sense."

"You need us to check her out?" Mace asked.

"I already know she's twenty-nine years old, a senior computer science engineering student at the University of Maine, and works part-time for a catering business. Her school record indicates she'd gotten permission to delay her program due to a family emergency. I haven't had a chance to find out anything else, and I... well, I..."

"You want her to tell you herself." Sylvie's soft voice captured his attention, and as he looked over, she'd captured the attention of all the other Keepers. "Most of you know what it's like to investigate someone that you later become interested in or that you're already interested in. While it suits your nature as a Keeper, it feels a bit ingenuous." She smiled, her eyes warm as they settled on Mace. "I certainly remember not being happy when I found out Mace already knew my background before I had a chance to tell him."

Mace walked over, placed his hands on her desk, and bent, kissing her lightly. "And I apologized, babe, but thank God, you understood it was necessary. "

She reached up and patted his jaw. "I didn't at first." As Mace stepped to the side, she cast her gaze around the room and then settled it back on Josh. "I'm not saying you shouldn't investigate her, but I also think you should encourage her to eventually give you the whole story. If she's been traumatized, she's going to feel like her power has been stripped away. Just make sure you're helping, not making it worse."

She looked back down at her desk, continuing her work, and he shot his gaze up toward Mace, who was staring at his wife's bowed head, a smile on his face, shaking his head. Mace looked over and chuckled. "And that, my friends, is the wonderful woman I fell in love with."

Cobb leaned over, his voice low. "I get what Sylvie is saying, and Josie would tell you the same thing. But remember, while you want to take care of her, you gotta take care of yourself, as well. You've got equipment in your home office and a fuck ton more in your bunker, and you've just told us she's a computer science engineering student."

"I hear you, man. I'll go careful and cautious."

Cobb dipped his chin in acknowledgment, and while Josh didn't want to stay away from Philippa for too long, he turned his attention toward Mace, who spent the rest of the meeting reviewing cases and giving out new assignments. One specifically brought out a few chuckles. Someone was needed for an upcoming security mission for a scientist taking a cruise and Mace had given it to Knox.

"Oh, perfect," Babs quipped, winking at her brother-in-law. "The perfect place for romance."

Knox scowled as he shot her a glare. "If I recall, you didn't exactly enjoy your cruise."

She laughed and shook her head. "Nope. Spent the

whole time trying not to barf all over the place. God, it was awful."

"Babe, but we got together because of that cruise," Drew called out, his brows lowered.

"Best thing about it, Flyboy!" She turned back to Knox. "And I'll be fascinated to see who reels you in!"

"Not me," he grinned, stretching his arms over his head. "No rocking the boat when on assignment. And a cruise is hardly where I'll find someone who'll get their hooks in me."

The others laughed, and just as the meeting was winding up, Mace added, "Josh, whatever you need, let us know. We've got your back, and that includes having Philippa's back if she needs us, also."

With the meeting over, Josh stood and called out his goodbyes. He'd monitored Philippa and knew she hadn't left. Anxious to get to his house, he had to admit he was also anxious to get back to her. *Why is she different than any other mission? She's not, she's just a woman I want to help.* He snorted as he drove down the road. *Now who's lying?* He'd never considered himself a coward and wasn't about to start now. *She's different. I want to see those blue eyes turn toward me, lit with a fire from deep inside, and not from cold fear.* The idea of what might flame between them stayed with him the rest of the way home.

6

Philippa hadn't lied this morning when she'd told Josh that she was tired. In fact, she couldn't remember the last time she'd been this exhausted. *I need to plan... something. But what the hell is the next step?*

Waking from her nap, she made the bed, glad to have something to do with her hands although it didn't still her thoughts. *The yacht. The storm. What I saw. A race to get away. Desperate to get to land. Dragging myself toward the light.* She stood, her hands on her hips, and closed her eyes. *And my rescuer, Josh, at the end of the tunnel.*

As much as she'd longed to stay in his comfortable sweatpants and sweatshirt, she knew it looked ridiculous. She showered and washed her hair, luxuriating under the warm spray. Once dry, she slipped her underwear and bra on, then pulled on her black pants and buttoned up her white blouse. Finding a comb in the bathroom, she managed to work it through her tangled tresses, braiding her long hair. Without a hairdryer and large roller brush, it would never be tamed any other way.

She still had no shoes, so she slipped his warm socks back onto her feet. Making her way downstairs, she found the laundry room and tossed in the clothes Josh had loaned to her. Their coffee mugs had been rinsed out but were still in the sink. She washed the few dishes and put them away before searching for something else to do.

She wanted to thank him for his hospitality, so she searched his refrigerator and pantry, coming up with the ingredients for simple spaghetti and meatballs. He must like that since he had the ingredients, she surmised.

As the jar sauce simmered in a pot on top of the stove, she baked the frozen meatballs in the oven. Once out, she turned the stove off, not knowing when he might come home.

Looking around, it was obvious his house was clean, and she had no idea if he had a housekeeper, but she didn't think it would hurt to run a vacuum and mop the kitchen floor. She continued the rote tasks, keeping her mind occupied and wondering what he'd found out about her. *He's an investigator. I don't even know what that means other than what I've seen on TV or read in books!* With no idea what he might be finding out about her, she knew there was little substance in her life to discover. *I'm a college student. I rent my apartment. I have some money, but I'm not rolling in it. I have a part-time job, but it's not my dream career.* She snorted. *Yeah, not a lot for him to find out.*

As she pushed the vacuum across the floor, she stopped suddenly, blinking as her heart pounded. Images flooded her mind and she was torn between wanting to run and not knowing where to run to.

Before she had a chance to consider escaping with no transportation, no ID, no money, and no phone, she heard a vehicle parking nearby. Fear gripped her heart, and she raced to the kitchen window, her breath rushing from her body when she saw it was Josh. *Oh, thank God!* As much as she'd discovered that lying was difficult, she needed to keep him from finding out more about her. *It's too dangerous for him to get involved in this mess!*

Nerves swept over her, but a smile slid across her lips as he walked through the door. He wore jeans that fit perfectly over his hips and thighs and a tight T-shirt that not only showcased the muscles in his broad chest but gave her a clear view of the beautiful tattoos that snaked down his arm. Everything about him screamed gorgeous, and yet what pulled her in the most were his eyes. Beautiful and kind. When his warm gaze landed on her and he beamed his smile in her direction, she felt as though she could breathe easily again. "Hey."

His eyes twinkled as he stepped closer. "Hey, yourself. Were you able to rest?"

"Yes, I was. Thank you."

"I had a feeling you were more tired than you realized."

Nodding slowly, she agreed. "I fell asleep immediately, so I know I was exhausted. But I woke feeling much better."

His eyes swept over her, obviously noting her change of clothes. Lifting his gaze, he said, "I wasn't sure you'd still be here."

She shrugged, uncertain how to respond. "I didn't want to just slip out. You've been very nice, so I… I fixed something for you to eat."

He looked over her shoulder toward the stove and sniffed, his smile widening. "That smells amazing, but you didn't have to cook for me." His gaze shifted, seeming to take in the sink and counter, and as he turned in a circle, he looked toward the family room. Coming back around to her, he shook his head. "Philippa, you don't owe me anything. You don't have to cook and clean!"

"I… 1 needed to do something." She clasped her hands together, twisting them slightly. She looked back up toward him, and he was staring at her hands. *I'll bet he misses very little.* Desperate to take the attention off herself, she begged, "Please, let's eat."

He gave in, and she breathed a sigh of relief. Plating their food, she carried it to the table while he grabbed a beer for himself. He held another one out, but she shook her head, wanting to keep her wits about her. "Water will be fine."

He held her gaze for a few seconds, then nodded, filling a glass with ice water. Sitting at the counter, she tried to think of something to say, glad when she didn't have to lie. "I really like your house."

His eyes twinkled as he chuckled. "It's different. Not at all what I imagined I'd end up with, but the first time I saw it, I really liked it."

"I think it has a lot of character."

"That's one way to describe it," he laughed.

It didn't take long for them to finish their food. She leaned back in her chair, lifting one leg and placing her foot on the seat, resting her chin on her knee. He pushed back his plate and smiled. "I can't thank you enough for the meal. I don't mind cooking for myself, but sometimes I get busy and forget until my stomach starts growling."

"Really, Josh, it was nothing. Just a small gesture to say thank you."

He held her gaze without saying anything, and she battled the urge to squirm. Finally, he stood, reaching for her plate, and they walked together toward the sink. While he rinsed the dishes, she put away the leftovers. He was still quiet, and she had no idea what he was thinking, but his silence made her nervous. Turning around, she found him standing with his hip leaning against the counter.

He stepped closer, and her head tilted back, refusing to not meet his eyes in spite of his intense gaze making the tension radiate through her body once again.

"If you really want to thank me, I've got something that I'd prefer even more than a meal."

She tilted her head to the side and waited silently, her heart threatening to pound out of her chest.

"Just tell me the truth. The truth about you. The truth about yesterday. The truth about what brought you to my shore."

Her breathing was shallow as she shook her head slowly back and forth. Thoughts flew fast and furiously through her mind as she tried to piece together another plausible lie, but she came up blank. Wincing, her fingers laced, clenched tightly. She gritted her teeth to hold the whirling thoughts in, but words slipped out unbidden in the barest whisper. "I can't. If I do, then you might be in danger, also."

If he was shocked at her words, he didn't act surprised. Instead, he simply nodded as though she'd confirmed what he'd suspected.

"So, you see, Josh, I need to leave. I hate to ask for anything else, and I promise as soon as I can, I'll pay you back, but I need to figure out where I can go to disappear for a little while."

Josh stepped closer until there were only a few inches of space between them, but she didn't feel crowded. Still looking up, she held her breath.

"When you set your sights on my lights and washed up on my shore, Philippa, you couldn't have picked a safer place. I told you I'm an investigator. But I am a helluva lot more. I work for an elite security company. All are former military. All are ready to give every mission one hundred percent. And we have the resources to keep you safe."

A rueful laugh barked out as she shook her head. "Do you have the resources to help me disappear?"

"If that's what's deemed best for you, then yeah."

At those words, she blinked. "I don't understand."

"You know I've already done some investigating. I can't force you to tell me anything, but I can let you know that there's very little I can't find out about you. Even what happened yesterday."

She opened her mouth to protest, but he kept talking, so she pressed her lips together tightly.

"But what will go a helluva lot further and faster is if you decide to trust me. Tell me what happened, and we'll go from there. You're no longer alone in whatever has you terrified."

She wanted to close her eyes and pretend the last twenty-four hours hadn't happened, but since that wasn't a possibility, she wanted to trust him. She wanted to believe in his ability to help her. She wanted to believe that he could keep her safe. Thoughts continued to battle in her mind, but finally, she choked on a sob, her hands lifting to press her fingers against her lips.

He wrapped his arms around her and pulled her tightly to him, her cheek resting against his steady heartbeat and her hands clinging to his arms. They didn't speak for several minutes as his strength seeped in, soothing and calming. Dragging in a hitching breath, she swiped her fingers across her cheeks to wipe the tears away. She finally nodded, her face simply moving against his chest.

"I can tell you agree to something, Philippa, but I'm not sure what. I need you to give me the words."

Letting out a cleansing breath, she leaned back and peered up at him, stunned again at the kindness in his eyes. "I'm in a situation that terrifies me, and I have no idea what to do about it. I'm in over my head, Josh."

"You're not alone anymore."

Those words washed over her, and she let out a deep

breath. "Okay, I trust you. But first, there's something you need to know."

His arms tightened ever so slightly, but his gaze never wavered. "Okay, I'm listening."

"My friends call me Pippa."

She watched as his smile slowly curved upward, reaching his eyes as they warmed, gazing over her. She had no idea what she was doing or how it would end, but for a moment, standing in his embrace with the security of his arms around her, staring up at the most handsome yet kind face she'd ever seen, she was ready to hand over her trust to him.

7

Josh stood at the front window of his house, staring down the drive as he waited for the other Keepers to arrive. He glanced toward the sofa, hating the way Pippa's hands were clenched in her lap once again. It seemed like ever since he'd met her, her hands had been clenched. But then, after what she'd just told him, he wasn't surprised. His hands were now fisted at his hips, as well.

"You don't have to be scared," he said, surprised he was able to keep his voice calm and steady when rage boiled on the inside. "The people you'll be talking to are not only my coworkers but my friends. You can trust them with your life."

She nodded but remained silent.

Forcing his fingers to unfurl as he walked over and sat on the coffee table facing her, he placed his hand on hers. She reacted to his touch, turning her gaze to him, and he was once more sucked into the desire to always stare at her face. With her cold fingers in his, he focused his desire, hoping to infuse some warmth into her cold hands.

When he'd called Mace, most of the Keepers were still at the compound, all instantly ready to come to his house. He'd already checked out enough of her story to know that she was not a threat, but Mace agreed that she'd be more comfortable at Josh's house.

At the sound of tires on the gravel drive, she startled, and he squeezed her hand before standing and walking to the door. Watching the Keepers alight from their vehicles and walk toward him, there were no smiles. Normally, they would be joking about the monstrosity that he lived in or asking if he was ever going to just move into the bunker. But right now, their expressions were serious... deadly serious.

He hadn't asked for any women to be present but felt relief at the sight of Mace escorting Sylvie and Babs walking alongside Drew. Tate, who lived nearby, had swung by and picked up Nora since Pippa had already met her.

Not wanting to leave Pippa in the living room by herself when the others came in, he simply offered a chin lift as they approached the front door and then moved into the room so he could stand next to her. Her eyes widened as the room began to fill with large men, all whose expressions had softened as they greeted her, but he could imagine that, in her eyes, they were intimidating.

Nora immediately crossed the room and approached Pippa. "I don't know if you remember me, but I'm—"

"Yes, of course, I do. You're Nora. Thank you so

much for everything you did for me." Pippa's voice was soft, her smile gentle.

Nora offered a sweet smile and pulled Pippa in for a hug, rubbing her back. Whispering, she said, "Don't be afraid. These are some of the best men I've ever met in my life. I promise, they're all here to help you."

As she let Pippa go, she shot another smile toward Josh and then crossed the room, taking the chair Tate held for her.

Josh looked around, seeing everyone fit easily in his big-ass house. *Thank God I put furniture in the living room.* As Pippa settled on the sofa close to him, he was glad she was still in a familiar place. *And with me.* Squashing that last thought, he focused on her situation.

Her body shook, and he reached over to place his hand on hers again, only this time, she held tightly to him. Twisting so that he could speak directly to her, she responded by keeping her eyes on him. "I'm right here with you, Pippa." Her fingers gripped his tighter, but she nodded.

"You all know that I discovered Philippa Everly on my property when my alarms went off. She was suffering from exhaustion, soaking wet, and I got her inside. With the help of Tate and Nora, we assessed that she was not in need of medical care as much as rest and food. And she was cognizant enough to let us know that she did not want the police or medical personnel involved. It was evident early on that she was scared, giving us the name of Eve Phillips, which I ascertained was false. I've convinced her that whatever her situation is, we can help her as long as we know the truth. She's told me her story, and I've verified much of it. I called Mace, who immediately agreed that we want to help her."

Looking down at her, he smiled. "And the first order of business is she's told me that her friends call her Pippa." Still holding her gaze, he added, "I don't expect you to remember everyone, but I want you to know who you're speaking to. I'd like you to meet my boss, Mace Hanover, and his wife, Sylvie. You've already met Tate and Nora. Nora doesn't work for us but as a nurse, and since she'd already met you, Tate thought you'd be more comfortable if she was here."

Pippa nodded, whispering, "Yes, thank you."

"Next to them are Drew and Babs. By the fireplace are Bray, Walker, and Cobb. To our left are Blake, Rank, Rick, and Knox. Levi is our liaison with the FBI. Clay and Carson are next to the doorway."

Pippa's hands were cold and shaking, but she nodded toward each Keeper as they were introduced. Turning back to her, he said, "Just tell them exactly what you told me. I promise every person here will do whatever they can to help keep you safe."

She turned her gaze toward him, and for a few seconds, everyone in the room disappeared. Shadows of fear filled her eyes and yet trust pushed through. While feeling the gut-punch from that gift, he vowed to chase the shadows away.

Pippa couldn't remember the last time she'd been in the presence of so much testosterone. In fact, she was sure this situation was a first. Josh had prepped her to just talk comfortably, telling about herself first and then what brought her to his shore. She'd been practicing what she would say for the past hour, but now that everyone's eyes were pinned on her, she found it difficult to know where to start.

As though he understood, Josh jiggled her hands slightly, drawing her attention back to him.

"You can just talk to them the way you did me. Start by telling them who you are and then we'll go from there."

Sucking in a deep breath, she nodded, licked her dry lips, then forced her gaze around the room, wanting to make sure she made eye contact with each of the people there to help her.

"As Josh said, my name is Philippa Everly. As he could already tell you, I'm twenty-nine years old, a senior software engineering student at the University of Maine. It's taken me a rather long time to get my degree, but I recently finished my last semester. I started right out of high school, but after two years, my dad had a stroke, and it was very difficult for my mother to handle all of his needs. I left school with every intention of going back but spent the next two years helping with my dad. My parents had a comfortable living, but it's amazing how quickly insurance can get maxed out. During that time, I worked part-time in a diner, in a bar, for a catering company—pretty much any service position I could get to bring in some money.

My father died, and I spent another year with my mom, helping her sell the house and move into a place that was easier for her to take care of. Then, I went back to school at the age of twenty-three, glad to be back, but had to retake some classes since I'd been gone three years. I was in school for another two years, and then my mom was involved in a car accident and disabled. So," she shrugged, "I moved back in with her. It was sort of a déjà vu situation. She lived for two years and then passed away. So, I went back to school, took more classes, and am finally graduating."

Her chest depressed as the air left her lungs, and she dropped her chin, shaking her head slowly. "I'm sorry."

"What are you sorry for?" Josh asked gently.

Looking first at him and then around the others, she scrunched her face. "I just realized I gave you a dissertation on my adult life, none of which is information you needed. I'm sorry, I don't seem to be handling this very articulately."

"Pippa?"

She looked toward Mace, his deep voice rumbling over her. Even if Josh had not introduced his boss, she would have been able to tell which man was in charge. While every man in the room was physically imposing with sharp, intelligent eyes, there was something about the intense, dark-eyed gaze of Mace that let her know he was absolutely the boss. "Yes?"

"Don't think that any piece of information you give us is not worth our knowing. Just even knowing who you are as a person has value to us. We know there's a vulnerability in needing our help, and you need to say whatever makes you feel comfortable. So, don't apologize for taking the time to really introduce who you are to us. You're free to say whatever comes to mind."

Her lips curved ever so slightly as she felt the discomfort ease. Josh gave her hands another squeeze, and she nodded, ready to continue. "Thank you for that, Mr. Hanover."

Sucking in a deep breath, she let it out slowly. "I suppose I needed you to understand why I'm twenty-nine years old and just now finishing my college degree, spending most of my employment in the service industry. It is not my interest but certainly has provided the necessary funds to help take care of my parents when they were living as well as my own expenses. And, as you'll find out in a few minutes, it was this job that led me to the events of yesterday."

Nora had stepped out of the room and came back with a glass of water, setting it on the coffee table in front of Pippa. Smiling with gratitude, she reached out and took a long sip, the cool water helping to settle her nerves as well as her throat.

"The last couple of years, I've worked part-time for a catering company. I found it easier to take only the jobs that fit into my schedule without having to commit to a certain number of days or hours each week. I really like the manager, have often filled in whenever they needed someone, and the money has been fine since they consider me trustworthy enough to handle some of the private parties where discretion is needed." She blushed as she shrugged. "By that, I mean that there are people who host private events for family or friends or coworkers, the alcohol flows, and they want servers that will stay in the background and won't post what's going on to social media. You know, like a politician who's at a party but his wife is not the one accompanying him." She jerked slightly, feeling the need to explain more fully. "I wasn't around drugs, prostitutes, or even strippers… not that I'm judging the last two. But I got paid very well to serve at these events because I stayed in the background, minding my own business. Although, now that I've almost got my degree, I've been anxious to get a job in my profession."

She took another sip of water, felt Josh's thumb rub over her knuckles, and whispered, "Yesterday. Yesterday changed everything."

"Start with the job you were on, Pippa," Josh nudged.

Nodding, she let out a deep breath before looking back at the others. "I wasn't scheduled to work yesterday, but my boss called me in the morning to ask if I could serve for a private party on a yacht. The girl who was supposed to work gets horribly seasick and told the manager she couldn't do it. I didn't have anything pending, so I agreed. They were leaving from a private dock in Camden, heading down to Brunswick where they were picking up guests, spending a few hours on the water, dropping the guests back off, and then we were coming back to Camden that night. It was a mid-sized yacht, a pilot, three men hosting, and I was the only server. I parked in the driveway and then loaded the trays of food and alcohol onto a cart and rolled them to the yacht and into the galley. One of the men introduced himself as Sid and said that I didn't need to serve them on the way to Brunswick, but I was told to get things ready for the main party. From their conversation, I also heard the names of Mark and Hank."

"What did you see when you docked in Brunswick?" one of the men asked.

"I was downstairs when we docked so I had no idea where we were," she shrugged. "I hurried up to the deck where I saw a small gathering. Looking toward the shore, I was impressed with the estate. There was a long expanse of manicured lawn leading up from the dock to a massive house partially hidden by trees. That was all I saw before I began serving the drinks.

"For the rest of the afternoon, as usual, I set out the food and drinks, stayed out of the way, kept my eye on the alcohol available and when I needed to replenish the food. To be honest, my mind wasn't on the event at all considering I've been waiting to hear back on a few job offers and also on a freshman-class lecture I was preparing for a professor that I'd worked for occasionally.

"I know I said I didn't pay attention to the event's discussions, but that doesn't mean I didn't hear anything. It became evident that it was some kind of political fundraising event, and I think the man named Mark was the one they came to see. I should be embarrassed that I didn't know who he was, but I don't have time or much interest in keeping up with politics."

As she stopped to take another sip, she caught the shared glances shooting between the others in the room. Licking a drop from her bottom lip, she turned toward Josh. "Is there something I'm missing?"

"Not right now, Pippa. It's fine. Just keep talking about what happened yesterday. Tell us about the guests."

She held his gaze, then simply nodded. "There were two couples, plus a single woman and two single men. That's all."

"And what happened when the event was over?"

"We docked at the same private estate in Brunswick, and as the guests were leaving, most of them pressed tips into my hand and were very generous. In fact, I made more in tips with that small event than I had in my last several catering jobs put together. The sky was beginning to roll with dark clouds, and I think everyone was anxious to get back to Camden. Sid, the man who had organized the event, thanked me, going so far as to say that I'd been such an efficient server he'd ask for me again. And then he tipped me more than I'd made with the other guests. I was stunned! The money I made in tips last night would take care of my next month's expenses while I'm waiting for a full-time job. He then told me that a rainstorm was coming in and there was nothing else I needed to do, so he told me that I could take some food up and sit with the pilot."

To this point, it hadn't been difficult to recite the events of yesterday. It struck her how ordinary, how boring it must sound. According to Josh, the testosterone-filled men in this room were all elite, former military, take-charge, feel-no-fear-kind of men who could chew up and spit out bad guys as though it were nothing. *Okay, that's my own overactive imagination.* She dropped her chin, her fingertips kneading the ache that blossomed behind her eyes.

"Do you need a break, Pippa?" Josh asked, his hand now gently rubbing up and down her back.

With her eyes still closed, she shook her head. "No. I need to keep going. It's the only way I can deal with what happened."

"Sweetie, sometimes the best thing in life you can do is unburden yourself to others."

At the sound of the sweet, southern voice, she looked up toward Babs. Dark hair hung to her shoulders with a bright fuchsia stripe framing her face. Pippa had the feeling this woman was a combination of southern belle and badass, and right now, she'd give anything to have a fraction of her strength. Gathering her courage, she nodded and smiled. "You're right. And I know that's what I've got to do. I just hope when I finish telling you what happened on that yacht, I'm not putting you all into the path of danger."

At that statement, the room erupted in scoffs, shaking heads, and outright snorts. Josh's hand continued to rub her back as he said, "We've already talked about that. You're not putting us in danger by talking to us. What you're doing is taking yourself out of danger."

She held his gaze, her top teeth pressing down on her bottom lip. Pippa had been alone for years, taking care of others, slowly making her own dreams come true. Seeing Josh's warm gaze penetrating through the cold, she wondered what it would be like to lean on others. *Or what it would be like to lean on just him.*

Sighing once again, she continued. "I arranged a tray of food and went up to the wheelhouse. I stayed for a few minutes, but the pilot wasn't very chatty and, quite frankly, with the rain, I preferred to let him concentrate on his duties. There were some items in the galley that I needed to pack up to take with me when we docked in Camden. If it was going to be pouring down rain, I wanted everything to be as portable as possible. So, I worked in the galley for a little while, made sure everything was clean and neat, and bagged up things that I would be taking with me. By now, the rain was really strong, and while the yacht was not rocking horribly, I was nervous and counting down the minutes until we could dock."

Her hands began to shake, and she clenched them together, looking down at her lap. With one hand, Josh wrapped her fingers in his, and with his other, he continued to gently rub her back. She realized that he'd leaned closer, his large body seeming to provide shelter. Swallowing deeply, she kept her eyes on their connected hands and continued. "There were three cabins, two of them very small. I went into one of the smaller ones, already having discovered they had their own private bathroom. When I came out, I truly had nothing to do until we docked. I sat on the edge of the bed and pulled out my phone. I decided to dictate notes for a class lecture that I was helping one of my professors prepare for. I heard voices coming closer and stopped dictating when I realized someone was coming. I could hear three voices as they went into the main cabin, and they were arguing."

Shaking her head, she said, "I didn't know what to do. If I stepped out so they'd know I was there, it could be embarrassing since they were arguing. But if I stayed where I was and one of them happened to come in, that would look like I was being sneaky and eavesdropping. As I was trying to decide my best course of action, the argument grew louder. I had no idea which one was talking, but I heard things like, 'You can't do that with their money,' 'Who's going to know,' 'You owe me.' God, it just kept going! And then suddenly, I heard someone shout, 'No!' and then a strange coughing sound." She squeezed her eyes tight, the sound reverberating through her body, and she began to shake. Josh's hand, which had been on her back, curved around her shoulder, pulling her in tight to his side.

"I didn't know. I didn't know. I didn't know." Forcing her eyes open, vulnerability slammed into her, and she couldn't stand looking at the others in the room staring at her.

"Look at me, Pippa," Josh ordered softly.

She jerked her head around, eyes wide, staring at him.

"Just talk to me. Forget everyone else, and just talk to me."

Clutching his hand, she stared into his eyes, wanting the warmth to embrace her. Keeping her attention on him, she said, "One said, 'Oh, my God, what did you do?' and the other one said to shut up and they needed to get something to take care of him. I heard the cabin door open, and then it was quiet. I peeked out, wanting to rush out and get back up top so they'd never know I

83

was there. I turned out the light and slipped out the door, but then, I saw one of the men lying on the floor of the main cabin. His eyes were... bulged... his mouth open, but he wasn't moving... his chest was still... he wasn't breathing. And he had a necktie tightly around his neck."

Pippa felt the out-of-body experience looking down from the ceiling, seeing the man staring up at her. Still shaking, she whispered, "He was dead. They killed him."

8

SENATOR MARK SINCLAIR'S CAR

Mark kept the engine in his luxury sedan running while he was parked at the back of the library. His gaze scanned the area, his stomach in knots until he spied Sid climbing from his vehicle. Walking over, Sid opened the passenger door and slid into the seat. For a moment, neither man spoke.

Finally, unable to take the silence, Mark growled, "Well? What the hell is going on? What have you been doing since last night?"

Sid turned and snarled. "Watch it, Mark. We're in this together up to our eyeballs, just like everything we've done since we were kids. Don't push me. I said I'd take care of it and I am."

Sucking in a deep breath, Mark let it out slowly. "Fine, fine, you're right. I just… last night was just… I mean, fuck, Sid. We could have tried to pay him off. Buy his silence. Did you have to kill him?"

Sid shook his head, incredulity pouring off him. "You were there. You heard him. He was going to go to the authorities. Hank—the man I never thought should have that job, but you insisted—was going to turn us both in. Hell, turn everyone in, and you know that would never have worked. Those men don't play. Jesus, we'd all be dead or wish we were. I doubt you'd get your three hundred dollar haircuts in prison."

Grimacing at the imagery Sid was stirring, Mark tried a different tactic. "Okay, you're right. I just need to know what's happening."

Sid rubbed his chin as he stared at Mark, his gaze intense. "The less you know of the particulars, the better. But I will say that our friend took care of everything. The cars are now untraceable. That happened last night. So, your place is clear, and it was done in a way that makes it copacetic if anyone looks at the security cameras at your lofty gated community."

"And they're sure they took care of it?"

Barking out a rude sound, Sid shook his head. "Are you going to question them? Because I'm sure as fuck not going to."

Both men fell silent again for another moment. Sid finally sighed heavily. "Look, Mark, we're on target. Your reelection is practically assured according to all the polls. We've gotten into bed with those who can take you places, and all you have to do is make things easier for them once you make it to Washington."

Nodding slowly, Mark's voice was barely above a whisper. "But Hank was a friend—"

"No, Hank was an employee. And when he became a liability, we took care of the problem. If he'd been loyal to you, willing to turn a blind eye, he'd still be here. But he made his choice, and so did we."

"Christ, you make murder sound like it was all his fault."

"Maybe because I see it that way."

Mark wondered what else Sid saw that way. The way that meant he'd take whatever he wanted. They'd been friends for almost as long as he could remember, and thinking back, he realized he'd always danced to Sid's tune. But it was too late to make a change now. After last night's fiasco, they were forever, irrevocably joined... all the way to the gates of hell.

9

Unaware that anyone had moved, Pippa startled when Nora walked back into the room with a hot cup of tea.

"I want you to sip this," Nora said. "You're very pale, and you've experienced trauma both emotionally and physically and need to take care of yourself. I've added sugar and honey to the tea." She looked over her shoulder toward Mace and then to Josh. "Can she take a break?"

"Absolutely," Mace and Josh said at the same time.

She started to protest, but several of the men had already stood, and others pulled out their tablets and quickly began tapping. She assumed they were searching for the veracity of her story.

Josh stood, gently pulling her to her feet. "Let's step out on the back deck so you can get some fresh air." She allowed him to escort her out and had to admit she immediately felt better with the ocean view just beyond the edge of his property.

"I feel like such a wimp," she admitted.

"You shouldn't—" Josh began.

"Absolutely not!" Sylvie said, stepping onto the back deck. "Josh, Mace wanted you to look at something inside. I'll stay with Pippa."

She felt Josh's hesitation and forced out a smile as she nodded. He squeezed Pippa's hand and went back inside. She glanced toward Sylvie, who had walked over to the railing, breathing deeply as a light breeze blew from the water. She joined Pippa, and the two women stood silent for a moment.

"I'm sure we must seem a strange group of people to you," Sylvie began. She turned and leaned her hip against the railing, facing Pippa. "I met Mace in the most unusual way. Believe it or not, my son was a witness to a murder—"

"No!" Pippa gasped, horrified at the thought that a child would have witnessed the same thing that terrified her.

"Oh, please don't think that I'm making light of what happened. It was several years ago, and I still sometimes wake up in the middle of the night. I was so scared that David would be scarred for life, but with counseling and the help of all these wonderful people inside, he's a well-adjusted boy. Mace stepped in to protect us, investigating when the police didn't believe David. I remember being shocked when meeting Mace's employees but so grateful for each one of them." She reached out and patted Pippa's hand resting on the railing and added, "The people in that room are not only the best employees but good friends. You should know that the instant Josh talked to Mace, every one of them was on board to help you. So, while I know you're overwhelmed with not only what happened yesterday but what's happening right now, please know that you're safe with all of us."

Pippa stared into Sylvie's beautiful face, and while she was not much older than herself, she could imagine Sylvie comforting her son the way she was comforting Pippa. "Thank you. I've always thought of myself as a strong person, but the events of the last twenty-four hours have shaken my confidence, zapped my strength, and caused me to doubt my sanity."

Sylvie nodded, her lips curving slightly. "Perfectly stated, Pippa!"

The two women hugged, and she felt calm descend, enveloping her. Stepping back, she sucked in a deep breath before letting it out slowly. "Okay, I'm ready to go back in and finish my story."

They walked inside, heading straight to the living room. Several men were tapping on their tablets and low murmurs of individual conversations filled the room, but it was Josh that captured her focus. The instant she entered, his assessing gaze roamed over her as though to ascertain her mental state. Realizing she had everyone's attention, she announced, "If you're ready, I'll finish explaining how I escaped and ended up here in the middle of the night."

Appreciative nods met her statement, and everyone soon settled back into their seats, she next to Josh, this time their legs touching as he sat close, his arm curled around her shoulder, and his hand covering hers. If it seemed odd this man that she barely knew was comforting her, she didn't care. All she knew was that he made her feel safe.

"I didn't know what to do other than get out of there. Call the police? I wondered if I could even do that when we were on the boat. Would they believe me? The men could easily come after me while I was waiting for help. I remember my heart pounding and it was hard to breathe. I rushed through the galley, then stopped. I wasn't sure if I should try to hide or keep going. I was terrified of hiding because I didn't want them to possibly find me, so after a split-second decision, I rushed up the steps and darted in the opposite direction from where I heard their voices. I was outside, in the rain, plastered against the side so they couldn't see me. I heard them go back downstairs, but I knew I couldn't stay there. It wouldn't take them long to wonder where I was, and if they asked the pilot if I'd been with him the whole time, they'd find out that I hadn't. I grabbed the railing and looked out, not having any idea where we were. There was lightning in the distance, and with the next flash, I could tell that we weren't that far from the shore. I also could see that the surf was not churning. And then I looked up and saw a light that didn't seem too far away. And my decision was made."

"That was incredibly brave, Pippa," Babs said, shaking her head.

A snort slipped out as Pippa replied, "Or incredibly foolish. But staying on that yacht, possibly being discovered after I'd witnessed a murder, would have been more foolish."

"So, you swam to shore?" one of the men asked, his eyes wide.

"I was prepared to, but there was a lifesaving buoy on the wall next to me and I grabbed it before jumping over the side. The water was cold, but I had no choice. I focused on the light in the distance, held onto the ring, and just kept kicking. I hoped I had enough time to get far enough away that they couldn't find me once they realized I wasn't on the yacht." She let out a heavy sigh and shrugged. "Honestly, everything happened so fast that I can't say I stopped to ponder my options."

Mace spoke, drawing her attention to him. "You were smart. You did the best thing you could have done even though it was a risk. I have no doubt that if the men had discovered that you hadn't been with the pilot the whole time, they wouldn't have taken the chance that you didn't know what they had done. And Pippa, I'm not trying to shock you, but those men would have had no compunction in killing you, as well."

Her breath squeezed from her lungs as she nodded, taking in their praise, feeling less out of control. "I'm sure you're right." She looked up at Josh. "I made it to the beach and crawled up the side of the hill, still wanting to get to the light. By then, I was wet, cold, and exhausted. I made it to a patio, and that's all I remember until you were there."

When she'd related the essentials of her story to him the first time, Josh had been angry at the idea that a murder had been committed while she was still on the yacht and then stunned that she'd had the intelligence and strength to escape, making it to the shore. But hearing it again in more detail, he was just as gut-punched as the first time.

He tried to think of her as just a mission but failed. He longed to pull her into his arms, not just to offer comfort but to promise to do anything to bring a smile to her face and a light to her eyes again.

While keeping his hands on hers, he'd continually rubbed warmth into them. She'd loosened her tight grip and had relaxed her fingers enough that he was able to slide his fingers between hers. The sound of the other Keepers talking barely registered as his focus centered on her. "You did great, Pippa."

She pressed her lips tightly together, her head jerking up and down. He wasn't sure if she agreed with his assessment or was simply acknowledging that he'd spoken.

"Pippa?"

At the sound of Mace's voice, they both turned toward his boss.

"Josh is right. You did great. You gave us information about yourself, and I'm sure it's no surprise that we've already checked to make sure you are who you say you are. You also gave us a succinct accounting of what happened yesterday which we've checked out, as well. The fact that you didn't waste days keeping this information to yourself is key."

Her head cocked to the side slightly, her brow furrowing. "Key?"

Squeezing her hand, drawing her attention back to him, Josh said, "Key to our being able to work this mission successfully. A longer time between a crime and finding out about it only gives the perpetrators more time to cover their tracks. Right now, the murder is a little less than twenty-four hours old, and the two men haven't had a lot of time to dispose of the body, consider how much you might know, discover who you are, or try to do something about that."

She nodded again, this time her movements smoother, and if he wasn't mistaken, the sharp intelligence in her eyes indicated she was starting to work the problem.

"I can see you're thinking, Pippa. I know you're smart, but you need to leave this up to us." As soon as the words left his mouth, he not only caught the narrowing of her eyes but the scoffs of the other Keepers in the room. Jerking his head around, he glared. "You don't agree?"

Walker threw his hands up in front of him, palms out. "Yes, I do agree, but she's already in this up to her eyeballs. Implying she should sit this out is—"

"Insulting," Pippa said, her eyes flashing. "I'm out of my element and wouldn't be able to figure things out on my own, but putting me in the corner isn't going to help. Granted, what happened last night was shocking and upsetting, but I'm not going to sit around and let someone get away with murder. And I sure as hell don't want someone to get the upper hand in trying to come after me. If they find me, then they find you, and that's the danger I told you I was afraid of."

Looking into her eyes, an onslaught of emotions pelted him, each vying for the top spot, and he sucked in a quick breath. Pride at her integrity. Awed by her courage. Excited at her interest. And terrified that her intelligence would make it easy for her to take risks.

"Your phone was in your pocket when you left the yacht?" Rank asked.

She nodded emphatically. "Yes, absolutely. I remember it was still in my hand as I raced through the galley and up the stairs. Once I was outside in the rain, I shoved it into my front pocket so that my hands were free. I hadn't carried a purse with me, only needing my phone and my driver's license, which had been shoved into my pockets but didn't survive the swim to shore."

"Did you drive to the dock yesterday?" Tate asked.

Josh inwardly winced as his fellow Keepers asked pertinent questions and his thoughts were completely muddled by the feel of Pippa's hand in his. *I gotta get my head in the game!*

He looked back at her as she answered. "Yes. I drive a—"

"Gray, six-year-old Nissan Altima," he answered for her.

She jerked her head around. "I should have known you'd already found that out."

While the Keepers were discussing the next step in the mission, he felt her body tense underneath his hand just before she gasped. "Pippa, what is it?"

"I can't believe I didn't think about this! The dictating app that I use on my phone is one that I created, and it syncs automatically to the notes that I keep for that professor." She clutched his hand tighter. "Josh, let me use a computer, and I should have the recording of everything that I heard!"

By the time her words penetrated, she'd jumped up from the sofa and tugged on his hand. Glancing toward Mace, he received a nod and murmured, "Be right back." He jogged into his study, wanting to make sure the computer he gave her would allow her to search without leaving a cyber footprint and held no LSI privy-only information. Stepping back into the living room, he was surprised to see her eyes bright as she hustled toward him. "I know you're excited about being able to do something, but in case someone is already searching, I need to make sure no one can see what you're doing."

She rolled her eyes before pinning them back on him. "Josh, I know what I'm doing. Computer science engineer and certified in cybersecurity. Believe me, my system is safe."

Once he gave her the information necessary to get into the laptop, he looked over her shoulder as she quickly brought up the file she needed. Seeing what she had done, he nodded, giving her shoulders a squeeze. "Your encryption is good. I can show you how to make it better, but for what you're doing here, it's really good."

She glanced up, her lips curving slightly. "Thanks. And I'm always interested to learn anything you want to show me."

She looked back down at the computer, and Josh's mind blanked as he stared at her bowed head, thick red hair, and lean, athletic figure. He knew she'd meant what he could show her with programming, but all he could think of was what he'd like to show her if the two of them were tangled up in his sheets.

"I've got it!" she called out, startling him out of his bedroom thoughts of her.

Jerking his attention back to the computer screen, he watched as she started the recording, turning up the volume. At first, it was her clear voice as she dictated ideas for the professor's lecture. Then there was a moment of quiet with the sound of movement in the background.

"This is when I heard them coming down the steps and moved toward the door," she explained.

The next sounds were muffled, but three discernible male voices were heard, their words harsh. There were no sounds in his living room as everyone present listened carefully. What Pippa had related was exactly what they heard. An argument about money, fundraising, and hiding campaign funds, followed by threats. More jostling came through the recording, and then a man cried out, "No, no!" just before gasps were heard. Finally, the two remaining voices talked in hushed tones, but they were clearly discernible.

"We've got to get something to take care of him."

"What the fuck did you do?"

"What needed to be done, and you didn't have the balls to do it. Now, shut up, and let's get this taken care of!"

"Damn, you got it!" Drew said, slapping his knee, grinning widely.

Josh's gaze shot to Pippa, ready to give his own

acknowledgment of what she'd recorded, even unwittingly, when he focused on her wide-eyed expression and pale face.

She twisted to look up at him, her wide-eyed gaze focused. "Oh, God, Josh… they killed him. Killed him! And I was the only witness."

He leaned forward to wrap his arms around her, sure that she was about to fall apart when her next words startled him.

"I can't let them get away with that. We've got to stop them."

10

"We're going to." Josh gave his definitive statement, hoping to allay Pippa's concerns. "That's what we do."

Shaking her head, her hair flew wildly about her face. "No! I don't just mean you but me, too. That's the *we* I'm talking about!"

"No way," he argued, standing over her. "You've done enough. In fact, you've done more than enough. You saved yourself. You managed to get a recording of what they said. You didn't fuck around but went ahead and trusted us with the information. Now, we take it from here."

It only took a few seconds for it to become obvious that the words he gave out as assurances were not taken that way. Red flooded her cheeks, and the way her gaze crackled with intensity, he was surprised his skin wasn't burning. She jumped to her feet, facing him, hands planted on her hips.

"What? You're just going to leave me out? I can't just sit around and wait."

Grabbing the back of his neck, he squeezed. "It's got nothing to do with leaving you out. I'm not saying you don't have valuable resources, but you're in a whole different league than we are. We got the experience and the know-how to go after these guys."

"Okay, teach me."

"Teach you?" Incredulous, his fists now jerked down to his hips, mirroring her stance. "It's not that easy. We have to jump in and start the mission immediately. We know how to run missions. We know how to investigate."

"So, you're saying I can't be an asset to your investigation?"

Flooded with exasperation, he threw out, "I'm saying you've already done enough."

"Pippa."

As Mace's voice cut through their argument, Josh looked around to see the grins on the faces of the other Keepers. *Fuck.* He gave his attention to Mace, seeing Pippa do the same.

"I get that you want to do something to help us. And no one is trying to shove you out because you're correct. You're right in the middle of this. But right now, we have no idea what these men know about you, what they might be capable of when it comes to you, or why they were so willing to murder their campaign finance manager."

Her eyes widened, and she reached out to grasp Josh's arm. He wasn't sure she was even aware of her need to use him for steady strength, but he wasn't about to complain.

"Do you know who was murdered?" she asked.

"We have our suspicions," Mace replied.

She remained quiet, and even though they'd only known each other a short time, Josh could tell she was already filtering through the possibilities. It was as though he could see the ideas rushing through her head as her lips pressed together, her gaze focused on Mace.

"Hank Carlsdale handled the finances for Senator Mark Sinclair. Sid Deerman is his campaign manager."

She gasped, blinking. "I... damn, I told you I wasn't into politics. I had no idea who they were."

Mace continued. "I don't doubt that you have programming skills. You've certainly already proven that, but you don't have the security clearance needed to assist with the mission right now. So I'm not benching you, but you're definitely on the sidelines until we have a chance to ascertain more information. And we'll come to you for any assistance we think you can give. My promise to you is that as LSI finds out information that we can share with you, we will."

The room was silent, and Josh hated that Pippa was the center of everyone's focus, hoping she wasn't embarrassed. He shifted, moving directly in front of her, his hands reaching out to rest on her shoulders. Her gaze turned up toward his, and relief flooded him as she no longer appeared angry. "Pippa, we're in this together," he said softly. As soon as the words left his mouth, he realized the multiple meanings. Yet he had no regrets. Whatever happened, he was in the presence of a beautiful, intelligent, strong woman who stirred interest in him that he'd never felt before.

Her gaze never left his, so many emotions churning amongst the blue. He'd never seen anything like that before as her eyes seemed to search his for understanding. She finally nodded slowly. "Okay, you're right. I need to step to the side and let you and... um... LSI do what needs to be done."

His thumbs gently glided over her collarbones as his fingers kneaded the tense muscles in the back of her shoulders. She released a long breath before turning and thanking the others. As he knew they would, they waved away her appreciation while offering smiles and chin lifts as they walked out the door.

Babs stepped over and pulled her into a hug, whispering, "I don't say this lightly, but you're totally badass for getting away from those men."

As Babs walked out with Drew, Pippa looked up toward Josh, making wide eyes while grinning. "She just called me badass. I don't know her, but I have a feeling that was a serious compliment."

"You're exactly right. Coming from Babs, that's the highest compliment she could pay you."

Nora and Sylvie walked over and hugged her as well, and once the door had closed, leaving just him and Pippa, she walked toward the kitchen, rubbing her forehead.

"You've been through a lot in the last twenty-four hours. Are you okay?"

She snorted, shaking her head. "Right now, I have no idea. My head is spinning with what I experienced yesterday and last night, telling the story and reliving it today, and now realizing the implications of everything."

The sound of an approaching vehicle met their ears, and he hustled to the door, throwing it open to welcome Horace and Marge. Pippa walked forward, her head tilted to the side.

"Pippa, I'd like you to meet two more members of the LSI team. This is Marge and Horace Tiddle. They're going to be staying with you while I go to work. Normally, there's a lot I can do here, but I need to go in with the others so we can collaborate together."

"I understand, and I'm fine here by myself. I don't need anyone to babysit me." She blushed slightly and looked over at the Tiddles. "Please, don't take offense."

Marge and Horace waved away her concerns, both smiling as their eyes moved between her and Josh.

"Until we know what's going on, we want you to be guarded. *I* want you to be guarded," Josh said. Seeing her gearing up to argue, he added, "When those men find out that you witnessed the murder, don't kid yourself into thinking they won't do anything they can to stop you."

Her face paled, and she blinked rapidly as her chin jerked back. "Do you really think I'm in danger at your house?"

Bending forward, he held her gaze. "What I think, Pippa, is that I don't want to take a chance on anything happening to you. Ever."

Once again, her gaze bounced between his eyes as though assessing the exact meaning of his words. He refused to look away, and she finally nodded slowly. He heard Marge and Horace leave the room as they walked down the hall toward the kitchen. Instead, he offered a quick hug while dropping a kiss onto her forehead. With a last goodbye and a promise to let her know what was happening when he got home, he turned and headed out to his vehicle, fighting the strong urge to pull her close and kiss her lips.

Pippa stood at the front window watching Josh drive away. She turned and faced the empty living room, her mind swirling with all that had been discussed, revealed, and speculated. *Me. My job. A murder. An escape. A rescue.* She dropped her chin to her chest, shaking her head. *A rescue because I landed in the lap of someone who works for an elite security company!* If anyone had ever felt like Dorothy in the Wizard of Oz when the tornado lifted her house and swirled her around before dropping her into a strange land, it was her.

Hearing noise from the kitchen, she headed in, wondering if she should play hostess to the older couple. Uncertain how they would be able to provide any security, she found them seemingly at home in Josh's house. Horace, with his gray hair cut in a military style, was barrel-chested, but upon closer observation, it was evident he was physically fit. Marge, with her steel-gray hair cut in a short bob, gave the vibe of being both friendly and no-nonsense at the same time.

Marge looked over her shoulder and smiled widely. "I hope you don't mind, but I brought over the makings for sandwiches. I also have a casserole, but I can see you ate earlier. Now, I know for a fact that Josh didn't cook this spaghetti." She pinched her lips and shook her head. "I'm not saying that he can't cook at all, but this definitely looks like it was prepared by someone with much more culinary skill than Josh."

Pippa offered a weak smile and nodded. "I needed something to do earlier, so I decided to cook. But after we ate, Josh wanted to know what happened. Then he quickly jumped in to call Mace." She sighed and shrugged. "Sort of a recipe for indigestion."

Marge smiled and patted her shoulder. "Do you have any objection to me making sandwiches now?" Marge asked.

She hesitated for a second, hating that Josh wasn't there to share the meal but certainly didn't want Marge and Horace to be hungry. "That's fine, but I can certainly do that."

"Oh, you can just sit and chat with Horace and me. After your ordeal, you really should rest."

While Marge began laying out the fixings, Pippa glanced over at the counter, seeing Horace's kind smile turned toward her. Unable to think of a reason why she shouldn't do as Marge suggested, she walked over and sat at the counter, too.

Uncertain what to say, she was reminded why she'd liked her job as a catering server: *I don't have to make small talk.* In fact, that trait was one reason why she wanted to go into computer science engineering. Math and technology challenged her mind, and other than a team she was working with, she didn't have to chat. Her hands rested on the table, and her fingers latched together although it dawned on her they weren't clenched. Knowing Josh was looking out for her had eased the tension.

"All of this must be a lot to take in."

Her head jerked up to see Horace looking at her. Now that they were close, she could see his smile was genuine, his eyes held a twinkle, and his body relaxed as he leaned back in the chair. It was a strange juxtaposition—hardened military bearing with a sweet grandfather's demeanor. She smiled in return. "I was just thinking a few minutes ago that I felt like Dorothy in the Wizard of Oz when the tornado swirled her up into the sky and then dropped her."

Horace chuckled, nodding. "For what it's worth, we're all really impressed with how you're handling everything."

"I have a feeling that most of you all have experienced a lot worse." She had no idea why she'd made that comment other than he and Marge appeared so accommodating. And she was more than a little curious about them and the other employees of LSI, especially Josh.

Marge turned from the sandwich-making and shook her head. "While we all have our various experiences, I don't think you can call one or another worse. What you witnessed was worse than what some people in the military ever experience."

"I'll tell you, I've seen many a person in the service throw up at sights like what you witnessed. Believe me, everyone at LSI is incredibly impressed with how you handled yourself."

Curiosity spurred her on to question more about Josh's world. "What is LSI? I mean, I know that there's probably a lot you can't tell me, but I'm really interested in whatever I can know. Especially since it looks like I'll be able to help with the investigation. Well, at least, I hope I can."

"While their cases and a lot of what they do are confidential, we can certainly fill in some information." Horace looked over at Marge, then pushed to a stand. "Looks like Marge has the food ready, so I'll tell you what. Let's get our grub, and while we eat, we can talk."

"Sounds like a good plan." The three filled their plates with sandwiches and chips. Soon, they settled around the counter on stools. It was hard to be patient given her curiosity, but she didn't want to pepper them with questions.

After a few minutes, Horace wiped his mouth with his napkin and looked over at her. "I'm figurin' that Josh gave you some of this information, so forgive me if I'm repeating myself."

"Oh, please, don't worry about that. To be honest, my brain has been so garbled that I'm not sure I remember much of what he said."

"Mace started Lighthouse Security Investigations when he got out of the military. He'd been in Special Forces and, while serving, met other people that shared his vision and ideals. He hired others that had the training and background to fit what he was looking for in an employee. And, as the name states, they run both security and investigations. It took time and money to build up his business, but LSI is employed by private as well as government contracts."

Her brow furrowed as she pondered what Horace had explained, her heart beginning to pound. "Okaaay," she said, dragging out the word. "I'm private, but I certainly don't have the funds to pay for the services of an elite security and investigation company." She blinked, her stomach threatening to revolt. "I need to call Josh. I need to tell him that I can't pay for any of what they're doing—"

"Whoa, whoa, there. Now, who said anything about you paying?" Horace asked, shaking his head. "Hell, the chance to catch a dirty politician who's involved in a murder? Mace and the others are chomping at the bit to get their hands in that!"

"Don't worry about payment," Marge interjected, leaning over to pat her arm. "You didn't employee LSI. They volunteered! Mace has always taken on certain cases simply because it was the right thing to do. And any time one of the employees has a need, whether it's family or someone they've become involved with, LSI steps in, taking care of each other. Goodness, that's how Mace and Sylvie got together. So, believe me, there won't be any payment at all."

"Sylvie explained a little bit about how she met Mace, but I'm not involved with Josh." She rolled her eyes, shaking her head quickly. "I mean, it's true I saw his light when I was getting to shore and came toward it. And he ended up rescuing me. And taking care of me. And giving me a place to stay right now. And calling in for help. And—"

Horace barked out a laugh. "If that ain't involved, I don't know what is!"

She blushed, scrunching her nose. "It's all still muddled in my mind, I guess."

Marge smiled, patting her arm again. "Don't try to un-muddle everything right now, Pippa. The last twenty-four hours have been traumatic for you. So, sit back, celebrate the fact that you were smart enough to escape, and thank your lucky stars that you landed where you did. Now, if you want my advice? Just hang on for the ride."

With that, Marge and Horace stood, taking their plates toward the sink. She followed more slowly, confusion still swirling, wondering if she'd be able to take Marge's advice. Looking over at the couple, she heaved a sigh and smiled. *Celebrate and thank my lucky stars.*

11

The LSI compound was a hive of activity. As soon as the Keepers arrived, Mace had called out, "The murder Pippa witnessed is slightly less than twenty-four hours old, and there's a good chance they don't know exactly what Pippa heard or saw. Assuming the dock they left from was from Mark Sinclair's house, Drew, you work with Rick and Cole on surveillance cameras. Check the neighborhood and see the comings and goings when that yacht docked. Where it docked, when it docked, anything you can get. Walker and Blake, get on her car. Is it still where she left it in the driveway or did someone take it? And if so, who? And Hank's vehicle, as well. Levi, still going with the assumption that this was Senator Sinclair and his campaign manager, get hold of your liaison with the FBI. Right now, they don't have a murder reported or a body, but we're going to work it and will feed them the information as we get it. They'll want to know if fraud is suspected, as well. Cobb, you're the point man for politics. Dig up everything you can on Mark Sinclair. Knox, work with him so that we also get a dossier on the missing Hank Carlsdale. Babs, see if you can find out who was on that yacht for the fundraising party from Brunswick. I know they weren't around when Pippa said the murder occurred, but we still want to know who was involved."

Josh sat at his station, staring up at Mace, aware that he hadn't been given an assignment. Ready to protest, Mace walked over to him. "Don't worry. I'm not sidelining you. We just need to have a talk first."

Hating the idea of wasting time, he followed Mace over to the side of the room, only slightly surprised when Carson was standing nearby. Mace held his gaze then inclined his head toward Carson. "Do you mind if he listens?"

"I can't imagine why I would," Josh replied, the tension in his shoulders tightening. The look on Mace's face sent concern shooting through him, and that alone pissed him off. "Boss, say what you gotta say because we've all got work to do."

"This is the first for you."

He blinked at Mace's words, not understanding his meaning. "First?" Hell, he'd worked missions for years, and this was not the first murder they'd investigated.

"This is the first mission where you've been personally involved with someone who's completely part of the investigation."

He swallowed, continuing to hold Mace's gaze, refusing to look away. "Mace, this isn't like the rest of you. I'm not involved with Pippa. I mean, I am—I found her, and she's staying at my house. But I've only known her since last night. So... I don't really think... it's not like I'm... there's not... oh, fuck." He dropped his chin to his chest, his hands landing on his hips. Sighing heavily, he shook his head and looked up again.

Mace stepped closer, his voice low. "What I mean is that you have a closer personal involvement with Pippa than with the typical witness, and that hasn't happened to you on a case before. Whether she stays an acquaintance, becomes more, or leaves your life completely when this is over, right now, I need you to be focused while admitting that emotions can get tangled in the investigation."

Josh winced at the idea that Pippa would walk out of his life at the end of the investigation. *Christ, I barely know her. Of course, she'll leave.* He tried to mask the emotion that gut-punched him. *Why the hell does that matter?*

Mace continued as though he knew Josh's thoughts. "Most of us have been there, and every one of those men will tell you that they never went into a mission expecting to come out with someone. But I watched you, and I watched her. She trusts you. So, you work the mission, but be honest with yourself that emotions can cloud your judgment. When that happens, you gotta trust that the rest of us will take care of her."

He gave a short nod, Mace's words swirling in his head with all the other shit that was bouncing around in his mind. His eyes cut toward Carson, whose expression rarely changed, but sharp eyes seemed to take everything in. "Any special reason you wanted company for this discussion?"

Mace's lips curved upward slightly. "Carson has had a successful security business as you know, but now that he's expanding, I've warned him about the propensity for a Keeper to meet extraordinary women while investigating." Mace shot Carson a grin before bringing his attention back to Josh. "It adds an element of uncertainty as well as heightened emotion to an investigation."

Carson rolled his eyes and scoffed as he turned to walk over to the others. Josh wanted to refute Mace's assumption that he was involved with Pippa, but the words stuck in his throat. *I feel protective for her considering she washed up on my property, that's all.*

Leaning closer, Mace added, "You might think ignoring emotions is the best thing for the mission, but we've all learned you can jeopardize everything if you lie to yourself."

Wondering how the hell Mace had read his mind, he locked his body in place to keep it from physically jerking.

Back to business, Mace said, "Dig up everything you can on Pippa. Bank accounts, addresses, friends, work, everything. If we can find it, we want to know before the murderers can."

With a chin lift, he acknowledged the assignment and hurried to his station. Firing up the programs he'd use, he squeezed the back of his neck, willing the tension to ease. He was used to careful analysis of the intel and prayed he could focus. For the next hour, he dug with intensity into Philippa Everly, pushing down the niggling sense of guilt he had in finding out everything he could about her without giving her a chance to consent. It was an odd emotion, one he'd never had while working on a case. Usually, he found out intimate details about people's lives when they worked missions with the end goal of the investigation as his sole motivation, without concern about what he was unearthing. Sighing, he realized that *this* was exactly what Mace meant.

Clearing his mind, he continued to dig. Mace had announced they'd convene in an hour to figure out their next steps before they'd go home for the night and actively hit the field tomorrow.

When they'd all gathered around the table, Mace turned to him. "Josh, you report first. Let's get the information about Pippa out of the way."

"So far, everything Pippa has told me has checked out. Philippa Everly. Twenty-nine years old. It's taken her a while to finish up her UM computer science degree because of family situations. Top grades. Added cybersecurity classes to her program. Both her parents are deceased. She's worked part-time, mostly in the foodservice industry, and for the last couple of years with The Maine Event Catering. According to her employee evals, she's reliable and efficient, resulting in her being given private events to assist with. She also works part-time for a UM professor as his assistant. Performance evaluations are all excellent. Neither of her bosses have any political connections nor can I find a connection with Senator Sinclair. Her bank account is modest. The insurance from her parents appeared to cover funeral costs with little left over. She lives alone in an apartment. Pays her bills on time. Spends little on herself. Her car was bought three years ago and was used at the time. Has very little social media. Email is mostly between her and the professor and classmates, dealing with assignments. She has no connection with politics or Senator Sinclair. Her biggest expense has been some computer equipment, but tapping into what I can see, it's all good stuff but not extravagant." He looked up from his dissertation and shrugged. "I can't find anything that would suggest what Pippa told us about herself or yesterday that's not true."

Mace dipped his chin in acknowledgment. "Good. Okay, what have we got on the docking point?"

Drew nodded toward Rick and a new Keeper, Cole, offering them the opportunity to report.

Rick said, "Senator Mark Sinclair's official office when in session is in Augusta. He has a family home in Camden, right on the water, with a yacht dock. It's in a gated community, but he's got several acres around him with woods, so it's private."

Cole grinned, adding, "Gated community means cameras. We were able to see Pippa's car go through the main gate at noon. Tapping into the caterer's online schedule, we can see that the yacht was due to arrive at the Sinclair house dock by then so she could start setting up."

"What about Sid and Hank?" Josh asked.

"Sid arrived the day before, and Hank came that morning. Checking the others who went through the gate that day, we identified Max Romano. He has a pass to get through the gate and is a licensed yacht captain, functioning as Sinclair's private pilot."

"Strangely, Sinclair's security around his house is shit. I guess he thinks that because he lives in a gated community he doesn't need much, but we were shocked to find that there's no direct camera view of the whole driveway or the dock," Rick reported.

"Shit… man's got a yacht and doesn't have cameras on it," Drew said, shaking his head.

"We can see a small section and can tell the pilot was the first to head in the direction of the dock, presumably to get it ready. Pippa made several trips from her car with a large rolling cart filled with boxes. Then Mark, Sid, and Hank came down from the house together, again presumably to board a little before one p.m., and the yacht must have pulled away from the dock about fifteen minutes later," Rick reported. "We have security on the water from his neighbor closer to the water entrance to the small community."

Drew looked toward Walker and Blake. "What's up with her car at her apartment? Did it return?"

"Her apartment is small but in a decent area. The parking lot doesn't have a camera but there's one just across the street at a little market. It actually gets the parking lot to the apartments as well as its storefront. We can see that her car has not returned to the parking lot." Walker looked around before continuing. "If we assume Hank's murder was not premeditated, then Mark and Sid would be scrambling to cover their tracks. They'd have to get rid of the body. They'd have to get rid of the evidence. They'd have to handle his automobile. They'd have to create a story. Then, Pippa's escape would have completely added a new element, causing them to try to figure out where she went, what she knew, and what she saw."

"Is Mark's wife at their Camden estate? If so, she'd wonder about the cars still in the driveway," Tate surmised.

"Negative," Babs called out. "She's at the house in Augusta with the children."

"So, Mark and Sid have some time to get rid of the vehicles, but I can't see them handling things well," Blake said.

"Maybe it *was* premeditated," Tate commented. As eyes turned to him, he shrugged. "Just mentioning the possibility. Seems like a lot of planning to have only a few hours to cover up."

"The recording sounds emotional, not premeditated," Clay argued.

"I've got eyes on the gate's cameras again," Walker announced. "I can see both Pippa's and Hank's cars leaving the gate about the same time. Pippa's drove out at just after midnight. Hank's was about five minutes later."

"So, if Hank was dead, and Pippa was on Josh's property then, who the fuck drove their cars? Mark and Sid?" Bray asked, his eyes on the others.

"If so, then where are their vehicles and how did Sid and Mark get back?" Mace asked.

"They had help... had to," Drew tossed out.

"Mob ties." Cobb's deep voice cut through the room.

Everyone swung their head toward him, knowing if

any of them understood political connections it would be Cobb considering his family and his fiancée's family were in politics.

"Mark Sinclair has a squeaky-clean reputation since becoming senator, but his meteoric rise is generally accompanied with big money. I've never met Sid, but he's been with Mark a long time and has rumors of being able to get whatever he needs to make sure Mark gets reelected."

"Anything on Hank Carlsdale?" Mace asked.

"As far as I know, Hank is clean. And as head of finances for the senator, the money should all go through him. I just started digging into it, but if we surmise that Sid is getting dirty money and Hank found out about it, that could be a motive for murder."

"But how would that translate into having someone help with the cleanup if it wasn't premeditated?" Blake asked.

Cobb snorted. "Someone to call. Someone who's used to taking care of business, especially the clean-up variety."

"What about the yacht captain? Max Romano?" Tate asked.

"He used to work for Camden Yacht Service, but for the last two years, he lists the senator as his employer on his taxes. It looks like he's the captain of choice when the senator wants to get on the water for an event where he can't be the one piloting. Still checking him out," Clay said.

Babs chimed in, "I can't find any way to see who was on the yacht from Brunswick."

"My FBI contact has been alerted," Levi said. "He's got nothing official to go on, but he'll do a little unofficial checking into Hank Carlsdale's disappearance. If the wife is expecting him, then she should file a missing persons report soon. The local police won't check until it's been twenty-four hours since missing."

Josh rubbed his chin, his mind turning over Levi's words. *Missing persons report.* Jerking his head up, he blurted, "There's no one to report Pippa missing. At least, not right away. The caterer probably wouldn't need to hear from her. She has no living relatives. She has no roommate. And they're at the end of the semester, so the professor wouldn't expect to hear from her soon."

"What are you thinking?" Bray asked.

"We're a step ahead of Mark and Sid. Hell, we're a hundred steps ahead of them. Even if they've got people to start looking for her, they only know she was a server for the catering company. We already know all about her. Plus, we can keep her safe while they're spinning their wheels looking for her. And, if they don't know there's no one to report her missing, then we can make sure a file gets into the police system. That would allow us to openly question whoever we want as though we were hired to find her."

Mace nodded. "Good idea. Hell, a fuckin' excellent idea. Okay, we want boots on the ground first thing in the morning. For tonight, I want a crew to get cameras into her apartment—"

"On it," Josh called out.

"From here?" Mace asked.

He was often the one in the compound leading the security when the others were out in the field, but he shook his head emphatically. "No. I want in. Rick can monitor from here. I want to be there."

"You can get some things for her while you're there," Babs said. "Just grab a few clothes and toiletries. She'll appreciate having them since she can't go back into her place for now."

He hadn't thought of that but was glad Babs had. Since he had no plans of letting Pippa leave his place until they knew all the danger had passed, she'd need some of her things. Deciding he'd call her on his way to her apartment, he'd find out exactly what she'd like to have. With a nod toward Babs, he looked over at Mace.

"Agreed," Mace said. "Any volunteers to assist?"

Josh grinned when everyone's hand lifted. Mace chuckled and shook his head, then jerked his chin back when he saw Carson's hand up.

Carson shrugged. "I know what my company does back in California, but if we're going to start working together, then I'd like to see how your team works in the field. If no one has an objection, I'd like to go."

"Welcome aboard," Josh said.

"Okay, Josh, Carson, and Walker. You three head over to her place tonight, get video and audio set up. If someone goes into her place, we want to know it. Josh, get anything you think she would need, but make sure the place doesn't look like someone's gone through it. The rest of you, back here first thing in the morning and we'll set up the next phase of the plan."

With Walker at the wheel and Carson riding shotgun, Josh climbed into the back of the SUV after they'd loaded the equipment needed to monitor her apartment. Calling Horace, he said, "Heading out to her place to set up cameras. It'll be a couple of hours before I get back. "

"Don't worry about us. We're fine. You want to talk to her?"

"Yeah, that'd be great."

After a few seconds, he heard Pippa's voice, a balm to the turmoil he'd felt since he left her.

"Hey, Josh. Is everything okay?"

"Yeah, I'll tell you all about it when I can. Right now, a couple of us are heading to your apartment."

"My apartment?"

"We want to get eyes and ears on the inside so in case someone comes looking for you, we'll know who it is. While I'm there, I want to grab some things so you'll be more comfortable at my place. Give me an idea of what you'd like me to bring back."

"Oh, please be careful, Josh. I keep imagining someone there looking for me."

"Don't worry about me. But what can I get for you?"

"Um… let's see. Just grab some jeans and shirts from my closet. There's a small suitcase in the corner. And there's a dresser in the bedroom. The top two drawers have underwear, so you'd better grab some. If you go into the bathroom, which I'm embarrassed to admit is messy, I have a travel bag under the sink. Just grab the shampoo and conditioner from the shower, and I have a makeup bag on the counter. My hairdryer is under the sink, also. Christ, that sounds like a lot! I'm sorry, Josh. Honestly, just grab anything. I'm not picky!"

"It's all good," he chuckled, glad to hear her sounding less scared. He had no doubt Horace and Marge were helping to keep her distracted.

"Will you be back tonight sometime?" she asked.

"Yeah, I'll be back. It'll be late, so go ahead and go to bed whenever you're tired. Marge and Horace will stay there until I get back."

"Okay." There were a few seconds of pause, and then she quickly said, "Josh?"

"Still here, Pippa."

"Please be careful. Come back safe."

He couldn't remember the last time someone had specifically told him to stay safe, and the words wrapped around him like a warm embrace. Knowing he needed to focus on the mission, he pushed that feeling down. "I'll be safe. Good night, Pippa." He disconnected before she had a chance to say anything else. Leaning back in the seat, he looked up and caught Walker's eyes staring at him in the rearview mirror. Knowing the fucker was grinning, he just shook his head and looked to the side, hiding his own smile.

12

Josh looked out the window as he, Carson, and Walker approached Pippa's apartment. Walker's assessment had been spot on. It was an older one-story building but in a decent part of town. She didn't live near the campus but about thirty minutes away, closer to the coast, which also meant closer to him. He wasn't ready to analyze why that tidbit made him happy, shoving it behind what they needed to do.

Rick had already altered the security video from across the street, not only disabling it so that they could get in and out unseen but making it look as though no time on the feed was missing. Josh had a feeling that no one would be looking at the security feed anyway, but they never took chances. On the way, Josh had centered his focus by explaining to Carson how he handled the missions from the LSI compound or his bunker. Carson's investigative background with special ops gave him the perfect experience for replicating what Mace had built.

Now inside, Walker took over with what they hoped to accomplish. "Josh, I know you're going to be getting personal items, so Carson, you're going to set up the cameras. By the time we're finished, Josh can test them here and then Rick can check the feed at LSI before we leave."

Given the go-ahead, they made their way to her apartment, an easier mission considering she lived in the end unit. The building looked as though it had been a small motel many years ago and had eventually been renovated into apartments. Entering, the layout was simple. The front door led to a living room and dining room combination with a kitchen at the back. The dining room was small but the space was filled with a large, heavy wooden table and chairs that seemed to have been made for a larger area. The living room held a small sofa that could have come from any discount store. The other side of the room was anchored by two matching wingback chairs with deep cushions that appeared incongruent with the other furniture.

A short hall to the side led to one bedroom and one bathroom. Beige carpet. White walls. Beige kitchen appliances. White countertops. No-frills, but it was clean, neat, and while he normally never thought about decorating, he noticed a few splashes of color that brightened up the otherwise drab interior. Throw pillows on the sofa in blues and greens. A blue, green, and yellow comforter on the bed, with matching curtains and pillows.

Hearing Walker and Carson talking about the equipment they were installing, he jerked back to the mission at hand, mentally chastising himself for allowing his mind to wander to Pippa's decorating instead of immediately collecting what she might need. *How the hell did the other Keepers do this? Keep someone safe that they cared about beyond the mission?*

Stealthily moving to her closet, he found the luggage she'd referred to and began filling it. Her clothes were hung neatly, and he quickly gathered several pairs of jeans and shirts, leaving plenty in the closet in case someone came looking. Next, he opened dresser drawers, grabbing handfuls of panties and a couple of bras and tossing them into the suitcase, as well. In the bathroom, the cosmetic case was exactly where she said it would be, and he gathered the items she'd asked for. Looking around, he left enough that the room still looked lived in, knowing what he was bringing back would make her stay with him more comfortable.

He stood in the middle of her bedroom after zipping the luggage and turned slowly, allowing his gaze to drift over Pippa's home, finding that he wanted to draw more of her in. He inhaled deeply, the light scent from her shampoo he'd packed filling the air, and he couldn't wait to smell it on her. He might not know a lot about the cost of women's clothing but could tell from her closet that she wasn't high maintenance. For some reason, her practicality made him smile.

A bookcase served as her nightstand, a reading lamp on top and the shelves filled with textbooks on programming, engineering, IT, and cybersecurity, and as he leaned closer, he discovered several romance novels tucked to the side. His grin widened, and he wondered if he should grab any of her books as he soaked up the images of her in her space.

Walker stepped into the room, jarring Josh back to the task at hand. He hoped his teammate had not noticed him lost in thought as he devoured everything he could find out about Pippa from her space. He set the suitcase on the floor and, clearing his throat, asked, "You ready for in here?"

"Yeah," Walker said, his gaze searching the room and not focusing on Josh. "That corner and over here." He pointed, then turned to Josh, waiting on his opinion.

Josh nodded, knowing Walker's security camera placement would be flawless. Carson walked in, continuing to help Walker, so Josh took the opportunity to get out of their way and take the suitcase into the living room. There was no desk, but her laptop was sitting on top of the dining table along with several notebooks. Spying a backpack, he placed the notebooks and the laptop inside, then perused the area to see if there was anything else he could take.

Walking around the small room, he sighed. *At least I should be fuckin' honest with myself. What I really want is to just understand more about her.* He couldn't deny the connection he felt to a woman he'd just met even if it flew in the face of practicality, something he prided himself on. A woman he barely knew. A woman whose life was in turmoil, therefore making it not the best time for anything other than making sure she was safe, and yet the knowledge that she was at his home made his breathing easier.

Another bookshelf, this one with a few picture

frames near the top, caught his eye. He walked over and spied a younger, smiling Pippa with a red-haired couple, the familial similarities making it obvious they were her parents. There were several photos of her growing up, one at the beach with a group of friends that looked to be several years earlier, but there were no recent pictures—and none with a boyfriend. It appeared her life had become focused and single-purpose. He let out a deep sigh again. *The similarities between us just keep coming.* He wanted to know a lot more about Pippa and hoped she felt the same.

He walked into the small kitchen and opened the refrigerator door. Peeking in, he grinned. He'd wondered if he would find lots of fresh ingredients to make homemade meals or super healthy smoothie ingredients or takeout leftovers, but what he discovered was that it was much like looking into his own refrigerator. A few store-bought microwavable meals. Milk and juice. A few fruits and vegetables. And a lot of empty shelf space, either from not going to the grocery very often or, more likely, from being busy with other things and simply forgetting. He didn't want to disturb too much in case someone came looking for evidence that she was still around but poured the milk down the sink and grabbed a small plastic bag to toss a few perishables that would become spoiled soon.

By now, Walker and Carson were finished, and he pulled out his tablet, quickly typing in codes. Looking up, he nodded. "Call Rick and Cole, tell them to test it."

A few minutes later, Walker gave a thumbs up. "All

good." Inclining his head toward the suitcase, he asked, "Have you got what you came for?"

"Yeah, I've got what she needs." As the words left his mouth, he hoped that was true in every sense. He wanted to be so much more than just her protector.

By the time he arrived back at his house, it was after midnight. Not surprised to find Marge and Horace awake in the living room, they told him that there were no problems to report. "You all can sleep in my bed tonight," he offered.

"Lordy, we're older, not ancient!" Horace grumbled. "We'll be just fine to leave. Anyway, it's only about ten minutes to the compound, and we'll stay at the cottage."

Marge walked over and gave him a hug. "I like her, Josh. She's got guts and smarts. I always did think the Keepers needed that particular combination."

Her words hit him in the chest, but he shook his head, hoping to hide his attraction to Pippa. "I'm just the rescuer, Marge. When all this is over, she'll go back to her life."

"Then you're a damn fool," Horace grumbled again.

"We'll see," Marge said, stifling a yawn. "Let me get this old man home before he grumbles his way into the night."

Laughing, Josh walked them to the door and waved them off, watching until they pulled out of his driveway. Closing the door, he set his alarm system, anxious to get upstairs and check on Pippa personally. Carrying the suitcase and backpack, he hesitated, then set them just outside the guest room. He wanted to knock on the door to see if she was awake. Or maybe gently open the door to see if she was sleeping. *Christ, stop hovering, man.*

He turned but had only taken a few steps when the guest room door flung open. Jerking around, his breath rushed out at the sight of her long, wavy red hair creating a wild halo. She was dressed in one of his T-shirts, and his gaze raked over her bare legs, moving upward, trying not to focus on the obvious fact that she wasn't wearing a bra.

Her blue eyes held his before her gaze dropped to the cases next to her feet and then back up. "You got into my apartment?" Her breathy voice raked over him, sending little tingles throughout his body.

He nodded, then cleared his throat. "Yeah."

"Was it okay? Had someone been there?"

"No, it was untouched. I went through each room and got what you asked for. I also brought your laptop and the notebooks from the table."

"Thank you," she said, her voice now barely above a whisper. Her gaze had never left his, staring intently, and yet he had no idea what she was thinking.

Shoving his hands into his pockets, he cocked his head to the side, keeping his eyes on her, now imagining her in her apartment. Studying at her dining table. Reading in bed with colorful pillows piled up behind her. Wandering into the kitchen to fix whatever was the easiest. What he didn't want to do was imagine her stepping out of her shower, her body wrapped in the blue towel he'd seen hanging on the towel rack, the delicate scent of her shampoo filling the air.

"Josh, are you okay?" Her voice was still soft as though afraid of waking someone.

"Yeah, yeah," he rushed. "Sorry, my mind wandered. Um... Marge and Horace left to go back home."

Her brow furrowed, and she tucked a strand of hair behind her ear but was unsuccessful considering the way the tress simply bounced around again.

"Could you not sleep?" he asked.

She pressed her lips together, slowly shaking her head. With a shrug, she said, "No, not really. I was worried about you."

"I was only in your apartment, Pippa. Were you afraid something scary might jump out of your closet at me?" he joked, hoping to keep her from seeing the nerves coursing through him. "Although, maybe something out of your refrigerator."

Her eyes bugged. "You looked in my refrigerator?" She popped her palm against her forehead in mock dismay.

"I just wanted to make sure you didn't have anything that might smell really bad before you go back. But I also didn't want to make it look like the refrigerator had been cleaned out, so I just dumped your milk and left everything else the way I found it."

She smiled up at him. "This might sound weird, but when I looked inside your refrigerator, the contents looked a lot like mine."

"It doesn't sound weird at all. I thought the same thing."

She laughed softly, and he was struck with how beautiful she looked in the moment of happiness. They continued staring at each other for a long moment before her smile slowly slipped from her face. "I was worried about you going to my apartment, Josh. All I could think of was what if they'd already found out my name and where I live? What if there was someone there waiting for me but you walked in instead? What if—"

"You can't live with *what-ifs* other than to use them to anticipate problems and work to mitigate them before they become a problem. That's why we're good at what we do. You need to trust me. We always plan our missions and go in ready to expect anything. Your apartment building is old, but there's a basic security camera across the street. We were able to tell by tapping into that that no one had gone in, so I promise, we were safe."

She was quiet for a moment, seeming to ponder what he'd explained. Her tongue darted out to lick her lips, and she lifted her chin, holding his gaze. "Can you tell me what's happening, Josh?"

"I'll be able to tell you more tomorrow, but don't be surprised if I'm gone when you wake up because it'll be an early morning as we do more investigating and planning. But I will just say that you're safe here. And we have eyes and ears on your apartment so that if anyone gets in, we'll know it."

She nodded slowly, thoughts racing behind her eyes. "And tomorrow? You'll let me know what the plan is for me?"

"That sounds like you trust us," he said, stepping closer as though pulled by an unseen magnet.

"I don't know that I have much choice, but to be honest, I'm glad I landed on your shore. Anywhere else, and I'd be facing this by myself. It feels nice to have you and the others to know what to do."

He lifted his hand and tucked the wild curl behind her ear, pleased when it stayed. "You don't have to worry, Pippa. I promise you're not alone. We're in this together, and I'm gonna make sure you're taken care of."

Her gaze didn't waver as her mouth opened slightly, her chest barely moving with her light breaths. Her pupils darkened, and the magnetic pull he'd felt a moment earlier strengthened. She leaned toward him as he took another step closer, placing his hands on her shoulders. They were so close it would only take a few more inches until his lips could taste hers.

Then doubt slammed into him. *She barely knows me, and she's been through trauma. I can't take advantage of this situation. I can't take advantage of her.* He lifted his head to place a kiss on her forehead, loving the feel of her warm skin underneath his lips. Stepping back, he dropped his hands after giving her shoulders a little squeeze. "Good night, Pippa. One of the Keepers will be here tomorrow morning before I leave. You don't have to entertain him. He'll be here to watch over you. I'll get home as soon as I can, and I promise I'll bring you up to speed on every-thing we're doing."

With that, he dipped his chin, offering a slight smile, trying to ignore the specter of hurt that filled her eyes. Turning, he headed into his room, then leaned his back against his door, hearing the soft click of her door shutting across the hall. Fighting the urge to bang his head against the wood, he sighed. He could tell she was interested, and if her gaze had dropped to his crotch, she would have seen evidence of his interest, also. *Hell, how can we be that attracted to each other in one day?* And while his fellow keepers had started relationships under her intense circumstances, he wasn't sure if it was the right thing to do… or feel… or pursue. *Why aren't relationships as easy as computer code?* Just as he suspected, no answer came to him. But thinking about the way her eyes had stared at him as she'd leaned forward, he smiled. *Tomorrow is another day—and maybe another chance.*

13

SENATOR MARK SINCLAIR'S OFFICE

"Betty, I promise to support the police in every endeavor to try to find Hank."

Mark Sinclair circled his large desk, reaching his hand out to the tearful woman. Gently assisting her from the chair, he wrapped his arm around her as they walked toward the door. "I've spoken to the police detectives that are looking into Hank's whereabouts, and it's my understanding that they might be able to involve the FBI. But you have my personal assurance that I want him found as much as you do."

Betty, normally perfectly coiffed and attired, dabbed the tears still falling. "But where can he be? He should have come directly home on Saturday night, and here it is Monday morning! I just can't imagine where he is. You know Hank. The police asked me if he was involved with another woman." She barked out an unattractive laugh. "My Hank? If he's not at work for you, he's with the family. He was supposed to go out with the kids yesterday and was so looking forward to it. There's no way he would just go off."

Mark nodded, patting her shoulder. "I agree, Betty. I've known Hank for years, that's why he's working for me. I wouldn't trust my campaign finances to anyone other than him. And that's exactly what I've told the police. The idea that he would just go off somewhere is ridiculous. But they're checking with the surrounding police and hospitals, just in case something happened."

As soon as he mentioned the word hospitals, he wished he could pull the words back in. Betty's tears started anew, and he continued to pat her shoulder as they walked out of his office. Looking at his secretary, he said, "Sharon, would you make sure that Betty gets home okay? I don't think she should be driving right now."

His secretary jumped up, shooting him a smile before moving over to Betty and gently maneuvering the tearful woman away from the senator.

"Betty, the police know to call me as soon as they find out anything. You take care, stay with your family, and I'll be in contact."

As soon as Betty and Sharon left, he waited a few minutes to make sure they weren't returning and then headed back into his office, shutting the door. The plush, burgundy carpet silenced his footsteps as he passed the heavy built-in bookshelves loaded with law books, history books, and photographs taken throughout the years.

He'd barely sat back down in the leather chair when a knock on the door sounded just before it opened. Sid

Deerman, his campaign manager, didn't wait for an invitation before he walked in, closing the door behind him. Irritation snaked through him at Sid's forwardness, but he pushed it to the background. They'd been friends for a long time, and he knew he wouldn't be sitting in the expensive chair his wife had paid a fortune for if it hadn't been for Sid's hard work and determination that Mark became a senator. But then, he also knew that Sid had an eye for Mark to run for president one day, and Sid would be expecting a position of great authority.

"How's Betty?" Sid asked as he settled into the chair that Betty had just vacated.

"About what you would expect for a woman whose husband has disappeared."

"And the police?"

"I gave them the same information that you and I agreed upon. I didn't waver from our story." With his elbows on the arms of the chair and his fingers steepled in front of him, he offered a hard stare toward Sid. "I hope that you didn't waver from the story either."

Sid's face twisted in irritation, making his hawkish features even more severe. "Of course, I didn't. I told them exactly what we decided would be best. This was my fuckin' plan, after all."

"And yet, we still have a problem that has not been resolved," Mark said, his voice hard. "What are you doing about that? I hope your *friends* will deal with this."

"You don't have to worry about my friends or me. You've gotten as far as you have because of us, and don't forget it. Anyway, I've got someone looking," Sid said.

He grimaced, shaking his head. "The fuck up should never have happened. We don't know where *the little bitch* is, where she went, or if she's even alive. Maybe the ocean took her."

"That would be the best-case scenario," Mark agreed. "But, in case she didn't die in a watery grave in the middle of the storm, you stay on it. Everything in our future rides on no one finding out what happened."

Sid jumped to his feet and sneered. "I know what's riding on *our* future, Mark. I spent years making sure of it." He turned and stalked to the door, looking over his shoulder before he opened it. "Just make sure you don't forget that we're both in this together."

Mark stared as Sid tossed out his parting comment and then left, closing the door behind him. Sighing heavily, Mark stood and walked over to the bank of windows, gazing outside without focusing on the scenery—and hoping the girl was at the bottom of the ocean.

14

Pippa should have slept well. In the past few days, she'd worked for hours, overheard an argument, witnessed a murder, had to escape by going over the side of the yacht that was thankfully not too far from shore, crawl through the rain to a place where she hoped she was hidden, and was then rescued, surrounded by some kind of a tactical security team, placed under their protection, and was now staying in a beautiful home owned by a man who made her heartbeat race more than anything else that had happened to her just by being near him.

If that wasn't a recipe for exhaustion, she didn't know what was. And yet, after having almost kissed Josh only to have him kiss her forehead before walking away, her eyes stayed open most of the night. Torn between frustration and embarrassment, she wasn't sure which emotion took precedence. *He must think I'm desperate.* She'd rolled over and over, searching for

143

comfortable positions, finally deciding that maybe she *was* desperate.

As she'd laid in bed, she'd attempted the tried-and-true way she'd always broken down her tangled thoughts into manageable pieces. *I feel safe with him.* That wasn't surprising considering he was tall, muscular, tatted, and might even be able to wrestle a bear with his hands, or at least a weaselly couple of politicians. *I can trust him.* He's smart and confident. He seems to know what he's talking about and has the backing of his coworkers to make things happen. *I'm attracted to him. Well, duh!* He was not only gorgeous, but she'd always found intelligence to be necessary for a potential relationship. And yet, he wasn't cocky. There was an element of uncertainty that ran through him that was endearing.

And his searching gaze always focused on her as though she was the center of his thoughts. And when her cheek had rested on his chest, all she'd wanted to do was stay there, holding him tight.

Hours later, all she'd done was make herself hot and bothered. She'd thought of him all evening while he was gone, and seeing him standing outside her bedroom door had made her want to rush into his arms. When he'd leaned in closer, she was sure he was going to kiss her. *God, I wanted that so much!* She'd lifted on her toes, anticipation growing, need pooling, and then his lips landed on her forehead. The kind of kiss you give your sister. Or cousin. Or maybe third cousin twice removed.

When sleep finally came, it was restless, filled with

dreams of Josh's body and hers naked, sweaty, and tangled in a bed.

Waking, she squeezed her eyes shut, groaning at the memories of her almost-kiss. *I'm an intelligent, rational, professional woman not given to throwing myself at men I just met. What must he think of me?* Rethinking all the things she'd gone through in the past day, she hoped he would simply assume her behavior was due to exhaustion.

Crawling from bed, she showered and dressed, then hurried downstairs. Josh was gone, replaced by one of the men whose name she couldn't remember. He offered her a wide smile that she had no doubt caused women all over the county, if not the state, to drop their panties with a come-hither expression of anticipation.

He handed her a cup of coffee, and she reached for it gratefully, returning his smile. "Thank you. This is exactly what I need." After a fortifying sip, she said, "I remember your face from yesterday, but I'm afraid I can't remember your name."

"Don't worry. I didn't expect you to keep us all straight. I'm Rick."

"Nice to meet you, Rick. To be honest, you look a lot like one of the other men."

He laughed and nodded. "That would be my brother, Rank."

Eyes wide, she couldn't help but startle. "Rick and Rank?"

"Actually, our last name is Rankin."

Blinking, she furrowed her brow, taking another sip

of coffee as she tried to discern if she'd heard correctly. "So, you two are Rick Rankin and Rank Rankin?"

This time, he threw his head back and laughed. "When you say it like that it does sound comical. Actually, I'm Richard, and his name is John. So, it's Richard and John Rankin."

When she blinked again, he smiled the killer smile once more. "His nickname in the Army was just Rank and that stuck. My parents always called me Rick. But yeah, as adults, our names together don't make a lot of sense."

As the caffeine hit her system, she shrugged. "Actually, names don't have to make sense. After all, I go by Pippa, and most people give me a strange look when they hear that."

She glanced around the kitchen, uncertain how the day was supposed to go. It had seemed a little easier when she'd had Marge and Horace to talk to. "So, um, am I supposed to stay out of your way? I'm afraid I don't really know how this security detail works."

"You don't worry about me. I just need to know where you are so that as I make my rounds checking on things, I'm always aware of your location."

She tilted her head to the side as she held his gaze. "And Josh?"

"What about him? If you're wondering if he's a good guy, he's the best. He's fuckin' amazing when it comes to the IT aspect of the security business, and he's one of the most sincere people I've ever met. What you see with Josh is what you get. Smart. Dedicated. Loyal. And a good friend. Believe me, you can't do any better than him."

She felt her cheeks heat with blush and muttered, "I actually just wondered when he was going to get back."

Now it was Rick's turn to blush. "Oh, shit. Um... well, he's meeting with the others and will be back just as soon as he can."

Desiring to escape with her cup of coffee before she said something incriminating like *Don't worry, I really am interested in your friend but hated to admit it*, she instead turned to fix a bowl of cereal and tried to adopt a casual tone. "I'll probably rest in my room for a while."

"Okay, sounds good. I'll do some perimeter checks and then settle in the living room to get some work done, also."

He turned and walked out of the room, and she poured the milk over her cereal. There was no doubt that Rick was great-looking. In fact, she wondered if that wasn't a requirement Mace advertised for considering every man that had crowded into Josh's living room the previous day had looked like they stepped off the cover of a magazine... *or one of my romance novels.* That thought reminded her that Josh had been in her bedroom, obviously seeing her reading material of technical books and manuals mixed in with romance novels. She wrinkled her nose and sighed. *Not that it'll matter what he thinks of me anyway. In a couple of days, this will all be over, and I'll be back in my apartment, looking for a CS job while waiting to get that diploma in my hand.* That thought didn't make her happy. *I was a loner, now with a team of people working to help me, and then I'll go back to my loner existence.*

For the next hour, she wandered around Josh's house, trying to stay busy. She hung up the clothes that he'd brought from her apartment, glad to have them. Placing her toiletries into the bathroom, she kept the counter neat and hoped he didn't feel like she was taking over too much space.

She created lecture notes for the professor to use for his next semester's freshman classes but saved them to a file since she couldn't email them to him. He would soon have a new teaching assistant since she was graduating, so that part of her life was coming to a halt anyway.

She wanted to contact her boss to explain why she hadn't brought back the empty trays but wasn't able to do that, either. She really liked her boss, but again, being able to finally get a new job with her degree, she was going to be giving up her food service job soon, also. She walked to her bed, turned around, then fell backward, flopping onto the mattress. So many changes were coming into her life, and she should be excited. Only, right now, all she felt was angst and uncertainty.

By lunchtime, she thought she was losing her mind and was grateful when Rick came into the kitchen as she fixed lunch. Looking over her shoulder, she smiled. "I know Josh told me that I didn't have to take care of you, but it doesn't make any sense for me to only make one sandwich." She pushed a plate loaded with a huge sandwich, chips, pickle, and a few store-bought cookies across the counter toward him. From the wide eyes and huge smile, she felt the gesture was appreciated.

Standing on either side of the counter, they dug in, eating in comfortable silence. Her lunch was much smaller than his, but she ate slowly, and they finished about the same time.

"This is really good, Pippa. Thanks," he said. "What do you think you'll be doing this afternoon?"

Snorting, she rolled her eyes. "Honestly? I'm bored out of my mind. But I'm also exhausted, so maybe I'll just take a nap."

"I think that's a good idea. You've been through a lot and need to take care of yourself. I'll be around, so you can rest easy."

Nodding, she watched as he left the kitchen again, and without anything else to do, she made her way upstairs. Lying on the bed, she rolled onto her back and watched the ceiling fan blades slowly turn while she thought about what Josh and the others were working on. As usual, she tried to break down the problem, seeing it the way an investigator would.

The state senator. His campaign manager. His finance manager. Hosting a fundraising event. *Not unusual. I served at a number of large, private fundraising events.* But the event on the yacht was not large. In fact, it was inordinately small to be considered a fundraising event. Unless the people on board were wealthy enough that the senator would court just them. *I wonder who they were...*

As she'd told Josh, she was used to being in food service and focusing on her job, not the clientele or their conversations. It was one of the reasons her boss often sent her for private events. She made sure the food trays were kept filled and alcohol well-stocked. She was never interested in their tedious small talk, conversations about family or friends, political opinions, or who was trying to outshine who. But now that she pondered the small event, she tried to remember more about it.

There were only seven guests. Two couples. A single man. A single woman. And another man, dressed in a dark suit with sunglasses, often standing apart from the others. *A bodyguard?* She remembered he never entered conversations. When she offered him a drink service, he only accepted water.

She closed her eyes and tried to remember any overheard snippets of conversations. After she'd escaped, it was as though everything fled her mind except the murder, but now her mind allowed a few more bits and pieces to filter in. *Financial contribution. Guarantee. What do I get for my money? Is there a return? Take out the opponent. Bank account. Investments.*

Sitting up in bed, she pounded her fist against the mattress. *None of this makes sense!* For them to kill their campaign finance manager, there had to be a connection to the money. Now that her mind was fully engaged, rest was not going to happen. She bounded off the bed and grabbed her backpack. Jogging down the stairs, she didn't see Rick, so she headed into the study. Opening her laptop, she made sure her searches were encrypted so no one could follow it back to her and began a simple search on Senator Mark Sinclair.

Married. Two kids. Attorney. Hair combed perfectly in all his pictures, his white smile gleaming. Same for his wife. Same for his kids. Looking at another picture, she snorted. *Looks like the dog was groomed, too.*

She read about his politics, finding the material dry and boring. She read about his background, finding that material only slightly less dry and boring, filled with stories of a self-made man who'd risen from a low-income background to wealth from hard work and dedication.

Not finding anything of interest, she used a program that she'd created in one of her classes that showed how banking information was not as secure as many people hoped. Glancing around to make sure Rick wasn't nearby, she started digging into the finances of the senator.

But no matter what she looked at, without a finance background, she was unable to see if there was anything suspicious. After another hour of searching, she leaned back in her chair, pressing her palms against her tired eyes, now wishing she'd taken a nap.

"Demetri, when will we get back to shore?"

"You've got women to talk to, food to eat, and plenty of vodka. What else do you want?"

"I'm bored."

"That is not my concern."

"I'm tired."

"Then take a nap."

"I can't do that here! You're so selfish. I don't even know why I bother."

Gasping, Pippa jerked her hands from her face, the

image of one of the couples from the yacht coming to mind. Tall, with dark hair, neatly trimmed beard, a white polo shirt, and navy slacks. He had a gold wedding band on his left hand and an ostentatious gold ring with a flat medallion on his right. A gold watch on his wrist. When he was with the other men, he laughed loudly and seemed attentive to his wife. Her blonde hair was pulled back into a low ponytail tied with a scarf. She wore a white silk blouse and pale blue pants and had blue sandals on her feet with red-painted toenails. She wore an excessive number of rings and bracelets, waving her hands as she spoke.

When Pippa had been down in the galley, she'd overheard them arguing. Not wanting to be caught nearby when they walked through, she quickly loaded her tray with more hors d'oeuvres and headed back up to the deck. When they reappeared, their arms were around each other and they smiled happily as though a cross word never passed their lips.

She was surprised the memory came to her and realized how much she actually saw and heard without really processing what was going on around her, focusing on the service. She opened her laptop and searched for any Demetri that lived in the Brunswick area. Time passed, but now that she had a purpose, she let time slip away, lost in her searches.

Hearing footsteps coming down the hall, she halted her searches, waiting for Rick to appear.

15

Josh sat at his computer station in the LSI compound, his fingers flying over the keyboard. He was able to focus as long as he kept his thoughts off the woman at his home. Easier said than done.

Pippa had stayed on his mind from the time he walked away from her in the hall in the middle of the night. Falling into a fitful sleep, he'd finally risen early with a raging hard-on, taking care of himself in the shower with thoughts of her joining him sending him over the edge as he sucked in air. *Christ, if that's what happens just thinking of her, what would it be like if I was buried to the hilt inside her?*

He managed to finish his shower, dress, and then stood outside her door, wishing she'd pop out like she'd done last night. Finally, feeling like a stalker, he headed downstairs, both glad that she was sleeping and frustrated that he hadn't seen her. Grabbing a cup of coffee, he greeted Rick as he bounded in through the back door.

Rick grinned, tossed his backpack onto the counter, leaned over, and snagged Josh's coffee. Taking a sip, Rick's eyes widened. "Damn, man, you *do* like your coffee strong!"

Grumbling at Rick's early morning cheer, Josh poured another cup into a travel mug and said, "I'll be back as soon as I can."

"Oh, take your time. I'll keep Pippa company."

Whirling around, he bit out, "You're here to protect her, not keep her company!"

Rick threw his head back and laughed. "I got you, man. Figured you were interested in the pretty Pippa."

Josh grimaced, refusing to rise to Rick's bait which reminded him so much of Rank's. Good men to have at your side, but no way was he going to admit to being interested in Pippa. Clapping Rick on the shoulder, he headed out to his SUV. Glancing toward his house in the rearview mirror, his gaze landed on the window in Pippa's room. Thinking of the woman sleeping inside, he smiled. Driving down the road toward the LSI compound, he thought of the threat to her life, and the smile turned into a hardened look of determination.

Once there, having already downed his first cup of coffee on the short drive, he fixed a pot of his special brew. Looking over his shoulder toward Tate, he called out, "Anything on her apartment?"

"No, not yet. No one going in or out."

Glad that her place hadn't been violated, at the same time, he was anxious for more evidence. Once at his station, he'd barely placed his hands onto his keyboard when Mace moved into mission planning.

"Anything on the guests that they picked up in Brunswick?" Mace asked.

Josh caught the others shaking their heads. Walker groused, "Brunswick is filled with multi-million-dollar homes on the coast, each with their own dock and a lot of them private. I'm tapping into security systems, but it's slow going." He looked over at Josh and said, "We need to find out from Pippa if she's remembered anything else or anyone's name that would help us narrow down who might have been on the yacht."

Nodding, he said, "I'll ask her."

Mace continued. "Working with our contacts and local law enforcement, we filed a missing persons report. Babs represented herself as Pippa's friend to file the report. Take Drew and go talk to her employer. See what you can find out."

"Got it, boss," Babs called out, winking toward Drew.

"Josh, eyes and ears on this one. I want two Keepers to go interview Mark Sinclair as private investigators following up on a missing person as a favor to a friend."

"You know I want in on that, Mace," Josh said. He felt the stare from the others, knowing his skills were generally used behind the scenes. Before anyone had a chance to object, he said, "You know you can trust me."

"Absolutely, we can trust you," Mace agreed. "That was never a question. You want in on this, you got it. Cobb, sorry, but you might be too well known with your political family. I want you in on the audio and video they'll send back. Blake, you're with Josh."

"For expediency, Blake and I can do field

surveillance for Babs and Drew, then head to the senator's office."

"Sounds good," Mace agreed.

"Fuckin' amazing," Carson mumbled from the side of the table, gaining the attention of the others. He shook his head and said, "You all work seamlessly as a team. Haven't seen anything like that since the Forces."

"That's why we're the best," Drew said, wiggling his eyebrows. "Ain't that right, babe?"

"You got that right, darlin'." Babs winked toward her husband and added, "Maybe I should go out to California with Carson and make sure his new team knows how it's supposed to be done."

Drew's smile dropped from his face, and he glared toward Babs. "Babe, you even think of going to California, and I'll tie you down."

"Promises, promises," she laughed.

Rolling his eyes as the others laughed, Mace looked toward Carson. "This is why I only choose the best. All Special Forces, most with CIA ops under their belts. We had some growing pains at the beginning, but then, we settled, got to know each other, and now function as a team. You've been choosing the right people, so it'll come together." Turning toward the Keepers, he ordered, "Keep digging into Mark, Sid, Max, and Hank. Turn their lives inside out, looking for everything you can."

Josh and Blake grabbed the equipment they needed, and once inside his SUV, followed Drew and Babs as they headed to The Maine Event Catering. Parked outside, he and Blake pulled up the miniature cameras

Drew and Babs wore, watching as they went inside the brick storefront in the strip mall.

Babs turned slowly once inside, giving a view of a reception area, photographs of food platters and cocktails decorating the walls. She approached the woman sitting behind the reception desk. "I'm looking for the owner, please," she requested, flashing her private investigator credentials.

The receptionist blinked as her smile faltered and her brow furrowed. "I'm sorry, what?"

"We need to speak to the owner pertaining to one of her employees who is missing." Babs spoke slowly, and Josh watched as the receptionist's expression slowly dawned understanding.

"Oh, my goodness! Well, that would be Lisa Salisbury." The woman pushed a few buttons on her phone and said, "Lisa, I have some investigators here that need to talk to you. I don't know. They just said they needed to talk to you." Hanging up, she smiled again. "I'll take you back."

Babs and Drew followed the woman down a short hall, passing a door leading into a large industrial kitchen. A woman came hustling over, her black hair pulled tightly away from her face and wrapped in a bun. She wiped her hands on her apron before jerking it over her head and tossing it onto the nearest counter. Approaching, her gaze darted between Babs and Drew. "I'm Lisa Salisbury. What can I do for you?"

"You have an employee, Philippa Everly?"

Lisa's chin jerked back slightly. "Yes, Pippa works for me part-time. What is this in reference to?"

"Have you heard from her since the last event she worked? The private yacht party for Senator Mark Sinclair?"

Lisa shook her head slowly. "No, I haven't seen or heard from her, but she's not required to report in. I thought it was a little odd because she usually brings the empty trays back the very next day, but I know she's getting ready for graduation, so I just assumed she'd bring them in a couple of days when she had a chance."

"So when one of your servers works for a private party, you don't usually have them report in when it's over? Even to tell you if everything went well?"

"They often will, but it's not required. I send out an online survey to our clients, and if there was a problem, they let me know. We pride ourselves that, usually, the comments are all five stars. Now, if something untoward did happen, then my executive servers, like Pippa, will call me to give me a heads up. She didn't, and I got my reply back from Mr. Deerman that everything was exceptional with the service." Her arms crossed in front of her, and she said, "Please let me know what's going on with Pippa?"

"Pippa has been reported missing."

Lisa's eyes widened as her whole body jerked. "Missing?"

"She hasn't been seen since the private party. So we would be very interested in seeing the email that Mr. Deerman sent to you so that we have a timeline of when he said everything was fine. And while we are private investigators who've been hired to look into this, I assume the police will be around shortly," Drew stated.

"Well, follow me to my office, and I'll make a copy of the survey. I suppose I should go ahead and make another one so that I'll have it when the police ask for it." Lisa walked into a small office across the hall, sitting behind a desk that was piled with papers, files, brochures, and her laptop. "I have to tell you this is so upsetting. Pippa is wonderful. I know I'm losing her soon to her chosen profession, and I'm very proud of how hard she's worked. She's destined for great things, but she'll be very missed. She's always on time, always reliable, never a complaint in all the years she's worked for me. That's why I have no problem letting her handle an event where I just need one server, especially for someone like a senator."

"And so you don't have any reason to think that Pippa just went off with someone or was involved in anything she shouldn't be?" Drew asked.

As Lisa reached for the piece of paper coming from the printer, she swung her head around, eyes wide, cheeks red. "Absolutely not! I've known Pippa for six or seven years. Believe me, she is the best of the best. If she wasn't graduating with a computer science engineering degree, I would offer her to be my partner in this business. She's that trustworthy!"

Babs held the email in front of her so that Josh and Blake could read it. A basic survey for the client that also included a section for comments. Sid Deerman had mentioned that Pippa had done an exceptional job and they were more than happy to have her serve at a future event. The time on the email would have been several hours after she'd jumped ship, which meant Sid was already covering his ass.

Thanking Lisa, Babs and Drew walked out and climbed into their SUV. As Drew pulled onto the street, Babs' voice came through the radio. "You get all that?"

"Yeah," Blake replied as Josh turned down another street. "We're gonna head to the senator's reelection headquarters. We'll meet up with you at the compound in a couple of hours once we've been able to talk to the senator."

Thirty minutes later, they were parking outside the senator's Camden reelection office. Stepping inside the plush reception area, Josh was glad Blake was with him. Tense, focused on keeping his fingers from clenching into a fist, he stood to the side as Blake beamed his smile toward the blonde receptionist.

"I'm sorry, we don't have an appointment, but we're private investigators checking into a missing person, last seen at a private event the senator hosted."

The receptionist's expression was similar to the one at the caterers—wide eyes, slightly open mouth, all pretense of their greeting having fallen to the wayside. "Oh... um... okay. Just a moment, please." She jumped up from her chair and hurried through a door, the sounds of multiple voices on the other side being heard.

The front door opened, and a group walked in, smiling and nodding toward Josh and Blake as they continued on with boxes and banners through the back door. Others came from the back, laughing and talking as they left the building. "Busy place," Blake muttered.

The blonde popped her head through the door and

smiled. "Follow me. The senator said he has just a few minutes to talk to you."

As they followed her into the main area of the campaign workroom, they spied a number of people at tables packing boxes with brochures and leaflets, answering phones, and talking amongst themselves. Entering another hall to the left, it was much quieter, and the receptionist led them to an open door, the senator's brass nameplate announcing whose office it was.

She stepped to the side, and Josh recognized Mark Sinclair. Polished appearance, white dress shirt with the sleeves rolled up his forearms, his tie abandoned, and his black pants neatly pressed. He looked exactly like he would in any of his commercials. And he wasn't alone. While Mark greeted them with a wide, white-toothed smile that could only have come from his dentist, the other man stood slowly, his eyes narrowing as he took in Josh and Blake.

"Gentlemen, come in, come in," Mark invited. "I'm Senator Sinclair, and this is Sid Deerman, my campaign manager."

"Nice to meet you, sir. I'm William Blake, and this is Josh Appleton." They held out their credentials, and Blake continued, "We're private investigators looking into the disappearance of a young woman that was with The Maine Event Catering service, taking care of your private boating party the other night."

"She's missing?" Mark asked, surprise showing in his wide eyes. "Pippa? I believe that was her name."

"Yes. We're trying to establish exactly when she went

missing, sir. What can you tell us from your event?" Blake asked.

"Please, sit down," Mark said, waving to the two chairs in his office placed in front of his desk and next to the one Sid was in. He settled behind his desk, shaking his head slightly. "She was an excellent event server. In fact, I told Sid that I'd like to request her at the next event we held. She's very quiet, very unassuming, made sure the trays were refilled with food and the drinks were flowing."

"When was the last time you saw her?" Josh asked, hoping his tone didn't give away his heightened interest.

Mark leaned back in his chair, rubbing his fingers over his chin, his brow crinkling as though he were giving the question great consideration. "After we let our guests off in Brunswick, it was just myself, Sid, and my campaign finance manager, Hank Carlsdale. We didn't need her service anymore, so I gave her permission to finish cleaning everything away and told her that she could certainly take some up to our pilot. I didn't see her again after that."

"And when you docked in Camden? You didn't notice her getting off the yacht?"

"I assumed she was gathering whatever she needed. Sid had already tipped her, and we knew that she was taken care of. I went ahead and disembarked first, and Sid and Hank were finishing their conversation. It was late, and I'd already said my goodbyes."

"You've heard, Senator, that Hank Carlsdale is missing, also. His wife has been speaking with the police, but it's my understanding she was unable to file the report until this morning."

Mark and Sid shared a long look. Mark blushed slightly and stared at his hands for a moment before lifting his gaze back to Josh and Blake, clearing his throat. "This is a bit delicate, so we hoped Hank would show up and that his wife would not have to file a report. But, you see... well, Sid saw them together." Looking back toward his campaign manager, he said, "Sid, you're the one that saw them, and if Hank doesn't resurface soon, I don't know how this is going to be kept secret."

Josh gave his attention back to Sid, watching as the other man gave a great pretense of blustering for a minute before finally speaking.

"Gentlemen, normally, I would ask that we'd all be discreet, but if Hank is continuing to act foolishly, as the senator said, I don't see how his behavior can be kept secret. Hank had what I would consider to be too much to drink, and he and the young woman seemed to have a little flirtation going on between them."

Josh barely managed to contain the growl that threatened to erupt.

Blake cocked his head to the side. "We've spoken to the owner of The Maine Event, and she gave us a copy of the survey that you completed a few hours after the trip where you had nothing but good things to say about her. Are you now saying that her behavior was not professional?"

"No, no," Sid said quickly, his surprise slipping through. "I mean, I never wanted her to lose her job—"

Mark shot a glare toward Sid. "You mentioned Hank's behavior, but you never said anything about hers."

"In all honesty, there was nothing that Pippa did that was inappropriate." Sid sighed heavily, looking as though the weight of the world rested on his shoulders. Turning toward the others, he said, "I didn't think anything about it at the time because Hank can be a bit of a flirt when his wife isn't around. He's harmless, and I always figured he was more talk than anything else." Glancing toward Mark, he added, "I haven't mentioned it to you because I didn't want to concern you when you have so much you need to focus on. I've talked to Hank before, and he always promises it's harmless flirtation, so I didn't think anything else about it. When we docked, Mark said his goodbyes and headed up to his house. I went up to the wheelhouse to speak to Max and watched as Pippa carried a box as she disembarked. Hank was with her. I heard him say that he would help get things to her car."

"And now they're both missing," Josh stated, keeping his expression neutral while his gaze stayed pinned on both men.

Mark's brow furrowed, and he shook his head. "This is all so distressing. Do you think they just went off together?"

Sid shrugged. "By the time I got up to the driveway, Hank and Ms. Everly's cars were both gone. Then Betty called to ask me about Hank not coming home. At that point, I assumed maybe he and Ms. Everly... uh...

hooked up somewhere. I haven't heard anything else, so I didn't mention it."

"And that was the last you saw of Hank and Ms. Everly?" Blake reiterated. "You saw them both leave the yacht and head toward the driveway, and when you followed them later, both of their cars were gone."

"Yes, absolutely," Sid assured.

"And do you still think that they're together?"

"Well, I have no way of knowing, but when Mark told me that Hank's wife reported him missing, I hoped he would show up soon. I have no reason to suspect anything else happened, especially since both he and the young woman are still missing."

"Gentlemen, if there's anything else we can help you with, please, let us know. I'm certainly very distressed that my friend and campaign finance manager has disappeared, and of course, I'm concerned about Ms. Everly, as well." Mark stood, his face flush, his eyes darting between them.

Josh recognized the indication that Mark had reached his limit with their presence. *Fucker's not hiding his nervousness very well.* Shooting a side glance toward Sid, he caught the tight jaw and lips pressed together of the man Josh felt sure had twisted the tie around Hank's neck, the same man who now cast disparaging accusations on Hank and Pippa to cover his tracks. Knowing his own jaw was clenched, he steadied his breathing and blanked his expression.

He and Blake stood, shook both mens' hands, and walked out, neither speaking until they were back in the

SUV. Blake turned to him and said, "Know you're pissed. Dig deep, man. We'll nail those bastards."

Josh simply nodded, not trusting his voice, but he was in total agreement. He was going to enjoy nailing those bastards.

16

By the time Josh and Blake returned to the LSI compound, he was still fuming. Knowing he'd have trouble concentrating, he was glad that Blake was driving. Since they were wired for audio and video, he wasn't surprised when they walked into the cavernous workroom and had the attention of everyone. Their expressions ranged from concern to mirroring his own anger.

He managed to stalk over to his desk without anyone speaking but had barely placed his fingertips on the keys when Mace's voice cut through the silence.

"Josh."

Still facing away from everyone, he closed his eyes for a few seconds, breathing deeply. Whirling around on his chair, he found the other Keepers' attention still on him. "Yeah, boss?"

"I know you're pissed. I don't blame you."

"You're going to tell me to keep my mind on the mission. I got that. You're gonna tell me not to go off half-cocked. I've got that locked down, too. You're gonna tell me not to do anything to fuck up the evidence we find that we'll turn over to the FBI? Yep, check. But, Mace, I just sat in the presence of two murderers who implicated Hank as a drinker and womanizer, neither of which is substantiated. And that he and Pippa left together, and that they're still probably off somewhere. They sat there acting like some entitled fuckin' boys' club wanting to keep Hank's wife from knowing they fuckin' murdered him. And Pippa? Hell, they didn't give her a second thought," he growled. By the time he finished, his breath came in pants and his hands curled into fists. "I know I have to deal with that shit. It's just that right now, I'm not sure how."

"Frankly, I thought you did good," Blake said, standing nearby. "You didn't bat an eye, not giving away anything. Fuckin' perfect."

He glanced up at Blake, his jaw tight. "I don't know how I did that when all I wanted to do was put my fist through Sid Deerman's face."

"The fact that you didn't put your fist through his face is exactly why you're a Keeper," Mace said. "Yeah, you're pissed. But I don't have to tell you to stick to the mission because you've already done it. So, what I'm going to tell you is good job."

Mace's praise wasn't unwelcome, but Josh was still struggling with his anger. The other Keepers offered him silent support, and throwing out a chin lift was the best he could do in response. Drawing in a deep breath, he let it out slowly before asking, "Where are we?"

"Louis Thatcher is my FBI liaison. I've known him

for years," Levi said. "We send him what we know, and he wants in on the investigation. While Mrs. Carlsdale is getting the local police involved with a missing persons report, with Hank being killed at sea, the FBI can take over jurisdiction. He's taking what we have and will interview Pippa."

Josh's eyes bugged from his head, and as he began to protest, Levi plowed on.

"Don't worry. It'll happen at your house. He knows we're keeping her hidden so that Mark and Sid stay off-balance by not knowing if she's alive or not. I told him you'd want to be there, so we made it for this afternoon."

With law enforcement now engaged, Josh knew the investigation would make it harder to keep her situation secret.

"There's more," Mace said, drawing Josh's attention back to his boss. "While you and some of the others were gone this morning, someone entered Pippa's apartment."

Josh's blood ran cold. He reached over and tapped quickly, pulling up the video to see for himself.

"Professional," Tate said.

Knowing that meant no identification and they would have been careful to avoid detection, he growled, "Goddammit!" Watching the screen, he viewed a man in all black with a black hood entering, then slipping through her place. He barely touched anything with his gloved hands, but he checked the refrigerator, looked into her closet, and opened a few drawers. "He was checking to see if she'd been back."

"That's our assessment, too. So, this is good," Mace said. "He sees enough there to make it look like she hasn't been back to clean out, and that means they still don't know where she is or if she's alive."

They continued to watch as the intruder left the apartment and slipped down the street away from their camera view.

"Got more," Mace announced.

Josh looked up at his boss, his eyes intense at the sound of Mace's voice.

"We did a fast but extensive background investigation on Pippa, more than what we had the other day."

Mace's voice rarely gave away any indication of what he was thinking, causing Josh to steel his spine, waiting to see what was going to be presented.

"She's clean. Absolutely, positively, exactly what she presented to us. Everything you'd already found out about her background, including employment, money, family, education… she's clean."

Cobb looked over, brows lifted as his lips curled upward. "And fuckin' smart. I mean, we knew that just from talking to her, but seriously, fuckin' smart. I told Mace he ought to hire her before she gets snagged by some government agency to do their hacking for them!"

The others chuckled, and Josh felt the air rush from his lungs, having not realized his breath had halted in anticipation.

Rank glanced over his shoulder toward his computer at the sound of an alert. Twisting around, he began tapping rapidly, finally chuckling. "Speak of the devil."

"What's going on?" Mace asked.

"I've been digging into the finances for Sinclair's previous campaigns. I set up alerts because I wanted to know if anyone else was doing the same. And someone is."

Anxious to see who was possibly trying to cover their tracks, Josh leaned forward. "Who is it? Where is it coming from?"

Twisting back around, Rank grinned. "It's coming from your house, Josh. The encryption is great, but Pippa can't know that we've got it set up to ping back to us. It looks like your girl is already doing some of our investigation for us."

"You gotta be fuckin' kidding me," Josh growled. "Is she crazy? She's supposed to be taking it easy, not investigating on her own! And where the fuck is Rick?"

Standing, he stalked toward the elevator that led to the ground floor. "I'm heading home. I'll ream out Rick and might possibly handcuff Pippa to a chair out of range of the computer!" The sound of laughter hit his ears as the elevator doors shut.

Pippa looked up, expecting to see Rick walking into the study. Instead, Josh came to the doorway. Her heart leaped, and she grinned widely, refusing to analyze how she could feel that way after knowing him for such a short time. "Hey!"

His lips curved, and relief that he also seemed glad to see her moved through her. Something else she refused to analyze. His gaze shot toward the laptop on his desk for a second before returning to her as he walked closer. "Hey, yourself." Instead of sitting in a chair, he hefted his hip on top of the desk, close but not crowding.

Her gaze drank him in, not caring if he did crowd her. She wanted to blurt that she'd missed him but bit back the words. For a few more seconds, they simply stared at each other.

"So, I thought you were going to rest today," he said.

"I'm fine," she assured. "Actually, I've been bored."

"With all the excitement you had, there's nothing wrong with being bored."

"I guess you're right." It dawned on her that she hadn't seen Rick since lunch. "Is Rick still here?"

"No, he was in the front when I relieved him of duty and sent him on his way."

"I felt bad having to have a babysitter. I'm sure there were other things more important that he could have been doing."

"Nothing is as important as you, Pippa," Josh said.

The words struck her heart, but she knew he was only speaking about keeping her safe because of the mission. Before she had a chance to ponder what she'd really like him to mean, he inclined his head toward her laptop.

"What are you working on?"

His voice sounded strange, but she knew he had to be tired. "To help with boredom, I was just looking up a few things."

"What kind of things?"

This time, his words held a cutting edge. *There's no way he can know I've been doing some investigating, not with the encryption programs I placed on my computer!* "Um… you know. Just stuff."

"Stuff? Just stuff?" His smile dropped, and his eyes seemed to bore straight into her, his body tighter than it had been. "Stuff like Mark Sinclair's fundraising? Background on Sid Deerman? Looking into the campaign finances? That kind of stuff, Pippa?"

Sighing heavily, she flopped back in the chair. "How did you know?"

"Christ, Pippa!" he shouted, standing and pacing to the middle of the floor before turning around and pinning her to the spot with his glare. "I know you're good, but you have no idea what we can do. We're already on this. We're already investigating."

"I just want to help!" She threw her arms up to the side.

"Help? You don't know what we do," he argued in return.

She wanted to scream in frustration. "Then show me. Teach me. I can't just sit around and do nothing while those murderers are out there. Hank has a wife. A wife who doesn't know where her husband is, and as much as it's going to devastate her, she deserves to know what happened to him. Mark Sinclair is out there raising money, and God only knows what Sid is doing with it. They deserve to be brought to justice."

He stalked toward her, halting just in front of the desk. Leaning over, his fists landed on top, holding her gaze. "That's what we're working on. We want to bring them to justice, too. But we're working methodically, and carefully, and with law enforcement. The last thing we want is for this to get fucked up. Hell, we've discovered someone was in your apartment!"

She gasped, knowing it might be possible but hoping it wouldn't happen. "God, I could have been there! Who was it?"

"Professional. We can't get an ID because they were dressed and hooded to cover their identity. Wore gloves. Fucking checked your place to make sure you hadn't been back."

"They didn't take anything?" She shook her head, wincing. "Not that I have anything to steal."

"No, just looked around. Checked refrigerator, closets, drawers. We left enough around to make it look like you had never come back. That's what we want, so as much as it creeps you out, it's good that they still think you're in the wind. Keeps them off-balance."

She slumped in her seat, emotions crashing against her heart. "I can help, Josh. Stop keeping me out of things."

He sighed heavily. "I know you're smart. I know you've got serious computer skills. But what you don't have is the knowledge and the experience to use them effectively in our line of work."

Her chin started to quiver, and she hated the idea that she was going to cry. Swallowing deeply several times, she finally took a shuddering breath and said, "I know you're right, and I'm sorry, but my mind just won't shut off. I hear their voices over and over in my head. I feel the same fear that I felt when I was there. I can still see Hank so clearly, and I'm not sure I'll ever get that out of my mind. And I've been trying to make sense of it all, searching for what they could have been talking about. What happened that made them commit murder."

His chin dropped so that his intense gaze was no longer boring into her.

She reached out slowly, placing her hand over his on top of the desk. "I'm sorry."

Lifting his head, he was no longer glaring, making her breathe easier. Instead, his gaze was full of the warmth that she'd already come to expect from him, filling her with the comfort she'd already come to crave. He walked around the side of the desk, managing to keep their hands connected, then gently pulled her to a stand. Wrapping his arms around her, he held her tight. With her cheek against his heartbeat and her arms surrounding his waist, she breathed him in, allowing his strength to seep deep inside. *This is the heartbeat I've longed to hear.*

"I'm sorry, too, Pippa. I didn't mean to sound like an asshole. It's just that when we could determine that you were here searching, all I could think of was wanting to get here to make sure you're safe."

She squeezed her eyes tightly shut, mortified that his coworkers knew she'd been snooping. "I promise I'll stop. The last thing I want to do is make things harder for you."

"I care about you. I can't explain how it is that we've just met and I feel so strongly, but you matter to me. I don't think I could stand it if something happened to you," he said.

She lifted her cheek away from his chest and looked up, his expression so sincere with a dash of nerves and hope mixed in. "I feel the same way," she confessed. The simple words were enough to make his arms tighten around her as he smiled, and her lips curved in response. "But if there's anything I can do to help, please, let me know. It's important."

"First, stay safe. Second, tell us anything you happen to think of, no matter how small. You never know what you might remember that will be just the clue that we're looking for to nail these guys."

Her body jolted, and she gasped. "Just before you came in, I'd remembered little snippets of conversations from the trip. Things that I didn't even know I over-heard. I'm so used to blanking out conversations that I was surprised they came back to me."

His arms dropped away from her back, but he reached down and grabbed her hands, bringing them between their bodies, holding them tight. Bending slightly, his face only a few inches from her, his voice was filled with intensity as he demanded, "Talk to me, Pippa. Tell me what you remembered."

"It had to do with one of the couples on the trip. His name was Demetri. And I know that because when he and his wife were arguing, that's what she called him. Demetri."

Before she had a chance to say anything else, he barked, "I gotta call this in." Letting go of her hands, he stepped back, jerking his phone from his pocket. She watched as he pressed a few numbers, then said, "Pippa is having memories coming back to her. Yeah, yeah. You got it." Shoving his phone back into his pocket, he said, "Grab your shoes. We're taking a road trip."

Blinking, she tilted her head to the side. "Road trip? But I thought I needed to stay here to be safe."

He grinned, reaching down to link his fingers with hers. "Where we're going, you'll be safe."

17

Pippa's gaze darted from the windshield to the passenger window as Josh turned off a back road. Security gates opened in the middle of the woods and shut behind them. The thick Maine forest was on either side, then slowly ended, exposing an expansive grassy area that led to cliffs overlooking the ocean. With another turn, a tall lighthouse came into view with a white-washed, red-roofed house nestled at its base. Air rushed from her lungs as she took in the beauty surrounding her. "Oh, my God, I don't know where we are, and I don't care. This is beautiful!"

There were cars parked around the house, and as they approached, she could see it was much larger than she'd originally thought. Josh pulled in next to some of the other trucks and SUVs, parked, then turned toward her. "This is part of where I work," he said. "Mace owns this and all the land around. We use this house as a meeting place."

Her head whipped around toward him, her gaze

focusing on his neutral expression, wondering how much he wasn't telling her. "I'm honored to be here," she said. "I can only assume I've been deemed not a threat. And that's okay, Josh. If there's one thing I understand from my cybersecurity studies it's that you can't be too careful."

He nodded, and she was grateful for his honesty. "I won't lie, Pippa. You've been thoroughly checked out in the last twenty-four hours by the Keepers."

"Keepers?"

"Those of us who work for Lighthouse Security Investigations are known as Keepers, from the old lighthouse keepers."

Understanding dawned, and she nodded slowly. "Guiding toward the light," she said softly. Reaching over, she placed her hand on his arm and squeezed. "Like the night I jumped from the yacht to head toward your light."

Their gazes locked, unspoken emotions swirling between them, crackling like electricity. Finally, he jerked slightly and said, "We're expected. We need to go in."

By the time she'd opened her door, he was already around and lifting his hand toward her. Glad for the connection, she slipped her hand into his, and they walked inside the house, directly into a large kitchen where Marge and Horace greeted her with friendly familiarity.

Marge's arms wrapped around her, and feeling the slight pat on her back was welcoming. Her mom used to hug that way—a hug followed by a pat. Blowing out a breath as they separated, Marge held her gaze for a moment, then offered a nod before looking beyond Pippa's shoulders toward Josh. "They know you're here. Go on in."

Josh's hands landed on Pippa's lower back, and she felt each fingertip like a brand. He guided her down the hall and into a massive room with a table in the middle and what seemed like dozens of chairs all around. She quickly recognized the other men and women, now knowing they were all Keepers. Glad that she'd already had a chance to talk with them at Josh's house, she felt less like a specimen under a microscope. Their smiles felt sincere, and she forced a smile onto her face, hoping to hide her nerves. Whatever she was remembering, Josh thought it was important.

Mace nodded toward a seat. "Pippa, glad you came. Have a seat and we'll get started."

It was on the tip of her tongue to say she didn't think she had a choice about coming, but considering she was excited to help move the investigation along, she glanced toward Josh as they sat next to each other, and the other Keepers filled in all around the table.

She hesitated, uncertain of the protocol, feeling the formality of being at one of their *meeting places* as opposed to the informality of Josh's living room. Grateful when Josh began to speak, she turned toward him just as his hand reached over and clasped hers. Without thinking, she linked fingers with him, once again glad for the connection.

"I know when I left you earlier, I was unhappy because Pippa was investigating. She understands the need for caution, and I have a better understanding of her security abilities. But then, she told me she was starting to have memories that have just come back to her."

Mace nodded toward her. "Pippa, just like before, talk to us."

Moistening her bottom lip, she breathed in deeply before letting the air out slowly, centering her mind. "I told you that I usually ignore the conversations that are going on around me. That's one of the reasons my employer often will send me to private events. I don't care about gossip. I don't have time in my life for eaves-dropping. Most party attendees are either discussing business, which doesn't concern me, or they're discussing politics, which I have no interest in. Or their small talk, which would be a waste of my time to listen to. Or they're talking about their lives, which, considering I'll never see them again, hardly matters to me. I simply focus on the food service." Shrugging, she offered a wide grin. "To be honest, I was often reciting computer code or class notes in my mind, preparing for a lecture or test."

"But what you may not have realized was that some conversations were overheard subconsciously. Is that right?" Babs asked.

Nodding, she smiled toward the enigmatic woman. "That's exactly right. I was downstairs in the galley preparing another tray when I overheard a couple arguing from one of the cabins. Actually, it was the cabin that I was in when Hank was murdered later on that evening. The man had a slight Slavic accent. It caught my attention, and since I'd heard him when I'd been on deck earlier, I knew who was in the room. He was tall, trim, with very dark hair and a dark beard. The strange thing is, I remember the gold he wore. A wide wedding ring and heavy watch. He also had a very large gold ring with a flat medallion on his other hand." She gave her head a little shake. "I know that's a strange thing to remember. I don't know why some things just seem to strike me as unusual. Anyway, his wife had blonde hair and also wore an excessive amount of jewelry. Well, excessive to me. Their argument escalated, and I didn't want to be caught listening if they came out of the room, so I took the tray back up to the deck. They returned to the gathering about five minutes later. They seemed all happy and smiling, so that little exchange just dropped from my mind with everything else that happened that evening. But what I really need to tell you that I remembered was that the woman called the man Demetri."

The air in the room immediately changed, the vibe electrified with intensity. As the Keepers' gazes jumped between themselves, Pippa sat in stunned silence, watching the unspoken thoughts flying around.

Bray looked down at his tablet on the table, mumbling, "Fuckin' Demetri Sidorov."

Josh's fingers gripped hers a little tighter, and she cast her gaze up toward him, her brows lowered. He leaned over, whispering, his breath brushing against her ear. "Russian mob."

Blinking, uncertain she'd heard him correctly, she

kept her mouth shut, but her mind raced. *Mob? Like Godfather-type mob?*

Flipping his tablet around, Bray asked, "Is this him?"

She stared at the face she recognized and nodded. "Yes. Only that's not the woman that was with him."

"Not surprised," Tate said, leaning back in his chair. "Sidorov is known for his mistresses."

Clicking to another photograph, Bray turned his tablet toward her again, his brow raised in silent question.

Pressing her lips together, she nodded. "Yes, that's who he was with."

"*She* is his wife," Bray said. "Crystal."

"Any other memories?" Josh asked, his head still close to hers.

She closed her eyes and scrunched her face, casting her mind back to before everything went to hell. "I was on the other side of the deck, checking the alcohol stock when Demetri and his wife came back. His wife called out to the woman in the other couple... Sasha. She called her Sasha. Physically, she was very much the opposite of Demetri's wife. Sasha was tall and dark, slender, the slight accent, as well." Opening her eyes, she received the same vibe bouncing around the room, and once again looked toward Josh.

Instead of explaining, he squeezed her hand again. "You're doing great."

Grumbling, she sighed. "If I was doing great, I would've remembered this yesterday. Think of the time I wasted!"

Mace shook his head, declaring, "You haven't wasted

any time. If it wasn't for you, no one would know that Hank was murdered. And don't worry about not remembering these things earlier. What you witnessed was traumatic, your escape was traumatic, and you're lucky to be alive. All of that took precedence in your brain. It's only now, as you're starting to relax, that you're able to bring up other memories. And believe me, for most people, it takes a lot longer than a day, if ever."

She had the feeling that Mace never minced words, and along with another squeeze on her hand from Josh, the tension in her shoulders eased. Bray turned his tablet around again, and she recognized the other couple. "Yes, that's them. There were two couples on the trip, then another woman who was there by herself, and then two men also by themselves."

"Sasha is Demetri's sister. She's married to Paul Markowitz."

"This greatly narrows our focus, Pippa," Mace acknowledged. "Is there anything else you can tell us?"

Before she had a chance to respond, Josh leaned forward and held her gaze, smiling with encouragement. "Don't try to force it. Just close your eyes and allow your mind to drift. And while you're doing that, just talk. Don't filter or think about what you're saying. Just talk out loud with your eyes closed. Let us be the ones who filter through what you're saying, pulling out what we might use."

Nodding, she smiled in return. Taking a deep breath, she let it out slowly, then closed her eyes. "I was below deck when I felt the yacht bump against a dock, or what I assumed was a dock. I knew we were going to pick up a small party in Brunswick. I could hear laughter and talking from above and had already set out drinks and hors d'oeuvres. I was carrying a tray up the stairs, paying more attention to not tripping on the moving yacht than on the people. At first, with everybody milling around, I didn't focus on anyone specifically. But now that I have in my mind what Crystal and Sasha look like, the other woman also had dark hair, almost black. She was average height but very curvy with an hourglass figure."

Keeping her eyes closed, she gave her head a little shake. "How strange that these things are so clear to me now. She was wearing a white blouse and white pants, and I remember she had a glass of red wine in her hand, and I thought that she must be very confident to move around the yacht with red wine while wearing white. I later saw her with some red on one of her sleeves and thought she must've spilled some of her wine."

"Could it have been blood?" one of the Keepers asked, but with her eyes closed, she wasn't sure which one had spoken.

"Maybe," she admitted, her teeth digging into her bottom lip. "But I didn't see anyone else with blood on them, so I'm not sure how it could be." She squeezed her eyes tighter, trying to force her memories.

"Keep going, Pippa," Josh prodded. It struck her that even if he had not been sitting next to her, she'd still be able to tell his voice as it wrapped around her.

"Of the other two men, both were quieter, but one rarely spoke. He stood in his suit the whole time with his sunglasses on. I even thought he might be a bodyguard although I had no idea why anyone would need him there in such a small gathering. I never heard either of their names. But I remember the other one stepping over to the table when I was placing food out, and just as some of the others laughed loudly, he rolled his eyes and grumbled something under his breath that sounded like, 'Idiots.' I had just picked up an empty tray and had to pass him on my way back down to the galley and caught sight of Hank on the other side of the table. Whether he was calling Hank an idiot or was referring to the other men, I honestly can't say."

"Can you bring up any snippets of conversations that may have had to do with money, finances, fundraising?" Mace asked.

When her main task was to simply refill the liquor stock and keep trays out with hors d'oeuvres, she preferred to work with her back to anyone in the room, or in this case, the gathering on the deck. She'd found that occasionally men with alcohol would attempt an advance, and if she never made eye contact with them, that seemed to help. Now, she wished she'd spent more time focusing on the group. She let her breath out again, allowing her mind to drift back to the trip.

"I remember one of the men talking about investments and returns, and that seemed to upset Hank. At one point, he said, 'You can't do that.' When I was coming up from the galley at another time, Crystal and Sasha were off to the side and the other woman said, "That's what my people want. Guarantees. If they pay for your office, they want the benefits."

Pain sliced through her head, and Pippa lifted her free hand, gently rubbing her forehead.

"Are you okay?" Josh asked.

She turned toward his voice before opening her eyes, surprised at how close he was and how his gaze stayed right on her. "I just have a headache, that's all." She looked out to the others and said, "I'm not trying to wimp out, honestly. But snatches of conversations were all I heard."

The others immediately assured her everything she told them had been important. Saying goodbye, she watched as the room emptied, most of the Keepers heading down the hall. Mace was the last to exit the room, and he turned toward Josh.

"Take her back to your place, but if you want to make a trip up top first, she might like that." Mace's gaze moved toward her before returning to Josh. "I know you want in on everything but also want to be where you can keep an eye on Pippa. Use your facility and include her." With that cryptic message, he offered them a chin dip before heading out of the room.

She thought they'd follow immediately, but Josh kept his hand on hers, and they waited for a moment before he finally said, "Do you feel well enough to climb some stairs?"

Eyes bright, she grinned. "The lighthouse?" At his nod, she squeezed his hand. "I'd love to!"

He led her out into the hall, and they walked through a doorway that led them to the steps of the lighthouse. Climbing the concrete steps, they wound their way to the top, passing by the huge prism lights and out onto the balcony that circled the glass enclosure. Behind them lay the thick, green forests that surround the area, and before them lay the ocean, the waves crashing against the rocks below.

She sucked in great gulps of fresh air, her lungs almost burning with each inhalation. The sun beamed down, and she closed her eyes as she lifted her face, allowing the warmth to settle over her. Still holding Josh's hand, she leaned her body slightly into his, craving the stability he offered.

"This is amazing! How on earth did Mace ever come to own a lighthouse?"

"There are a lot of lighthouses on the coast, many of them no longer used. Mace used to come here as a kid, having been raised nearby. When his grandfather passed away years ago, he left the family land to Mace. When this lighthouse was decommissioned, he bought it and all the property around it. The symbol of the lighthouse meant something to him and became the symbol of his business."

"Lighthouse Security Investigation," she said softly. "I think it's wonderful." She turned slightly, looking up at Josh, and admitted, "I think you're wonderful, too. I owe you so much."

His arms wrapped around her, he shook his head. "No, you don't. And I don't want you to."

"You don't want me to be grateful for you rescuing me?" She understood modesty but didn't understand why he didn't want her gratitude.

"It's not that I... what I mean is that you shouldn't... if we're going to be living together, well, working together…" He grimaced as his words floundered.

She tightened her arms around his waist, keeping her gaze pinned on him. "Hey, Josh, it's just me. You can just talk to me."

His gaze lifted to scan the horizon over her head for a moment before he dropped his chin and his eyes seemed to search hers. He lifted one hand to hold a strand of hair flying in the breeze before finally speaking. "I understand your gratitude, Pippa. It's just that it's not necessary."

She waited, but no other explanation came. With a last look over the great expanse from the top of the lighthouse, he kept a tight hold on her hand as they descended the stairs. A sense of disappointment moved over her, difficult to define but very clear in the way it made her feel. *Why did I think he was going to say something profound about us being together? Staying together when all this is over? But then, I haven't either. Maybe it's time I stopped being afraid. Or maybe being afraid just keeps me safe.* Sighing, she climbed back into his SUV after saying goodbye to Marge and Horace, her heart heavy.

18

During the short ride back to Josh's place, neither he nor Pippa spoke. His mind was filled with what she'd said, but the last thing he wanted was for her to feel that she owed him a debt of gratitude. Sure, he understood she was grateful that he'd found her, but she'd escaped on her own and made her way to his shore by her own grit and determination.

His attraction to her was growing, and by the way she looked at him occasionally, he wondered if she felt the same way. But he didn't want her to feel confused because of gratitude. Pulling up to his house, he put the vehicle in park, but neither opened their door. He shifted to face her, finding her actions to mirror his own.

"Pippa—"

"Josh—"

They both smiled, and her understated beauty struck him. "Ladies first," he offered.

She ducked her head, tucking a wayward strand of

hair behind her ear. She looked out the front windshield toward his house for a moment, not speaking. In the two days he'd known her, he'd already learned that she was cautious, not one to prattle aimlessly. Waiting, he knew she'd speak when she was ready.

She looked back toward him, a light blush tinging her cheeks. "I am grateful that you rescued me, Josh. Even more grateful that you didn't call the police or take me to the hospital when I begged you not to. And I know it was sheer luck that I landed at the doorstep of someone who has the skills and career to help." She pressed her lips together, then finally blew out a heavy breath. "I'm no good at flirting or always knowing the right thing to say, so I'm just going to be honest. When I'm with you, I feel something, and I'm positive it has nothing to do with gratitude."

"What do you feel?" His heart beat faster, the sound pounding in his ears, surprised she couldn't hear it.

"The night I jumped over the side of the yacht, it was raining, but the worst of the storm had passed. In the distance, there was lightning, and I remember being glad that I was able to swim toward the shore without worrying about being in the middle of a horrendous storm. And yet, the air felt electrified. I chalked that up to adrenaline, and maybe that's what's happening now. But every time I'm with you, I feel that same jolt of energy… like an electric current is running between us. I've never felt that with anyone before, and I don't feel it with anyone else except you."

"I'm no good at flirting, either, Pippa," he confessed. "I never understood games of the heart." Offering a rueful chuckle, he shook his head. "I used to watch some of the other Keepers, all good men, most happily married now. But when I first knew them, quite a few of them rarely left the bar alone. I understand sex for the sake of a physical release or just fun, but I usually found it dissatisfying to either watch a woman get dressed and walk away right afterward, or she didn't, and I wished she would."

Pippa laughed, nodding. "It's hard, isn't it? Or maybe I just always made it harder than it should be. But it seemed like men were either intimidated by intellect, wanted to go out with me because they needed help in their classes, or met me when I was serving alcohol and assumed I was looking for a quickie in the coat closet."

"Shit, Pippa. No woman should have to put up with that!" He placed his hand over hers, still resting on his arm, appalled she'd had those experiences.

"It is what it is and not that uncommon, unfortunately." They were silent for another moment before she said, "I just wanted to explain that I feel something for you that has nothing to do with gratitude. I don't expect anything back, but I haven't felt this attracted to a man in a long time—if ever." She squeezed her eyes tightly shut, dropping her chin. "I've just totally fucked things up, haven't I? Now, you probably don't want me here—"

He halted her words with his knuckle under her chin, lifting her face up toward his. "You didn't fuck anything up, Pippa. Hell, you managed to cut through all the garbage that was rolling around in my head."

With her chin still resting on his hand, her brow furrowed. "I don't understand. What garbage?"

"The minute you opened your eyes and looked at me, I felt struck by lightning. It sounds like some dumbass saying, but it's absolutely fuckin' true. But there was no way I was going to take advantage of you. You need a place to stay, and I want you here. You need someone to watch out for you, and I want it to be me. But I sure as hell didn't want you to feel like you owed me anything out of gratitude."

They stared at each other, lips curving upward, the air inside the vehicle crackling. He wanted to kiss her but knew they had work to do before they could get into passion. "I want to show you something." Her eyes brightened as her brows lifted, and he laughed, shaking his head. "No, not that. But it's still something you're going to want to see."

He hated to let go of her hand but did so, circling around the front before assisting her down, glad to link fingers with her again. "We'll go around the house to the backyard." He led her down the cracked concrete path until they came to the place where he'd found her.

She gasped as she looked around. "This is where you found me, isn't it? I remember crawling up from the beach, still going for the light of your house. But when I got here, there was a small light, and even though it was concrete, I remember being so tired and just wanting to sleep." She tilted her head to the side, asking, "Is this what you wanted me to see?"

"No. This is." He stepped to the wall and flipped open the hidden panel, tapping in a code before placing his hand on the scanner. A click sounded, and the heavy door leading into the bunker unlocked. Turning toward her, he grinned at her wide-eyed expression. "Other than the Keepers, you're the only one who's ever been in." With their fingers still linked, he led her inside, the door closing behind them, the lock sliding into place.

She looked around, confusion filling her eyes as she turned them back up to his. "What is this?"

"An old World War II bunker."

She blinked, her body visibly jolting. "You can't be serious!"

"Absolutely. The east and west coast are dotted with them, kind of like lighthouses. The fact that this was in the backyard is probably why the old house didn't sell for a long time. When I saw it, I saw potential." It suddenly struck him how odd this might seem, but now that they were inside, he showed her the rest. "Come on."

He led her into a large room filled with computer equipment. He tried to ignore her gasp, afraid to look at her in case she really did think he was crazy. But if she was ever going to *get* him, she had to understand what made him tick. *God, I hope she gets it.*

"Whoa…" she breathed.

He took heart in hearing the curiosity and wonder in her voice, chancing a glance in her direction. "I set it up as a secure location for LSI to be able to have a second site in case it was ever needed." As her bright gaze wandered around the room, he turned his body toward hers and reached down to grab her other hand, holding them both tightly, drawing her gaze up to him.

"I'm able to let you come in here because LSI has already checked you out. They have the means without the government red tape to find out what they need. You being here means that LSI trusts you. *I* trust you. If you're going to do searches and try to find out what you can based on your memories, you need to do it here where the security is absolute and no one will know what you're doing."

Her eyes widened, and her mouth opened slightly as she simply stared up at him. He leaned forward and whispered, "Breathe."

As the air rushed from her lungs it blew sweetly over his cheek, and he battled the desire to see if her lips would taste just as sweet.

"Josh, I'm incredibly flattered, but I just finished my degree. And even though I specialized in cybersecurity, I doubt there's anything I can do that would come close to what you and the other Keepers can do."

"I'm the only one of the Keepers with a computer science engineering background, Pippa. The others have various specialties, and because they're all highly intelligent, they picked up a lot of what they need to do. But we're in a time crunch to bring Mark and Sid to justice by offering what we can to the FBI. Your memories have thrown things into a completely different light."

"I don't understand. Was it the other people on the yacht?"

He nodded, forcing down his desire to kiss her. *Work. It's time for work.* Leading her over to several chairs at computer stations, they sat, facing each other.

"The names you gave us made all the difference. Before that, all we had to go on was the recording, which was good but didn't tell the whole picture. For all we knew, Mark, Sid, and Hank had an argument that got out of hand, and one of them killed Hank. But Demetri Sidorov is mid-level Bratva... Russian mob. His sister, Sasha, is married to a man who's been brought in, working for Demetri. Until now, Mark Sinclair has appeared squeaky clean. But with him hosting a private event, looking for money from the Bratva, it brings a whole new twist to what you witnessed."

He watched as thoughts moved through her eyes, certain that she was filtering through the information, analyzing each piece. And just like he knew she would, she suddenly jerked, reaching out to grab his hands. "A politician with visions of going all the way to the top without the scruples of where the money comes from or if it's reported correctly would be compromised. A puppet for whatever the mob wanted."

"A PEP." He caught her head jerk and expounded. "A politically exposed person."

Shaking her head, she said, "I've never heard of that term."

"When talking about finances, a politically exposed person is at higher risk for bribery and corruption. A lot of financial institutions will look at a PEP to carefully monitor that their fundraising and finance accounts are correct."

She nibbled on her bottom lip for a minute before nodding slowly. "That's why they needed Hank. If Hank was honest, following laws and regulations, he wouldn't have wanted to go along with anything that he was hearing."

"That's what we're thinking." He stared at her as a crease formed in her brow, and her lips pressed tight together. He had no idea what she was pondering, and that made him nervous. "Look, Pippa, you don't have to do any—"

"When do I start?"

He blinked, caught by surprise with the determination in her question. "Are you sure? I realize that bringing you here probably wasn't fair. Everything you're doing puts you more at risk."

"Josh, I know that I'm at risk. Right now, I need to keep out of sight so no one realizes that I'm alive. But I'll go crazy if I'm just sitting around, wondering what's happening. I'm absolutely honored that you're asking for my help. So, point me in the right direction."

His grin spread widely over his face, finding her even sexier than he had before. "Okay, let's get started."

For the next two hours, he walked through some of the computer programs and systems he'd developed and put into place. Not wanting to overwhelm her, he wasn't surprised at how quickly she picked everything up. And as they worked side-by-side, several more memories came to the surface. Every time she was able to identify another piece of the puzzle, they dug deeper while informing Mace at the same time.

As she described the single woman and two men, he keyed in the information, then showed her the program he used to start coming up with possible identifications, based on the assumption that all the guests on the yacht were part of the Bratva.

"Found the men!" she called out. "Two brothers, Peter and George Balk. Digging deeper, it appears they changed their name from their birth name of Balakin."

"Damn, girl, that's fuckin' awesome. Let's get the program to dig up everything it can on them." For a moment, Josh forgot what he was doing, staring at Pippa as her fingers flew over the keyboard, her eyes alight.

She glanced over at him, then did a double-take. "Why are you staring at me? Am I doing something wrong?"

Shaking his head, he said, "No. Not at all. In fact, you're doing great. You're doing everything right." She held his gaze, tilting her head slightly to the side in silent question, and he sighed. "All of the Keepers take turns working security, learning the programs, spending time in our main work area, but they all prefer being out in the field. I don't mind fieldwork at all, but I know that we're safer and smarter when we go into a mission with all the information we can possibly gather. Anyway, the program on the Balk brothers can run during the night and we'll have the information in the morning."

He hesitated, but she nodded slowly, giving him hope that she understood. Clearing his throat, he continued. "It's just that I was already attracted to you, but seeing you here working, excited with what you're learning and doing... well, it's pretty fucking amazing, not to mention sexy as hell."

She threw her head back and laughed, reaching out to grab his hand. He rolled her chair closer, spread his knees, and settled his thighs on either side of hers. Her eyes sparkled as they held his gaze, and she leaned forward until their lips were a whisper away from each other.

"If you're like me," he began, "I could stay on the computer all night. But that's not really what I want to do tonight. "

"Yeah?" Her lips curved upward. "What would you like to do instead?"

Emboldened by the desire in her eyes, he grinned. "Head back up to the house. Strip out of our clothes. As for the rest of the night, discover everything we can about each other."

Her eyes still gleamed, but she didn't reply, and his heart beat a staccato rhythm in his chest as he wondered if he'd misread her interest. *Shit! I just propositioned a woman who's been through a traumatic experience only a couple of days ago. What the hell was I thinking?* Just when he opened his mouth to apologize, she placed her fingers on his lips.

"Don't you dare take back what you just said, Josh. Don't you dare apologize. I can't explain why I'm so attracted to you after only knowing you for a couple of days, but I am. And it's not because of the rescue. It's not because of the crazy past forty-eight hours. It's because of you. Just you."

As her fingers slowly slid from his lips, his heart still pounded but in anticipation, not regret. "Then you liked my suggestion?"

"Yeah, all except one thing."

"What's that?" He tried to remember what he'd said that she'd object to.

Grinning, she said, "That we'd have to wait until we got back to the house. When I walked down the hall earlier to go to the restroom, I saw that you have a room with a bed down here."

He chuckled, shaking his head. "Yeah, because sometimes I'm running a program that's hard to walk away from, so I end up sleeping a few hours down here. But that's not for us, Pippa. It's a little more than an army bunk. You deserve a lot more. A bed. A real bed—"

"All I want is you. I don't care if it's a bunk, the floor, a wall. Just you. Now."

She leaned forward, her tongue darting out to lick his lips.

At the feel of her tongue on his mouth, all his resolve went to hell. "Fuck!" Bending his arms around her, he stood. She wrapped her legs around his waist, grinding her hot core against his already straining erection. "Hang on," he mumbled, backing her up against the closest wall. She did as he ordered, tightening her arms and legs around him. The electricity he always felt around her intensified, crackling the air. With her breasts tight against his chest, he pressed his hips forward, both now grinding together. *Christ, I could come just dry-humping her.* He wanted their clothes off, but trying to do it with their bodies clinging together was not going to make it happen fast enough. *Yeah, this wall isn't cutting it.*

Turning, he stalked down the hall and into the room

MARYANN JORDAN

where he kept the bunk. Glad that it had a real mattress and clean sheets, he bent to set her gently on the side, his chest heaving at the sight of her beautiful face staring up at him. She lay back, and he leaned forward, planting his palms on the mattress next to her. "Are you sure? I gotta know that you're sure."

Still grinning, she grabbed the bottom of her shirt and started pulling it up, wiggling to get it over her head. She tossed it to the side. "If that's not answer enough, then I'll say it. I want you."

He bent slowly and placed a kiss between her breasts at the top of her bra. Slowly trailing his lips up over her collarbone and neck, he finally sealed his lips over hers, finding them just as sweet as he'd imagined.

19

Pippa's head was swirling but she was ready. Not just ready for what she hoped was going to be blow-me-away sex but ready for everything Josh had to give. In fact, she'd _been_ ready. Sure, gratitude might have caused what she felt when she first met him, followed quickly by the shock that he was in the investigative business. Next came awe at the way his friends and coworkers jumped in to help. And she couldn't discount the fact that she considered humble intellect to be sexy as hell. Throw in the toys in his bunker, and she was on excitement overload.

But more than any of that, it was the way his eyes lit with intensity when he looked at her. The shy smile that curved his lips. Confident but not cocky. Brilliant but not in-your-face. Kind but not patronizing. And holy moly, his body. Muscular. Tall. Tats down one arm that made her want to start at his fingertips and lick all the way to his shoulder, studying each one, discovering what each one meant to him.

And now, all she wanted to do was get their clothes off as fast as possible. Her core was aching, her breasts were heavy, and her legs fell apart, welcoming his weight. But the second he put his lips gently on her chest, slowly kissing his way up until finally sealing his mouth over hers, she wanted nothing more than to make their time together last as long as it could.

He held his weight off her chest with his forearms planted next to her, his palms cupping her cheeks as he angled her head to take the kiss deeper. She opened her mouth, granting access, thrilled when he accepted. His tongue glided over hers, thrusting as it explored her mouth, and she gave this to him readily until her own desires took over and she thrust her tongue into his mouth, as well.

He groaned, and she swallowed the sound, loving that she could make the strong man moan. Her arms circled around his shoulders, her fingers digging into the warm skin covering hard muscles. Applying pressure, she pulled him closer, wanting to feel all of him covering all of her.

"Too heavy," he mumbled against her lips before diving his tongue back in, the sweet velvet feeling sending more tingles through her already-electrified body.

"Uh-uh," she barely managed to protest, tightening her hold. She lifted her hips, and the feel of his erect cock trapped in his jeans made her want to free both of them from all constrictions.

He must have had the same thought as he dragged his lips away from hers and stood, staring down. His gaze was so intense, the light in his eyes now dark. His hands reached to his belt, and every sound seemed to echo in the concrete bunker. The click of the metal buckle. The slide of leather. The button releasing. The metal zipper as he slid it down. The slight release of air from his lungs as his cock was no longer constrained. It only took a few seconds and yet it felt agonizingly slow.

Breaking out of her trance, she reached to the front closure of her bra, popping it open, allowing the cups to fall away. She couldn't imagine how his eyes could darken anymore, but they did as he stared at her naked breasts, the cool air tightening her nipples to painful buds.

His thumbs had hooked into the waistband of his jeans, but he stilled their progress as his gaze roved over her naked torso. "Christ almighty. Jesus, Pippa, you're fuckin' beautiful."

She'd never felt beautiful before. Of course, there'd been men who told her she was pretty. She'd always felt like the girl next door. A plain-Jane next to the model-gorgeous women who always seemed to have stylish clothes, trendy hairstyles, and perfectly applied makeup. But the way Josh was staring down at her, she felt as beautiful as he seemed to think she was.

His hands left his waistband as he grabbed the back of his T-shirt and dragged it over his head, dropping it to the side of the bed. He reached into his back pocket and jerked out a couple of condoms from his wallet. Bending, he replaced his hands on either side of her on the bed and gently kissed one nipple before dragging it deeply into his mouth. She gasped at the zinging electricity that moved from his lips straight to her core. She wrapped her arms around him again as his mouth shifted between her breasts.

The ache in her sex was building, and she slid her hands to his lower back to press his hips to hers, desperate to ease the need for friction. He lifted slightly and grinned down at her, his hands snagging her pants and panties as he dragged them down her legs. His nose nuzzled her sex, inhaling deeply, and she shivered, uncertain she'd ever seen anything as sensual as his blatant appreciation.

Her shoes dropped to the floor, and he sent her pants and panties following. Kneeling, he shouldered her legs as far apart as they could go and dove in like a man starving. It had been so long since she'd had a man go down on her, she jolted in surprise at the feel of his tongue licking her folds. *Jeez, I should've groomed!* For a second, she allowed self-doubt to cloud her mind, then his tongue slid in, and all thoughts were flung to the far corners of the earth as her entire being focused on his mouth and her core and the sensations threatened to drown her.

Her fingers dove into his hair, the nails dragging along his scalp as he licked and sucked before adding a finger deep inside, finding the spot that had her body quivering. His mouth found her clit, and she raced toward the edge of the cliff, her coil tightening until she finally cried out her release and flung over the edge of the precipice, not caring where she landed, sure that he'd catch her. Or that she'd die happy and fulfilled from orgasm overload. To say she'd never felt that way would not have been an exaggeration. Past lovers now proved to be fumbling fools, and she wasn't sure anyone could ever surpass what Josh had just allowed her to experience.

Her rubbery legs fell open, and she wasn't sure she had control of any muscles at this point. He stood and leaned over her, his lips quirking upward on one side. It was the first cocky expression she'd seen on his face, and she would've teased him about it if she'd been able to find her voice. Instead, as she lay naked, he leaned over and kissed her hard. As his tongue delved back into her mouth, she tasted her essence, another new experience for her.

Barely aware that he'd toed off his boots, he lifted slightly as he shucked his pants and boxers to the floor, kicking them off to the side. Lifting her head, she stared as he palmed his impressive cock. *Oh, yeah, my past lovers were definitely lacking.* Grinning, she lifted her hands, beckoning, heart dancing as he rolled on a condom and crawled onto the bed over her.

Lining the tip of his cock up at her entrance, he pushed in slowly, almost reverently. A hiss of air escaped through his clenched teeth. "Fuck, Pippa, you're so tight. I don't want to hurt you."

"Josh, the only way you're going to hurt me is if you stop. I'm not sure I'd ever recover from the pain of having you this close then losing you before I found out exactly what we could experience together."

Closing the gap so that his chest was lightly resting against her breasts and his face was directly in front of hers, his breath puffed against her face. With his top teeth landing on his bottom lip, he shifted his hips, driving his cock balls deep inside. She gasped at the intense pressure but clutched him tighter, not wanting him to stop. His gaze held hers, and he must've been satisfied she wasn't in pain because he began thrusting, each movement sending shockwaves throughout every nerve in her body. Clutching him tightly, she lifted her hips to meet his, and they moved as one.

She'd never had two orgasms without the aid of her vibrator and couldn't believe when the coils inside tightened once again. Digging her fingers into his muscles tighter, she groaned until finally crying out his name as fireworks exploded behind her tightly closed eyelids. Continuing to cling to him, she loved their connection but knew down to her very being it wasn't just about sex. She knew she'd take whatever she could get from Josh but prayed this wasn't a one and done.

Watching Pippa come apart in his arms ranked as one of the sexiest things—no, *the* sexiest thing—Josh had ever witnessed. And the next thought that slammed into him was that he hoped this wasn't the only time he got to experience that feeling with her.

He continued to stare, his movements slowing as he gave her body a chance to drag out her release. Her eyes blinked open, holding him captive as her lips curved upward. Her fingers dug in tighter to the muscles of his upper back before one of her hands slid down to his ass, gripping him tightly.

He bent and took her lips as he thrust his hips forward, his movements faster with a desperate desire to lose himself in her tight warmth. His fingers clutched her wild curls as the burn in his lower back began. Finally, he planted himself fully inside her, his orgasm shutting down his brain as his body released each drop into her. As though every ounce of energy had also been expended, he barely managed to keep from crushing her, rolling so that she was now on top.

While he sucked in gulps of air, her slight weight rested completely on him, her cheek pressed against his sweat-covered chest. Her legs tangled in his, her wild hair flowing to the side, the strands resting against his shoulder. He wasn't sure he could move and was damn sure he didn't want to. Ever. The mission could disappear. The world could disappear. He had food, water, a small bathroom, and this bed in his bunker. Right now, with her in his arms, he had everything he could want.

As their bodies cooled and their heartbeats steadied, she shifted, lifting so that she could rest her chin on her hands propped on his chest and peer down at him. She smiled widely, the sight piercing his heart.

"Was that just me, or was that completely *wow*?" she asked.

He chuckled, her body moving along with his chest. It struck him what he'd been longing for, what he'd been missing in the last women he tried to date. Honesty. Humility. Ease that knocked out the feeling to always be something more than he felt he was. He didn't bother trying to tuck her hair behind her ear, knowing it was going to bounce free. Instead, he threaded his fingers through the tresses and held them back so that he could have an unadulterated view of her beauty. "It wasn't just you. It was more than *wow*. It was fuckin' fantastic."

She heaved a sigh, and if he wasn't mistaken, it was out of relief. How the fuck could she be afraid it wasn't every bit as good as it was? He could only surmise her past lovers had not gotten her there. And thank God, he did.

She shifted her body slightly, her lips landing on his. The kiss was soft and slow, then she lifted and slid off his body, tucking herself into his side.

His arms tightened around her for a few seconds, knowing he needed to deal with the condom but hating to separate from her. Finally, he sat up. "Duty calls." He stood and walked to the small, utilitarian bathroom across the hall, took care of the condom, and washed his hands. Walking back in, his feet almost stumbled at the sight of her lying on her side, her elbow bent and palm propping her head. *Naked and fuckin' gorgeous.*

And on her beautiful face was the most stunning smile. She pushed upward, sitting on the edge of the bed. "So, what now?"

"We could work all night on the mission, forgoing sleep and food. I know because I've done it many times before. But that's not what I want to do. As much as I want to get to the bottom of what's going on, we're only part of the team."

She stood, completely naked, and like every man's wet dream, walked toward him. Stopping just before their bodies touched, she leaned her head back and held his gaze. "What do you want to do?"

Glancing behind her at the bunk that would now always remind him of her, he shifted his gaze to her eyes as he lifted his hand and cupped her cheek, gliding his thumb over the soft skin. "I want to blow this bunker and get back up to the house. And once there, I want to give you what I think we both want and what you deserve." She tilted her head to the side in the adorable way she questioned without speaking. Grinning, he said, "What I want to give you is another orgasm. What you deserve is to be cradled in a real bed."

A small giggle slipped out, and she leaned just close enough where her breasts crushed against his chest. Lifting on her toes, she placed a light kiss on his jaw. "Then take me home, Keeper."

It didn't take long for them to get dressed and for him to check on his computer programs that would run through the night. Stepping outside under the starry sky, he reset the security before grabbing her hand, and they raced up the hill and into his house.

Once there, they wasted no time getting naked again, and he gave her what he wanted and what she deserved.

20

The early morning sun blasted through Josh's east-facing windows and unadorned sliding glass door leading to a balcony. Blinking at the light, she lifted her head. Pippa first looked down at the man lying next to her and grinned. Her gaze traced the tattoos on his arm from his wrist to his shoulder, creating a work of art. She'd never thought much about tattoos before, but now, seeing them on Josh, she wanted to stare at them, discovering their meanings as she traced them with her fingers. On his other shoulder, he only had one, but it was beautiful—a lighthouse all in black and white except for the golden light beaming from its lamp.

Dragging her gaze from his body, she twisted her head to the side, grimacing as her eyes narrowed against the sunlight. While the view over the water was breathtaking, it was obvious that Josh desperately needed some kind of window covering. Blinds, curtains, shutters, hell, even a sheet taped over the window.

Remembering the night she'd spent in his arms, she

grinned again, rolling away from the window and plastering her body against his side. With his eyes still closed, his lips curved and his arms reached out to pull her close.

"Damn, Pippa. You. Naked in this bed. The best thing I've ever woken up to."

She laughed, kissing him lightly before snuggling her head on his shoulder, her fingers running lightly over his chest. "I'll bet I can make it even better." Without giving him a chance to respond, she kissed her way down his chest, over his stomach, her lips surrounding his cock, sucking him deep.

His body jerked, and his fingers clutched her hair almost painfully before loosening slightly. "Fuuuuuck, babe," he groaned, his hips bucking upward.

Loving that she could give him the same pleasure he'd given her the previous night, she licked and sucked, her hands fisting the base of his cock. She lost herself in the action, driving them both to distraction. Giving head had always seemed perfunctory, much like the oral she'd been on the receiving end of in the past. But just as Josh had taken her to new heights last night, she discovered that giving was as good as getting with Josh.

"I don't want to come in your mouth," he groaned, his hips jerking again.

She kept going until he reached down and snagged her under her arms, pulling her upward. Now straddling his hips, she licked her swollen lips as she looked down into his intense gaze, her hair providing a curtain around them. Lifting on her knees, he settled the tip of his cock at her entrance, and she slid down, both moaning at the same time.

Her fingers clutched his shoulders as he held onto her hips, and they found the new rhythm. Her breasts bounced as she lifted and sank on his cock. Just as she was tiring, he slid one hand to her mound, his thumb gliding over her over-sensitive clit. She gasped just before her body shuddered, her orgasm firing shock-waves throughout. As the shudders ebbed, she wasn't sure her arms could hold her up.

He grasped her waist and lifted her slightly before pistoning his hips up and down, taking his thrusts harder and deeper than she'd been able to. Soon, his face and neck muscles tightened and his fingertips dug into her ass as his own release shot deep inside.

She fell forward, eliciting an "umph" from his lips, but was unable to move. She blinked in the sunlight again, finally murmuring, "You need to get window coverings."

He started to chuckle, and then the sound halted in his lungs. "Shit, Pippa. That's not the only covering I don't have."

She lifted her head and peered down, her brow furrowed as her sex-foggy brain tried to decipher his words. Tilting her head to the side, she waited.

"I'm so sorry," he began. "I didn't use a condom."

Eyes wide, her mouth dropped open. "Oh, shit." Blinking several times, her mind raced. "Um… I think this is where I'm supposed to tell you that it's all okay because I'm on the pill and I'm clean. I mean, I am. On the pill and clean. But I know that was risky. Shit."

"I swear, I'm clean, too. We get tested constantly."

Nodding her head in quick jerks, she let out a breath. "Okay, good. We should be good. We should be safe."

"And I give you my word that I won't forget again."

Just hearing him use the word 'again' made her smile. "I like knowing that we can do this again." His smile widened, curling around her heart. Chuckling, she shook her head. "I've never done that before."

"You never went down on anybody before?"

Rolling her eyes, she pinched his stomach, finding almost no body fat. "I never lost myself in it before."

His gaze held her, but his smile slowly eased. "Then I'm honored you lost yourself with me. Because I gotta tell you, I feel the same way."

Josh looked over at Pippa standing in his kitchen after insisting on fixing him breakfast. He'd once again assured her that she wasn't there to take care of him, but she'd shut him up with a kiss. Considering he could barely walk, much less think, after a round of shower sex, he'd stopped talking and just enjoyed the view of her in his kitchen.

They ate in silence for a few minutes, sitting at the counter when she finally turned toward him. "I know this wasn't your childhood home, but most of us pick places to live that either remind us of home or definitely don't remind us of home. I look at this house and keep trying to picture a young Josh."

He swallowed, then looked around, trying to see his house through her eyes. "This house is nothing like the house I grew up in, but I wasn't trying to find the opposite." Turning back toward her, he shook his head. "My parents have a little house. It was just the three of us, and they made decent money, but it wasn't extravagant. But my dad always said he fell in love with the house for two reasons—it had a bright, sunny kitchen that my mom loved and a huge garage in the back for him. He was a mechanic and loved to tinker on cars, even on his days off."

She smiled and reached over, placing her hand on his as it rested on top of the counter. "Then you did find a house like your parents."

Jerking his head back slightly, he lowered his brow. "I don't understand."

"You found a house with a World War II bunker in the backyard that you've turned into an investigator's computer dream."

Chuckling, he had to admit, "You're right. I guess I never thought about it that way."

"And the house just happened to come with it."

He started to agree, then looked around at the large windows facing the water or woods, the updated kitchen, the finished wooden floors, and large rooms. Glancing toward the empty dining room now that they'd just eaten at the counter, he suddenly thought of dining room furniture. He'd never missed it before, but now, it made sense. "Guess I could use some more furniture," he muttered, smiling as she laughed softly.

"Oh, I don't know. Eating here works fine."

He held her gaze, her easy acceptance of his house, including his lack of fancy furniture—or in a few rooms, any furniture—made his heart beat faster.

He then thought of the master bedroom upstairs with its windows and sliding glass door that opened onto a deck and the way he'd loved waking up to Pippa this morning in that room. Turning back to her, the breath seemed to catch in his lungs at the idea of admitting that to her. But he'd never been one for skirting around the truth. Turning his hand over, they linked fingers. "I don't know that I've ever realized it, but this is a house that didn't just come with the bunker but is a place I can see myself living for a long time. Sharing with someone I care about. Someone who likes its uniqueness as much as I do."

"You want to know what this house reminded me of when I first saw it from the outside?"

He cocked an eyebrow. "A Victorian dollhouse?"

She blinked, and her brow furrowed as she shook her head.

"Sorry, but that's what most people tell me," he explained.

"For me, it reminded me of a playhouse I had. Not just a little dollhouse, but an actual playhouse. While your dad liked to tinker with cars, my dad enjoyed woodworking as a hobby. He taught mathematics at our local high school, but I sometimes think he would've been just as happy if he'd worked with his hands building things all the time. Of course, he used to tell me, 'Pippa, this is geometry in real life.' Anyway, he built a playhouse in our backyard. Big enough that I could stand up in, with a bookshelf and a small desk. I used to spend hours reading in there. Being an only child, it wasn't that I couldn't do that in the house, but somehow, having my own space gave me the freedom that I craved. He gave me a place to escape when the taunts from other children about being a smarty-pants or teacher's pet or brainiac made me want to get away." Ducking her head, a blush tinged her cheeks. "It probably sounds dumb, doesn't it?"

He shook his head, squeezing her fingers. "Not at all. My dad and I built a treehouse. And yeah, it had bookshelves and a desk. And I know what you mean about the taunts. I have no doubt it was harder for you. I think it's always been harder for smart girls."

She shrugged and sighed. "I think taunts sting no matter who you are." They were quiet for a moment until she added, "It's funny that we both had such similar places to escape, and you were able to find one as an adult."

He leaned closer. "And you found this place, too. This place—and me." Closing the distance, he kissed her lips, knowing it wasn't the right time but wanting to say more. *More like it doesn't matter that we've only known each other for a couple of days because what I feel for you is real. More like maybe it was all that, but you made your way to my light. More like I'm not sure this house will feel the same when you leave, and I sure as fuck would love it if you didn't leave. Yeah, that'd scare the shit out of her.*

"So, what's on our agenda for today?" she asked, dragging his thoughts back to what they needed to do.

"I need to go into the compound for briefings. Nora

said something about stopping by your place to get a few more things. I think Babs is going with her."

Huffing, she let go of his fingers and threw up her hands. "Can't I even go to my place to get some more things? I could go with Nora and Babs before working in the bunker today."

He shifted around on his stool, caging her knees in with his. Reaching out, he snagged both her hands, holding them close. "Look, Pippa, it's not that I'm trying to make you a prisoner, but we've got to keep you hidden for a little longer. If no one knows you're alive, then it keeps you safer. Once the women leave, then you can go down to the bunker and patch into me. I'll have you look over some more of Sinclair's finances. I've got to go in for a meeting but need you safe. I can't think if I'm worried about you."

She tilted her head to the side, but instead of staying silent, she asked, "You'd worry about me?"

Leaning closer, he nodded. "Yeah, I would. I don't know what the hell is going on between us, Pippa. I've never done this before... fallen so far, so fast. But I can't believe what I'm feeling for you is just based on the extraordinary circumstances that brought us together. At least, not for me."

"Me either."

His eyes widened, his gaze searching her face.

"Josh, I thought maybe it was just me. This crazy wild ride of the last several days. But I feel something when I'm with you that I've never felt before and sure as hell don't feel with anyone else. So, whatever this is, I want us to be able to move beyond the investigation so that it's just us. Just a man and a woman navigating their way to finding each other."

He closed the distance, pouring everything he had into the kiss, letting go of the past and the doubts, embracing whatever this was building between them. It was only the sound of wheels on the driveway that caused him to separate, dragging air into his lungs as they both smiled at each other.

Babs and Nora walked in through the kitchen door, their gazes darting between them. While Nora placed a few bags on the table, Babs laughed, saying, "Well, all right. I can see that you two gave in to what the rest of us were already noticing." Clapping Josh on the shoulder, she added, "It looks good on you, man. Get outta here so I can share lots of embarrassing stories about you with Pippa. Oh, and since she's stuck here, I've called for the others to come to visit. Just wait until they fill her full of their stories!"

Shooting Babs a warning glare, he kissed Pippa goodbye before heading out to his SUV, his heart lighter but his determination to see the mission quickly come to an end even stronger. He wanted her safe so they could move forward without the thread of her needing his protection tethering her to him.

21

Josh's eyes were pinned on his computer screen, the pictures of George and Peter Balk staring back at him.

"Got anything on them?" Clay asked, clapping Josh on the shoulder as he sat down next to him.

Josh flashed the program to the large screen for everyone to see. "Pippa's identification of the two Balakin brothers, now going by the last name of Balk, is proving that there is a connection between them and Demetri." Glancing toward Levi, he nodded.

Levi took over. "It seems George, as the oldest, has worked his way to a lofty position in the transportation industry as one of Demetri's top men. Peter, as the younger brother, appears to be an enforcer, probably on the yacht as extra eyes and ears. My guess is that when Pippa overheard George say, 'Idiot,' he was referring to Sid hiring her instead of someone from inside their organization or even having just refreshments with no server. Sid's determination to always make Mark look like a big fuckin' deal may have been seen as problematic."

Mace stood and looked around the room. "This morning, LSI received a call from the head of the Bureau. They officially want our assistance. Of course, you know the drill. Whatever we find, we turn over to them. They get the glory, and we get satisfaction."

"And the pay!" Drew said, his smile wide.

Mace turned to Carson. "With LSI's backing into the new LSI West Coast, expect this to happen on occasion."

"Impressive as fuck," Carson said, nodding.

Josh turned his attention back to his computer screen, understanding the importance of what Mace had said but more interested in the alert sounding. They'd placed a tracer on Sid's vehicle, and he was now following its course. When Josh was sure of what he was seeing, he called over his shoulder, "Got Sid on the move to Portland. Mark isn't with him, but he's headed to the Western Waterfront District."

"Right where the freight and the industrial harbor is," Mace said, his eyes on the map that Josh had sent to the widescreen they all could view.

"And right where Sidorov and Markowitz have their warehouses," Bray added.

From the tracer placed on Sid's vehicle, they were able to watch on the map as he entered through the gates leading to private warehouses on the harbor. Josh glanced toward Mace and asked, "You ready for audio?"

The new tracers they'd gotten their hands on had the ability to pick up audio from inside the vehicle. To keep the battery power up, they kept them off until necessary. Considering Sid's car had stopped and now was slowly moving, again, Mace nodded. "Bring it up."

"... brother is not happy. You fucked up and now expect us to take care of everything."

"We didn't know Carlsdale would disagree with the plan. I sure as hell didn't know he'd threatened to expose everything. That would've been an even bigger mess for you to clean up."

"If you'd left things alone, we could have taken care of him and the girl. We already had plans to take care of her, and it would have been no problem to have taken care of him, as well."

"Mark panicked! It was him. It was all him. I was ready to stick to the plan."

Long seconds of silence ensued.

"Why have you come?"

"I have no idea who's watching. Mark is nervous, afraid of his own shadow at this point. So, I told him I'd handle everything. I can't trust phones or emails, so I had to come in person. I don't care what you've done with the body, but the girl has to be found."

"If she hasn't been found, then she's probably already dead at the bottom of the ocean."

"But if she's not?"

"You told us she wasn't on the boat so she would have no way of knowing if Hank left the boat or not."

"We... we weren't with his body the whole time. She could have seen something."

"You're even more stupid than we thought. But, we took care of her car, along with his, crushed beyond all identification. I have eyes out looking for her, but no one has seen or heard from her. She has nothing on us. You are the ones who *acted foolishly. Sidorov wants you to take care of it. But listen well... Sidorov will expect full cooperation from your boss. Full. Do you understand what this means?"*

"Yes, yes. I'll make sure he does. I promise, no more problems from us."

The sound of a door closing met their ears, and they watched the screen as Sid's vehicle slowly moved away from the warehouses on the harbor before heading north again.

The Keepers looked at each other as Josh turned off the audio, hands shaking, unable to speak with the fury coursing through his veins.

Mace nodded toward Levi. "Send this to Agent Thatcher."

"So, that answers what happened to Hank and Pippa's cars—probably taken to one of the mob-owned junkyards. Identification removed, then crushed," Josh said.

Tate cocked his head to the side, leaning forward in his chair. "And Hank's body? Think it was in the car when crushed? Would that be how they got rid of it?"

Shaking his head, Drew said, "Too risky. Too risky to be caught on the way with the body in the back. My guess? Mark and Sid panicked and dumped him in the water."

"Fuck," Cobb cursed, shaking his head as well.

"And Pippa?" Josh asked, his stomach tight, fury filling every cell of his being. "They were going to *'take care of the girl?'* Christ! They always planned on getting rid of her!"

"I doubt Mark and Sid planned on it. That plan was

probably put into play when Demitri and company got on the yacht and realized someone else was there. They couldn't afford to be identified," Mace said.

"But your girl was smart. Analyzed the situation, recognized the risk, and made a decision," Walker responded.

Josh's breakfast threatened to reappear at the thought of the fate that would have awaited Pippa if she hadn't seen the light at his place and jumped into the water.

"She's our mission as well as the investigation. Once Mark and Sid are brought down, the Bratva won't have any interest in her since she has no information on them."

"Don't worry," Drew said, clapping Josh on the shoulder. "You know Babs will take care of her."

"It's my understanding the other women are dropping by, also. That's enough to make anyone worry."

Tate joined in. "According to Nora, Pippa fits in with the rest of our badass women. She'll be just fine."

Josh nodded but remained quiet. Sighing heavily, he scrubbed his hand over his face and turned back to the computer screen. Pippa had proved she could handle herself in an emergency, but he had no idea how she'd feel about the women of LSI invading.

―――――

Pippa walked through the opened sliding glass door to the deck overlooking the water, a full coffee pot in her hands. She hesitated for a few seconds, listening to the sounds of conversation and laughter from the women outside. Babs hadn't been kidding when she'd said others were coming. Of the group, she'd only met Sylvie and Nora. As the others were introduced to her, she'd battled the desire to remember all their names and faces and the gut-wrenching realization that when the investigation was over, she might never see them again. But more than that, it was the idea that she might not see Josh again. Sure, he'd said he felt something for her, but... *maybe it's all the drama swirling around us.*

Good breeding won out in the end, and she was determined to remember their names. Rank's beautiful Helena looked like a society princess but was down to earth. Walker's wife, Julie, was a wholesome beauty who worked at one of the local high schools. Clay's wife, Christina, was a petite musician with boundless energy. Levi's wife, Claire, a teacher at a local college, had a smile that lit the room when Pippa met her. Cobb's wife, Josie, was a social worker whose beauty was only eclipsed by her caring personality. Bray's fiancée, Marie, was a doctor, instantly concerned with how Pippa was doing. Blake's wife, Sara, had hair similar to Pippa's, and she'd already told of her harrowing escape in French Guiana, where she'd had to cover up her red hair to keep from being recognized.

The women seemed so close, and yet it was strange how Pippa didn't feel like an outsider. Somehow, they had the ability to swap stories of how they'd met their Keepers, talk about what they had in common, and make her feel as though she fit right in with them.

They'd all brought food, but she fell naturally into

playing hostess even though they were at Josh's house. None had seemed surprised at her taking on the role. She pushed that thought down, not wanting to give too much headspace to the reminder of how much she'd love to stay when the mission was over.

Glancing down at the coffee pot in her hand, a long-buried memory drifted to the forefront of her mind. When she was a child, her parents enjoyed having others over. Teachers in her father's department. Newly hired teachers. Neighbors. But after her father became sick, it was almost impossible to host social gatherings. Her mother was never the same after her father passed, and it wasn't many years before she became ill.

Pippa's life had revolved around school and work for the past several years, socializing mostly in an educational setting and spending time at work trying to just earn money and not become involved in what others were doing. *Look at me now. Less than a week since I fled a crime scene, and here I am, playing hostess to ten brilliant women.*

"Need some help?"

Pippa looked up quickly at Julie standing nearby. "Sorry, my mind just wandered."

"Don't worry about it," Julie said. "We've all been there."

"I have to admit everyone's stories are shocking." Pippa looked over to see all eyes on her, but instead of feeling nervous, she realized their smiles were encouraging. "But then, if you'd asked me a week ago if I would be where I am right now after having seen what I saw and done what I did, I'd tell you that you were crazy."

Laughter rang out as everyone nodded. Sylvie stood and walked over, taking the coffee pot from her hand. "Pippa, honey, whatever happens, don't doubt that you fit right in."

She sucked in her lips, a question dancing in her head, then decided to lay it on the line. "Marge mentioned the other day that it takes a special woman for a Keeper. I understand the concept now that I've had a chance to see a little of what they do. I suppose it's kind of like being a military wife where they could be called out at any time. But," she shrugged, "I still got the feeling that Marge meant something more?"

She watched as the women's gazes darted amongst each other before knowing smiles crossed their faces. She wondered who might speak first, thinking perhaps it would be Sylvie, but it was Babs who took over.

"I was recruited by Mace from CIA special ops," Babs said, catching Pippa by surprise. "So, I guess I can speak to the mind of a Keeper. They're not looking for a clingy, little woman who just wrings their hands every time something doesn't go their way. Yes, it's in their nature to protect. But they also need someone who can keep up with them. Mentally. Intellectually. Emotionally. Someone that understands the demands of their career and yet has their own interests, as well." Babs twirled her finger around at all the women sitting on the deck. "Each of you may have met your significant other while being rescued, but none of you sat around crying, 'Poor me.' You jumped in, did what you needed to do, showed extraordinary courage, and never gave up. And that's exactly what Keepers needed when they were all special ops. And they need that in their significant others. Someone who'll watch their six."

Pippa hoped her mouth hadn't hung open as she'd listened to Babs' words, but one look around told her that the other women were equally surprised.

Sylvie clapped, nodding. "Damn, Babs, I couldn't have said it better myself." Turning back to Pippa, she said, "Does that answer your question?"

Nodding, Pippa smiled, her cheeks hurting from the wide grin. Moving to sit with the rest of them, she looked forward to the opportunity to know them better. *And maybe, just maybe, when this is all over, I'll truly be part of them.*

22

Josh was ready to go home. In previous years, he would stay at the compound until the wee hours of the night, working on intel. Since equipping the bunker, he'd often head home when the others left, just to disappear into his bunker until falling asleep. Now, all he wanted to do was go home and see Pippa.

But it was thinking of her and wanting her safe that kept his ass in the seat. After seeing the gate's security cameras at Mark's neighborhood, they knew that both Hank and Pippa's vehicles had left Mark Sinclair's property. Since they were obviously not driving them, someone had removed them out of sight, but the odds of it being Mark and Sid were nil considering they weren't seen coming back in.

Turning to the others, he scrubbed his hand over his face. "What if the enforcer, Peter Balk, got off the boat with Demetri in Brunswick, immediately got into his vehicle, and drove to Camden? Middle of the night, he can make it in an hour. The plan could have been for him to deal with Pippa. Probably to... Jesus... kill her and then drive her vehicle back through the gate, making it look like she'd left. He'd dispose of her body, drive her car and take it to a designated junkyard." Sighing heavily, he added, "Shit... Hank's car."

"Yeah, he'd need someone else to get Hank's car at the same time," Drew agreed. "So, two of them?"

"But why?" Tate asked. "They wouldn't know about Hank before they left Brunswick."

"Travel in pairs," Cobb surmised. "Maybe someone in the Bratva training. Maybe just for extra muscle."

"So, the enforcer has someone with him," Rick surmised. "They probably figured it would be easier for one to drive Pippa's car out of the main gate. When they got there, they needed both of them just to take care of Hank's car, as well."

Blake nodded slowly, rubbing his chin. "So, while they're on their way to Camden, Mark and Sid take care of Hank. Now the enforcer has got to deal with two vehicles and no bodies. His plan changes to deal with Hank's car the way they were originally going to deal with Pippa's, only now he has to make a second dump."

"Makes sense. If they ran into any trouble, they would have been able to take care of it easier with the two of them," Carson said. As the others looked toward him, he added, "Just call it past experience more than intuition."

Josh squeezed his eyes tightly shut, leaning his head back. "This is fuckin' killing me. Shit, I don't know how you all did this."

"You just keep working the problem to keep her safe," Mace advised. "That's all that matters."

"Do you think Hank's body got dumped into the ocean?" Carson asked.

"Maybe," Josh replied. "It would make sense. They panicked. Don't want to deal with a body on land. It was dark. It was raining. They could weigh it down and toss it overboard. There's no way they'd want to take Hank's body very far, risking everything."

"Send everything to Thatcher," Mace ordered Levi. Looking around, he said, "Since we're now officially working with the FBI, I say we make a little midnight trip to Sinclair's yacht. Who's in?"

Josh chuckled. As usual, there was no shortage of hands in the air. Mace turned his attention to him. "Get home and into the bunker. We'll want Pippa in on this. She can guide us through the yacht. It'll make it quicker."

Pippa stared at the computer screen, fascinated at what she was witnessing. Josh had audio and video from Rank and Walker, who'd slipped in through the woods and boarded Mark's yacht. She'd never watched video through night-vision goggles before, making her focus more intently on what she was viewing.

Josh glanced over toward her. "Talk them through it."

Nodding, she spoke into the microphone. "At the bottom of the stairs from the main deck is a living room. To the left is a hall leading to the galley. On the right is the hall to the three cabins. The first one on the left is where I was, and the one on the right is where Hank was strangled." She watched them as they followed her lead, seeing their view through their night vision goggles. "Yes, right there. His body was just inside the doorway."

"Drag marks on the carpet," Rank reported. "Plus, the back of the door is scuffed as though kicked."

"Hank's feet were close to the door." Wincing, she looked toward Josh.

"Focus, babe," he said softly. "Nothing you can do for him now other than help nail Mark and Sid."

She nodded, sucking in a deep breath, then let it out slowly. Josh was right—she needed to keep her head focused.

"Going to get a recording of the vessel's locations. We know it was near Josh's when Hank was killed based on the time Pippa went overboard," Walker reported.

She watched as Rank and Walker looked around before they ascended the stairs again then continued upward to the wheelhouse, waiting in silence as the two Keepers easily discovered the yacht's computerized logging. They transferred the information to a drive, then pulled out a small box, plugged it in, and she blinked as Josh began downloading the information. "Wow, you really do have the best toys."

He grinned and leaned over for a quick kiss before their attention moved back to Rank and Walker as they exited the yacht, slipped through the darkness, and disappeared into the woods. Once they were safe, she twisted around in her chair, placing her hands on Josh's knees.

"You okay?" he asked.

She nodded slowly. "Yeah, you're right about focus. I can't change the past. And being here with you makes all the difference."

"They'll get the info back to the compound and then can start trying to determine the location of the yacht when Hank was killed based on the time you gave us and how close you were to this property when you jumped off. So, there's nothing we need to do right now until that information comes in tomorrow."

His smile widened as he kissed her again, this time longer and wetter. Leaning back, she batted her eyes with exaggerated flirtation. "So... what's next on the agenda for tonight?"

His tongue darted out to trace her lips. "I can think of one or two things for us to do, but I don't know if that will go on an official agenda."

"Then maybe we can just make our own agenda," she mumbled against his lips. "We could call it our naked agenda."

He stood quickly, scooping her up into his arms. She squealed at the sudden motion, then laughed. He carried her outside, then set her down to check all the locks and alarms on the bunker. She linked fingers with his, and they raced back up to the house. While he locked the door, she began stripping as she headed upstairs. By the time they fell into bed, they were both very ready for their "naked agenda."

It felt strange to work in the bunker without Josh but only because she preferred his company. Glancing around at the concrete walls, piped-in air, regulated temperature, and utilitarian furniture, Pippa knew many people would feel claustrophobic. But for her, she was thrilled with the chance to do the work she loved in an environment that was already established.

When she'd added cybersecurity to her degree, it was originally to have another avenue to pad her resume. But after having the chance to see the type of work that Josh and LSI accomplished, a fire had been lit inside of her that made her itch to combine her computer science degree for investigations. *Okay, perhaps the fact that I'm in the middle of this mess has some-thing to do with that!* But even with that acknowledg-ment, she loved the programs at her fingertips.

Glancing back at the screen, she sighed. *Okay, maybe not so much loving the financial spreadsheets of Senator Sinclair.* Josh was needed at LSI today for his work on other cases as well as hers, but he'd hooked her up with Cobb. Josh had explained that both Cobb and Josie came from political families, so he'd be able to answer any questions she might have.

Earlier, when the numbers had begun to run together, she'd taken a break and walked around the bunker. Glancing into the room with the bed, she'd grinned, memories flooding back. *Was that just a few days ago?* Once again, time had ceased to matter between her and Josh.

Sitting back down in front of the monitors, she shifted her focus for a few minutes to the social media account of the senator, containing plenty of pictures of him and Sid. Josh had told her what they'd said about Hank and her. Hot fury ran through her at their duplicity. *They're involved in something illegal, and Hank didn't want to go along with it. They killed him, planned on killing me, and have the audacity to say we went off together!*

Flipping through the pictures online, her fingers halted over the keys as an image snagged her attention, one of the many photographs of the smiling senator shaking hands with constituents at a marina. It was a woman standing off to the side that captured her attention. She could clearly see that the woman was from the yacht. With digital focusing, it appeared most people were wearing a stick-on/peel-off name badge. Enlarging and focusing more, the name didn't match the person. Shana Larkin, Bakerton Distributors. *Bakerton.* Using facial recognition, she discovered the true identity of the woman: Sonya Lipovsky.

With a shove, she rolled her chair to another station, quickly pulling up the financial logs she'd looked at earlier. Scrolling through what felt like thousands, she found what she was looking for. Sonya Lipovsky had been a major campaign donor for Mark Sinclair. But the money didn't show up in all the public records. Pressing her lips together, she leaned back. *They're a front... maybe for laundering money... maybe for payoffs for political favors... maybe...*

Typing in Bakerton Distributors, she ran into a

cyber roadblock, uncertain how to proceed. Hoping that Josh wouldn't mind her calling, she quickly dialed.

"Hey, Pippa. What's up?"

For a second, she blanked out everything other than the way he seemed happy at her call and the way her heart leaped at the sound of his voice.

"Pippa?"

"Oh, sorry. I didn't know if this was a bad time or not, but I wanted to let you know something I'd found out. I didn't know how to call Cobb directly or if I should." She shook her head slightly, hating the way she babbled.

"No worries," Josh assured. "I'll put you on speaker since Cobb is right here."

"I need to find out more about Bakerton Distributors. They're a major campaign donor to Mark Sinclair, but when I follow the trail of money, it seems to get lost. And I run into roadblocks when I try to find out more about them."

"Pippa, this is Cobb. Any special reason you're suspicious? Anything in particular I need to look for?"

"I came across a picture of Mark at a campaign event. What caught my eye was a woman standing in the background, and when I enlarged the photograph, I could see that her name tag said she was from Bakerton Distributors and her name was listed as Shana Larkin. But I recognized her. She was the woman from the yacht that night. I used facial recognition and identified her as Sonya Lipovsky."

She could hear whistling in the background and wondered what was happening. Josh jumped on and said, "Great job, babe. Let us work it from here. I'll let you know what I find."

They disconnected and she sat for a moment, a sigh slipping out. She loved working but wished there was more she could do. *I feel like I've been a student forever. And even when I get a job, I'll be the newbie, still learning.* She dropped her chin to her chest. *I'll be the oldest newbie in the history of the world.*

Standing quickly, she stalked to the bunker door, the need for fresh air to blow out the depressing cobwebs overwhelming. Securing the bunker, she walked around to the back of the house where the large deck overlooked the water. Bypassing the deck, she walked to the edge of Josh's yard where the grass ended at the path curving down toward the thin strip of beach. With his house behind her and tall trees around his property, she could only see nature. Closing her eyes, she lifted her face to the sun and spread her arms wide. Breathing deeply, she felt a calm return.

Casting her gaze back over the water, she watched the boats in the distance, a couple of sailboats, several commercial fishing vessels, and a few smaller boats closer to the shore. A yacht moved into her line of vision, and the little sliver of peace she'd just found fled at the reminder of Mark's yacht and what had occurred less than a week ago. Even with the sun still beaming, a shiver ran up her spine. It ached to drag air into her lungs at the idea that Hank's body was somewhere near where she'd jumped into the water and the realization of how close she'd come to joining him there.

Suddenly, feeling exposed on the open embankment

in front of Josh's home, she turned and hurried onto the deck and let herself into the house. Glancing at the clock, she sighed, wondering when Josh would come home and hating that her confinement kept her from participating in her normal life.

23

Josh jogged up the steps leading into the kitchen, going back on a foot when Pippa leaped into his arms. He'd never been greeted with such exuberance but wasn't complaining. Her legs wrapped around his waist, her arms held his shoulders tight, her body pressed close to his, and her lips sealed over his mouth, threatening to steal his breath as well as his heart.

Kissing her back, all thoughts fled other than wanting to be inside her as fast as they could get their clothes off, but he'd hit the LSI weight room while one of his programs was taking its sweet time to run through all the databases. He knew he needed a shower, but as he stalked toward the stairs with her hot body grinding against his crotch, the idea of shower sex slammed into him.

Carrying her easily up the stairs, he continued through the master bedroom and into the bath, only letting go with one hand to reach in and flip on the water. She leaned back slightly, an adorably confused expression on her face.

"I need a shower," he announced, figuring it was an unnecessary proclamation since he was still sweaty. "Want to get clean with me?"

Her top teeth landed on her bottom, upwardly curving lip, and she slowly nodded. "Only if we can get dirty first."

Grinning, he bounced her slightly in his arms, and she took the hint, dropping her legs. Still holding her close, he slid his hands down to the bottom of her T-shirt and drew it upward, watching as each inch of skin was exposed. His fingers glided over her silky skin, his senses already firing on overload. Her scent. Her feel. Her smile. The light in her eyes.

Tossing her top to the floor, it was joined by his as he snatched it over his head, and her bra was quickly added to the pile. She was already barefoot, and he leaned over to unlace his boots, toeing them off.

Now only a foot apart, both naked from the waist up, they halted, each drinking their fill as their gazes roved. Then suddenly, as though a switch had been flipped, they bolted into action, each shucking their pants and underwear until they were naked. Leaning past her, he pulled a condom packet from the drawer next to the sink. Seeing her lifted brow, he chuckled. "After our first time, I stored them all over the house. Figured it would be good to have them close by."

She threw her head back and laughed. "Always prepared. Such a Boy Scout."

Hating the scant distance between them, he wrapped

his arms around her and pulled her close. He stepped inside the shower, allowing the water to hit his back. "This Scout wants you close so hop up, babe," he softly ordered.

With her hands on his shoulders and his on her hips, she acquiesced, wrapping her legs around his waist, again nestling her sex against his eager cock. For only a second, he hesitated as the mechanics of shower sex seemed uncertain. Wanting leverage to make sure she was comfortable, he pressed her back against the now-warm tiles. If her smile was anything to judge by, she was good to go, but he had to check. "Babe, I've never had sex this way, and I don't want to hurt you."

"Remember what I told you our first time?" she asked, her lips nibbling along his jaw.

His brain, close to short-circuiting, had no problem remembering. "You said the only thing I could do to hurt you was to stop."

She nibbled her way around his lips, dragging her tongue over his stubble. "Same thing applies right now."

With her back against the wall and her legs spread wide, he slipped one forearm under her thigh, exposing her even more. Holding her with ease, he settled her down until he was fully sheathed deep inside her sex. His eyes nearly rolled back into his head at the feel of her tight muscles gripping him. The need to move battled the desire to stay connected exactly as they were. Finally, she wiggled, and he took the hint. Her body was crying out for friction, and he wanted to give everything he could to her.

Pumping his hips, he thrust deep before sliding his

other forearm under her thigh, opening her even wider. Her fingers dug into the muscles of his shoulders, and with her ankles crossed around his hips, he was barely aware of the pounding of the water against his ass with her heels digging in.

Dark tendrils of her hair, wet from the steam, lay about her shoulders and curled around the tops of her breasts. He bent slightly to suck deeply on one nipple before kissing his way over to the other.

Moans escaped her lips as the air fled her lungs with each thrust, and each puff of air that hit his face spurred him on to take her over the edge. Neither leaned in to kiss, and he wasn't sure they'd be able to with the way they were gasping. Her groans melded with his grunts, the sounds almost desperate as they clung to each other.

Finally, she flung back against the tile, but before he could ask if she was okay, her eyes widened as her grip tightened and, through gritted teeth, she cried out. Certain that he'd never seen anything sexier than this woman falling apart in his arms as his cock thrust deep inside, her inner muscles had just eased their grip when he roared out his own release.

Continuing to pump until he was drained, he pulled one arm from underneath her thigh and pressed his hand flat against the tile next to her head. Uncertain he could move and certain he didn't care, he rested his forehead against hers as they dragged in ragged breaths.

Once rational thought began to creep past the heady glow of orgasm, he moved his other arm, gently slid his cock from her sex, and kept her steady until her feet were on the floor of the shower and her legs held her upright.

"Is this much sex normal?" she asked, laughing before holding his gaze, the mirth slowing.

Neither spoke for a long moment, but volumes between them were said as their eyes devoured each other. He pulled her in close, and as she rested her cheek on his chest, he cradled her in his arms. "It's never been like this, Pippa. I've never felt like this."

She leaned back, peered up at him, and he could have sworn tears were in her eyes. "Me either." She swallowed deeply, "And that scares me."

He knew exactly what she was saying, and the depth of his feelings for her so quickly scared him, too. Not willing to give false promises, he simply said, "Whatever this is… whatever we feel… I'm not willing to give up on it. I want to see it through, ride it out." He saw questions move through her eyes but kept going, not wanting her to voice them. "What I do know is this isn't just because of the mission. We may have met in the most unusual way, but that doesn't make this any less real."

He held his breath as her eyes searched his, but her lips curved in a beautiful smile, and his heart squeezed with the hope that he'd see that smile every day. Stepping out of the shower, he blurted, "I've got something for you."

She tilted her head to the side, her towel slowly moving over her body.

He reached down to his pants pocket and pulled out

a small box. Opening it, he picked up a silver chain from which dangled a silver lighthouse charm.

She gasped. "Oh, my God, Josh. A lighthouse. It's beautiful."

"It's special, babe." He fastened the chain about her neck, allowing the charm to nestle just above her cleavage. With his forefinger gently touching it, feeling the heat of her skin already warming the metal, he smiled. "There's a tracker inside. It will allow me to always know where you are... just for protection. The other Keeper women have one, as well."

Her top teeth landed on her bottom lip, but they curved upward anyway. "You can keep up with me?"

He cleared his throat, suddenly uncertain. "I have a confession to make."

Once more, her head tilted in silent question.

"The first night you were here, I knew something major was happening to you and I put a tracer in the waistband of your pants, just in case you left and I needed to find you. I know it was invasive, but babe, I wanted to protect you and wasn't sure you would be able to protect yourself." Her eyes bugged, and he plowed forward. "Of course, you've been in different pants since then, so I haven't had a tracer on you. But," he shrugged, "it seemed important to confess that to you."

She held his gaze then looked past him toward the mirror. He shifted around so that he was behind her, his arms wrapped around her waist. Staring at her naked beauty with the lighthouse necklace dangling between her breasts, his breath caught in his throat. "You're so fuckin' beautiful, Pippa."

"I was just thinking that we looked beautiful together." Her voice was soft, and her smile filled his heart once again. *Yeah... I want to see that smile every day.*

"Cobb? Can we find a connection?" Josh knew the tone of his voice when he'd asked the question was the reason Cobb's left eyebrow lifted. Sighing, he tossed his pen down. "Fuckin' hell, I'm sorry."

"I've got Pippa on your end in the bunker, and we're close. But you know the FBI isn't going to sanction going after a state senator if we don't have the tie-in to nail him down," Cobb replied.

"What's really going on, Josh?" Tate asked. "You're always the cool, level-headed one. Follow the trail, that's what you always say, and then you go digging to find it."

He glanced over, seeing the other Keepers' attention on him. He wanted to shake his head and tell them nothing, admit to nothing. But that wasn't how LSI rolled. "It's Pippa. She's been great about everything considering what all she's been through. But it's getting harder, and her mood this morning during breakfast was… not so great."

Drew nodded. "Let me tell you about—"

"Honeybunch, love of my life. Shut the hell up." Babs shot Drew a glare. "If you say one word about women and moods, you'll be sleeping on the couch!"

Drew's eyes widened, and he made a motion of

zipping his lip. When the others stopped laughing, she turned toward Josh. "Look, there are no secrets around here. I could tell yesterday that you two were already an item."

Josh wanted to protest but kept his mouth shut, knowing the others would see right through him. Plus, Babs was on a roll, and he'd learned early on it was best to let her keep going.

"She's fit for a Keeper, and you know I wouldn't say that about just anyone. She managed to save herself, keep her cool, and jump right in to figure out what's going on. Hell, she's practically a Keeper herself. But she's been in hiding for five days. Her professor, boss, fellow students, landlord, and anyone else she used to talk to don't even know she's alive. For all they know, she ran off somewhere. So, even though the two of you have started something good, part of her has to wonder if it's even real because her life is on hold."

Josh nodded, amazed at how succinctly Babs put into words exactly what Pippa had intimated this morning. "She hadn't planned on going to her graduation since she didn't have family there, but she wants to find out about getting her diploma. And she said she has some applications out but can't even access them to see if she's being called for any interviews. So yeah, when we're inside our little bubble in my house, it's great. But when she starts thinking of everything else, she wants the mission to move on."

"We all do," Mace said. "For the case, but mostly for you and Pippa. And I give my word, we're working on this."

Josh's phone vibrated, and he looked down and grinned. "And here she is." Connecting, he said, "Hey, babe."

"I think I've got it!" she cried.

"Putting you on speaker."

"Take a look at the subsidiaries of Bakerton Distributors. The smallest one in terms of IRS reporting is connected to C. Solari. That's Crystal Solari. That's Demetri's wife's maiden name."

"Holy shit!" Cobb exclaimed. "I can't believe we missed this."

"Not just us," Blake reminded him. "The FBI did, too."

Josh grinned. "Good work, Pippa."

"That's not all," she continued. "That subsidiary has offshore accounts. And one of the names listed on the account is S. Deerman. That has to be Sid!"

"That's where he's laundering the money coming from the Russians," Mace said, moving forward to stare at the financial records up on the screen.

"Josh?"

"Yeah, babe?"

"This doesn't tie in Mark, though."

"Don't worry about that. We're getting closer." It was on the tip of his tongue to say that she would soon have her life back, but that thought stabbed at his heart. *What if it didn't include him?*

24

"I've been looking at Hank's campaign accounts, and I can't see where he did anything wrong. I know you had someone there look at his personal accounts, and... well, I wonder if his wife would know anything." Pippa and Josh sat at his counter eating lunch after he'd run home to check on her.

"Like what?"

"Like if Hank had any suspicions of what Mark and Sid were doing."

"The FBI talked to her yesterday. They even took his home computer and laptop. According to Thatcher, they didn't find anything on it. We even tried to talk to her this morning."

"What did she say?" A surge of excitement filled her. Finding the link between Sid and the money trail had been the only elation she'd felt since Josh had left that morning.

He stopped chewing and shook his head. "Sid got to her."

Gasping, her hand snapped out to land on his arm. "Oh, my God—"

"No, no! Fuck, Pippa, I'm sorry! I just meant that he talked to her."

Her breath rushed from her lungs, relief for a woman she'd never met spearing through her. "Oh, thank God." When her heart stopped racing, she lifted her gaze back to Josh. "What did he say?"

"She wasn't talking about her husband. Sid Deerman had told her that he'd possibly gone off with a woman server from their trip."

"That asshole! What a horrible thing to say to her." She closed her eyes, and the vision of Hank standing on the deck nibbling on hors d'oeuvres came to mind. He'd seemed quiet, mild-mannered. Probably secure in his job and yet next to the enigmatic senator rather plain. The idea that his wife still didn't know what had happened to her husband but had been lied to made Pippa wonder if she could keep her lunch down. "I need to do something, Josh. I can't just sit here any longer. I need to talk to her."

Josh stared at her as though she had two heads. "No way, babe. You can't—"

"I swear if you tell me 'I can't' do something one more time, I'm going to lose my mind!" She glared even as she knew her threat was empty. Sighing heavily, she blinked back tears. "Sorry... I'm just..."

He wiped his mouth before turning on the stool to capture her knees between his thighs. Placing his hands on her shoulders, he sighed, as well. "Okay, listen, babe. I know you're going stir-crazy. And all I want to do is wrap you in a protective cover until this fuckin' mess is over."

"Josh, I know you're worried, and I don't want to do anything to put myself or any of you in danger. But I'd love to help. She deserves to know. And I'm the only one who can tell her. Josh, please. Think of how you'd feel if someone you love was missing and you didn't know if they were alive or dead or had run off with someone. You'd need that closure."

This time, he stared at her for a long time, anguish slashing across his features, his fingers flexing on her shoulders. Finally, he said, "I'll talk to Mace. But it's his call, Pippa. He says no, then it's no."

She nodded her head in jerks, then watched as he pulled out his phone and moved to the other room. Wondering if she was crazy for even considering the idea of coming out of hiding, she pushed those thoughts away. *Hank's wife deserves to know.*

Two hours later, she found herself in the back of an LSI SUV, having promised to do exactly as she was told, when she was told, and how she was told. She didn't even care that Josh was super bossy, knowing he just wanted her protected. She sat in the back between Josh and the FBI agent, Louis Thatcher. Knox and Blake were in the front, and during the forty-five-minute drive, she listened as they discussed the case, including the instructions they gave her.

Pulling into the driveway of the modest home in an older neighborhood where each brick house was unique and mature trees filled the yards, nerves suddenly struck. Not wanting to give voice to her reservations, she wished Josh and Blake good luck, watching them head to the front door with Thatcher. Knox stayed behind the wheel, but Blake pulled out his tablet. With a few taps, she watched the video and audio from Josh's mini-camera.

A middle-aged woman, her face haggard and eyes red-rimmed, answered the door. Her gaze narrowed on Thatcher, her expression immediately hardening.

"Mrs. Carlsdale? I know we spoke earlier, but we have new information to share. This is Mr. Appleton from Lighthouse Security Investigations, working with us on the case of your husband."

She stood in the doorway, not letting them in. "And I believe, Agent Thatcher, that I've given you everything I can. I've been informed that my husband's situation may not be as I had feared."

"Mrs. Carlsdale, we know that Sid Deerman has spoken to you, but his information is incorrect."

"And why should I believe you?"

Pippa held her breath as she waited to see what Josh was going to answer.

Finally, he replied, "Because the woman in question has been with me."

Betty's eyes narrowed, her gaze assessing.

Before she had a chance to say anything, Josh continued. "We have her with us if you'd like a chance to talk to her."

A gasp slipped from her lips as her gaze darted beyond the men on her doorstep and moved to the dark tinted-windowed SUV. She remained perfectly still for a moment and then offered a curt nod, stepping back.

Blake climbed from the SUV and opened the door for Pippa. "Remember... straight in. Answer questions and don't give personal information."

Pippa nodded and stayed right next to him as they followed Josh and Thatcher into the comfortable living room. She immediately noticed family pictures on the wall and shelves, and her heart squeezed.

Thatcher turned and said, "This is the woman who was on the yacht trip with your husband. She was the server and has been with this investigator since that night."

"So, you didn't leave with my husband?"

Pippa shook her head after glancing toward Josh. "No, Mrs. Carlsdale, I didn't. What I can tell you is that your husband was a perfect gentleman during the entire event. He barely drank, thanked me for providing food, and mostly just seemed to be listening as the others were talking."

"So, you have no idea where he is?"

Thatcher had prepared her, but staring at the ravaged expression of Hank's wife, she swallowed deeply. "No, I can't say that I know where he is. But I can tell you that I've been with this man," she said nodding toward Josh, "since that night." She watched as a tear slid down Betty's cheek, and she reached out, taking the other woman's arm. Ignoring the instructions she'd been given, she acted on impulse. One hurting woman to another.

Leading Betty over to the sofa, Pippa gently pulled her down next to her, turned so that she was facing Betty slightly, and held the other woman's hands together on their knees. "Please understand there's a lot I can't say because of the FBI investigation. But just know that if Mr. Deerman told you that your husband left with me, he's lying."

Betty held Pippa's gaze for a long, silent moment before sucking in a deep breath and letting it out slowly. "There's a lot you're not telling me, and I understand even though it's killing me to not know everything. But there's also a lot you're telling me."

Pippa nodded. "Yes, what I'm telling you is that Sid. Is. Lying."

"A man who lies about something like this is protecting himself," Betty said.

Surprised, Pippa remained quiet but nodded again. Betty looked away, turmoil obvious as she grimaced several times. Finally, she pulled her hands away from Pippa's and stood. She left the room, and Pippa glanced to the others, seeing their gazes on Betty's retreat. Remaining where she was, she took to her feet as soon as Betty reappeared in the room.

Ignoring the men, Betty walked straight to Pippa. Standing in front of her, she held her gaze. "My husband was an honorable man. I've always known that, and I'm ashamed that I, in my distress, allowed someone else to try to convince me differently. I don't know what's going on, but a few months ago, Hank told me that he was storing information on a drive and that if I was ever in doubt, to turn it over to the authorities. I laughed, thinking he was being overly dramatic. But now, I think it's important that I give it to you."

She lifted her hand, and Pippa reached out to take

what was offered. Betty dropped a thumb drive into Pippa's palm. Breathing deeply again, Betty turned to look at the men standing nearby, her chin quivering as another tear slid down her cheek. "Agent Thatcher, I need to know what happened to Hank."

He stepped closer, and she reached out to grab Pippa's hand again. "Mrs. Carlsdale, we don't have proof, but there's been a report that your husband may have been killed. The agency is taking it seriously, and we are actively working to determine if the report is true, and if so, where he is."

She swallowed deeply, and Pippa held on tightly, hoping to offer strength.

"Then I won't keep you from your investigation, Agent Thatcher. But I do expect to be kept in the loop of everything you find out."

"Ma'am, you have my promise." He handed her his card then glanced toward Pippa, offering a slight chin lift before stepping back with Josh and Blake.

Turning so that she was directly in front of Betty, Pippa held her gaze and squeezed her hands. "There's little I can do right now, but please, as soon as the investigation is over, I hope you'll call me."

"Thank you," Betty whispered, returning the fingers squeeze before letting go.

Pippa pressed her lips together in an attempt to quell the threatening tears. Turning, she walked directly toward Josh and was quickly surrounded by the three men as they left the Carlsdale residence and hurried back into the SUV.

Josh wrapped his arm around her, and she rested her

head on his shoulder as Knox began the drive back to LSI.

"I know that was hard, babe," Josh said softly.

Knowing if she spoke the tears would come, she simply nodded.

Blake glanced to the back, his assessing gaze scanning her before shifting over to Josh. "She's fuckin' amazing, you know?"

"You don't have to tell me," Josh replied.

"Hell, I didn't think I was ready, but after seeing that, I hope my time is next," Knox called out from the front seat.

"Your girl has got it going on, that's for sure," Thatcher said.

Sitting up straighter, she huffed. "You all do realize that I'm sitting right here, right? I can hear everything you say, right?"

Josh chuckled, and she whipped her head around to glare. He pulled her back into his embrace. "Looks like you're one of us now, Pippa. So you'd better get used to the teasing."

A small grin slipped across her face. As heart wrenching as her meeting with Betty had been, she loved the camaraderie of the Keepers.

25

Josh stood by the side of the bed for several minutes, staring at Pippa as she slept. When they'd gotten home yesterday, she shunned the congratulations coming from the other Keepers, falling into a quiet sadness that permeated her whole being. Tearful, she'd admitted that being with Betty, knowing Hank was dead and not being able to confirm that fully for her, had been difficult. He'd held her close, hoping to offer what strength he could.

When she'd turned to him in the night wanting to make love, he'd hesitated until she'd said, "I want to feel alive... alive with you, Josh." With that, he would have given her anything. They'd made love—slowly, gently, tenderly, with whispered promises and vows. When they fell asleep wrapped around each other, he knew he wanted her in his house, in his bed, and in his heart.

Now, after she'd slept through an early morning call he'd received, he couldn't bear to leave without a kiss.

Bending, he gently placed his lips on hers, smiling as she blinked her eyes open.

"Sorry, babe, but I've been called in. I just wanted you to know."

She sat up, rubbing her eyes before reaching out to place her hand on his arm. "What's going on?"

"Seems like your efforts with Betty worked wonders for the investigation. Cobb analyzed the drive with the FBI, and it was as we hoped—a backup of the suspicions that Hank had. He'd noticed problems with the money for a while and was trying to gather evidence."

"Oh," she sighed. "If he had just gotten off the yacht without showing his hand, he might still be alive."

"You're right, but I think Sid and Mark courting the Russian mob was just more than Hank could take," he said.

"But why do you have to leave at…" she turned to look at the clock on the nightstand, "four o'clock in the morning?"

"We're taking the boats out this morning, and I need to get the computers up and running."

"Boats?" she asked, a crinkle forming between her brows.

"Seems like more is happening. Thatcher called Mace to tell him that with the coordinates from the yacht that we copied, your witness statement, and the proximity of my property, the FBI has an area offshore they want divers to check out for Hank's body."

"But how do they know his body was tossed overboard?"

By now, she appeared fully awake, and her eyes were

bright with interest. He smiled, his heart full as he knew what he'd been missing and what most of the other Keepers had found. Someone that *got* him and his work. And someone who wanted to be part of that world. "Christ, I'm falling for you, Pippa," he blurted, not caring if they'd only met six days ago.

She blinked, her mouth falling open as a little gasp slipped out. "Seriously?"

Now uncertain of her reaction to his honest declaration, he plunged ahead. "Yeah, babe, I am."

Her lips curved until her smile speared the left side of his chest.

"Well, good because I've already fallen and was afraid it was all too soon."

Shaking his head, he kissed her again, this time deeply. "Nothing too soon about love." He stood, and she tossed back the covers and leaped out of bed, rushing to stand in front of him.

"Wait!" she cried. "You haven't told me about Hank!"

"Oh, yeah. Seems the FBI picked up Mark Sinclair last night for questioning. He fell apart and started singing. Says the whole scheme was Sid's idea, and he was unaware of the money laundering. He admitted to panicking and helping Sid toss Hank's body overboard but said it was Sid who strangled Hank."

"Oh, my God! What about Sid?"

"Seems he's in the wind."

Her brow scrunched as she tilted her head to the side.

"The FBI is looking for him, but he's gone into

hiding for now. Don't worry, they'll get him. He can't run forever."

Eyes wide, she breathed, "Wow." With her hands on his shoulders, she lifted on her toes and offered her mouth, an offering he readily accepted. As she settled her heels back onto the floor, she asked, "So, what are you doing this morning? Working the computers in the bunker or at LSI?"

"Neither. I'll be on one of the boats with the information our former SEAL guys need for their dive. Based on our approximations, we have about a five-mile area not too far off the coast that we're going to look at."

Sucking in her lips, she glanced toward the bedroom's sliding glass door that overlooked the water. "But couldn't his body have drifted, or floated out to sea, or... I don't know."

"We've got cameras specifically fitted for undersea vision. Our guys will only go in if there's something we ping."

"Why can't the FBI or Coast Guard do this?"

He laughed, then bent to kiss her lightly. "You sure woke up with a lot of questions."

"Hmph," she groused, narrowing her eyes. "Well, don't wake me up if you don't want me to know what's happening.

He kissed her pout away. "We're contracted with FBI and are their support right now."

"Maybe I could help."

"Not this time, babe. We've got what we need. All you need to do today is relax, enjoy the sunshine on the coast, and think about where you'd like to go when I take you out on our first date."

Her eyes widened and her smile beamed. "Really? A date?" Laughing, she added, "I guess we went about things backward, didn't we?"

Holding her close, he mumbled against her lips. "Might have been backward but no less real." Their kiss wasn't light as they poured everything they felt into the connections—finally, they separated, breathing hard.

"You need to go," she whispered, "so you can come back."

With a final touch of their lips, he turned and headed out to his vehicle, glad for waking her up before he left and wondering if that could be a new habit for them.

With Clay in the wheelhouse of their thirty-foot boat, Josh was below deck, staring at the cameras and running the computer equipment as they traveled slowly in a grid over the area where they were most likely to find Hank's body. Blake was in the wheelhouse of their other boat, and between the two crafts, the other Keepers, Carson, Thatcher, and several more FBI agents watched, as well.

"How long do you think this will take?" one of the agents asked.

Josh caught a glimpse of Thatcher shooting a glare toward the young agent.

"As long as it takes, Roselli," Thatcher barked. "Why don't you go up on deck and make yourself useful?"

Josh stifled a grin, knowing there was no way the young agent had been former military. *Hell, I could wait all day just knowing in the end, we'll prevail.*

"Sorry about that," Thatcher said.

"Don't worry about him. Young and green," Bray said, standing nearby.

Josh shot a quick look toward Thatcher before shifting his gaze back to the screen. "Got anything else from Sinclair?"

"Not yet. As soon as he realized we didn't have a body, he lawyered up."

"Well, let's hope we get one for you today," Josh said.

Carson stood nearby, his expression tight as he stared at the cameras along with Josh. "I can see why Mace recruits from the pool that he does. I had a few bodyguards that were little more than bouncers with no military training when I just had a security business in LA. It didn't take long to find out that they had more brawn than brains. Thought being a bodyguard to someone famous was going to get them a movie contract. Some of them couldn't believe it when they actually had to work in a job where no one paid any attention to them."

Josh openly grinned this time and nodded, keeping his eyes trained on the two camera feeds coming in. "Sounds like the new LSI business will be right up your alley. As Mace says, hire the right people who will get the jobs done without looking for glory, and the contracts will keep rolling in."

The sound of a signal brought his attention to the camera from his boat. Immediately tapping on his keyboard, he worked the program to focus the image, leaning closer to the screen. "Keeper One has a signal and a visual."

"Copy that," Blake radioed in return.

Thatcher leaned over Josh's shoulder. "Can you tell what it is?"

Moving the camera around for a better angle, he enlarged the image, continuing to focus. "Looks like rope tied around a tarp. The size and shape would approximate a human body." Without looking up, he asked, "What do you want to do?"

He gave Thatcher a moment as the experienced agent nodded slowly. "I agree with your assessment. Radio for the divers."

"Keeper One, come alongside us. Keeper One and Keeper Two, Agent Thatcher is calling for the divers."

The other Keepers on his boat pulled up their tablets, taking a look at the object to be retrieved. Rank, Walker, Tate, Cobb, and Rick were all former SEALs, and while the others were certified divers with Special Forces, Mace had tasked those five Keepers to be their divers for this mission.

The two boats pulled alongside each other, and Josh felt his vessel rock slightly as the five divers gathered on one boat.

Mace called over the radio, "LSI Six, divers ready."

"LSI Six, copy that. Sonar places object zero-point-eight kilometers below the surface. Use snag-line with jackstay. Direct from the surface."

As the five divers radioed their understanding, he felt the vessel rock again slightly as they made their way into the water. Each had a camera and lights attached to their full-face masks, so now Josh and the others were monitoring five more camera feeds along with the two from the boats.

"We're in luck that it's not too deep," Thatcher said.

"We were able to get tide and current directions from the Coast Guard, but the fact that they tossed the body when the winds were blowing toward the shore really helped."

"Why do you think they didn't turn to go deeper out to sea? That would have been the smart play," Roselli said, having made his way back from the deck, obviously not wanting to miss the action.

"You got to think like the murderers. Panicked. Scared. An un-premeditated murder means no plan had been made for disposing of the body. They most likely wanted to wrap it up, tie it up, and put some kind of weight on it so it would go below the surface, and that's all they thought about. Other than that, it was get it the fuck off the boat," Thatcher said to the nods of the others.

For the next hour, they watched as the divers swam in a pattern, finally calling out that they'd discovered the object. Bringing it slowly to the surface, everyone made their way to the deck as the tied, blanketed object was hoisted to the deck.

The Keepers stepped back, allowing Thatcher and the other agents to come forward. They immediately began collecting evidence, photographing, bagging, and tagging as they carefully loosened the ties and pulled the blanket back, exposing Hank Carlsdale's face.

Roselli was the only agent with a smile on his face as he fist-pumped the air, excited to be on the case. The other agents and Keepers stood quietly, chins to their chests as they acknowledged that while the case was moving forward, a good man who'd tried to document a crime and do the right thing had died.

"At least his wife will have closure," Carson said softly as he stood next to Josh. "And hopefully, your girl will, too."

Josh's mind was filled with thoughts of Pippa. While her interaction with Hank had been brief, after witnessing his murder, she would always be intrinsically connected to Betty, and her heart would ache for the other woman. *But, at least she'd be free... no more hiding. And they could move forward together.*

26

Pippa walked out onto the deck facing the water, breathing deeply. Her thoughts stayed firmly on Josh—what he was doing, what he was finding, and if the sea would give Betty any closure. Slowly turning in a circle, she allowed her gaze to drift over Josh's yard that still needed to be mowed, the woods around his property providing shade and shelter, the stone path that led down to the bunker where they'd spent time working and loving, and the blue, Victorian house that stood proudly on the knoll, as individual and unique as Josh himself. And she felt peace. She felt at home. Two things she hadn't felt in a very long time. She refused to ponder the short amount of time that she'd known him, choosing instead to focus on how right the world felt when she was with him.

The day was warm, and she pulled her long tresses into a ponytail, having slipped on a T-shirt and jeans. Her feet were bare, and she loved the feel of the sun-bathed wood of the deck beneath her toes.

Closing her eyes, she tilted her head back, loving the warmth of the sun on her face. The sound of water slapping against something hard met her ears, but as she looked out over the water in the distance, she could only see boats away from the shore. Curious, she walked toward the path that led down to the beach, the very one she'd traversed up to Josh's place six days ago.

As the beach came into view, she saw that a boat had anchored just off the surf, but there was no one around. Wondering if someone had decided this was an excellent fishing spot, she walked closer to the edge of the short cliff and peered downward.

"You weren't an easy woman to find."

At the voice coming from behind her, she whirled around, gasping as she stared into the face of a man she'd hoped to never see again. Sid Deerman. She jerked her gaze around, seeing no one else in the vicinity. Looking back at him, she stared in incredulity that he'd come out of hiding, knowing the FBI was searching for him. "What are you doing? Why are you here?"

He stepped closer, and as she took a step backward, she teetered slightly on the edge of the drop-off leading to the beach. As her arms windmilled to maintain her balance, he rushed forward, tackling her to the ground. She tried to escape, slapping, hitting, kicking in every direction, but his weight kept her movements to a minimum. A sharp prick jabbed into her neck, and she screamed, fearful that he'd stabbed her. The sting eased as her world slowed and his voice sounded farther and farther away. She stared up, blinking at the sunlight before her eyes closed. Her

last thought was wondering if she'd ever see Josh
again.

"How far away from your place are we?" Drew asked,
leaning back on one of the benches on Keeper One.

Hank's body had been taken to the harbor where
Thatcher and the other FBI agents were met by the
medical examiner to begin the process of evidence
gathering before transporting him to the hospital for
the autopsy. Now, the Keepers were kicked back and
relaxed as they made their way toward the LSI
compound where their two boats would be docked.

Josh looked toward the shore, recognizing the area.
"Not far. Just around the bend, about five miles north of
the lighthouse." He looked toward the others and
grinned. "Next get-together is at my place."

The others grinned their agreement, and Josh
blinked as spray splashed over them, the cool welcome
against the warm day. His phone vibrated, and he pulled
it from his pocket. Surprised at the tone of the alarm, he
recognized it as the alert he'd set for Pippa's locator
necklace. "What the fuck?"

"What's wrong?" Tate asked as the other Keepers
immediately focused their attention on Josh.

"It's Pippa. Her tracer alert is notifying me that she's
moving off the property."

Blake twisted to look over his shoulder. "She's
leaving?"

Jumping to his feet, disbelief filling him, he shook

his head. "No way... not without telling me first." *Not after everything we've said. Not after everything we feel.* Absolute resolve flooded him. "She wouldn't leave. Not voluntarily."

"Maybe one of the women came by to take her out," Levi volunteered.

"She would have let me know," he muttered, pulling up her location on his tablet. More disbelief raced through his veins as he tapped furiously. "Fuckin' hell! She's on the water!"

"What the hell?" Drew leaned over to look at the locator program on the tablet also.

"Someone's got her," Josh called out, his heart pounding as his mind raced through the possibilities.

"Bratva?" Clay asked.

Mace shook his head. "The Feds don't have Sid, and he's the one who killed Hank."

Levi pulled out his phone, immediately calling Thatcher.

The two Keeper boats circled around as Josh worked to get a lock on her location, his fingers shaking. *Shit, I gotta pull it together.* Breathing hard, he worked to steady his pounding heartbeat. Zeroing in, his breath whooshed out. "Christ almighty! She's moving away from the shore from my place, heading this way," he called out. Looking up, he cast his gaze around, desperately searching. He spied fishing boats and several personal boats of various sizes nearby. Dismissing the ones heading away from them, he shouted, "Shit, who the fuck is it?"

"Why the hell would Sid take her then bring her this

way when we're out here?" Drew, like the others, was on his feet, his gaze scanning the boats on the horizon.

"Our good luck and his dumb luck," Tate said.

"There!" Cobb shouted, pointing to a twenty-foot motorboat with a single person visible moving quickly in their direction but also angled out to sea.

"Change course," Mace called to Clay, who nodded in response, picking up his radio.

"Keeper Two. Change course. South-southeast. Keep motorboat in sights. Suspect Sid Deerman with Pippa as hostage."

Josh could hear the cursing from the others in his boat as well as the other LSI vessel, but grabbing the binoculars, all his focus was on the one visible occupant. "Where is she?" Looking back at his tablet, he knew they must have the right boat. *Pippa must be lying in the bottom of the boat.*

"Why the hell is he going farther out? Why not get away closer to the shore?" Blake yelled.

He's gonna dump her. He's gonna fuckin' dump her! As the thought hit his mind, he struggled to breathe. "He's... dump her..."

"Shit, he dumps her then takes off, he knows he'll get away 'cause we'll go after her!" Drew shouted over the sound of their motor roaring.

"Fuck that!" several Keepers cursed at the same time.

"Suit up!" Mace ordered.

The Keepers who'd dived for Hank immediately grabbed their diving gear as Blake and Clay raced after the smaller motorboat. As they closed the distance gap, Josh could now see a figure lying in the boat. Sid looked over his shoulders, his eyes wide and wild. With his hand coming off the steering, he whirled as he bent, his arms reaching out.

Josh watched in horror as Sid struggled to lift Pippa over the side. He moved to the side of the boat, ready to launch into the water after her if Sid succeeded. Her movements appeared sluggish, her weight heavy, keeping Sid from tossing her over the side. Sid stood and faced the approaching LSI boats, his face now twisted. Grabbing the steering again, he turned his boat around and gunned the motor, now coming straight for them.

"He's going to ram us!"

"Fuckin' suicide!" someone yelled, but Josh was barely able to hear over the pounding of his heartbeat.

"Take him out!" Mace yelled.

Weapons were in position, but Knox, a former sniper, lay on the top of the wheelhouse, his weapon aimed toward the approaching vessel. One shot rang out, echoing over the water, and Sid fell backward as Pippa struggled to sit up. Pippa toppled to the side as the speedboat continued forward.

"Shit!" Josh yelled, seeing her staring down at the undoubtedly dead man. At the speed they were traveling, they'd never be able to jump into her boat to bring it under control. And he had no idea if she knew how to slow the vessel down. Racing to the helm, he grabbed the radio, flipping it to megaphone. "Pippa! Pippa!"

27

Jostled hard, banging her head against a solid object, Pippa struggled to open her eyes, then blinked as the bright sun sent a piercing pain through her skull. Rolling to the side with difficulty, she battled nausea as her body bounced again.

The world seemed to fly by as her hair whipped about her in a frenzy, and she gasped as water doused her. Each movement took great effort, her body slow in obeying her mind. Sucking in great gulps of air, she focused on a man standing nearby, his hands on a steering wheel. Forcing her limbs to move, she pushed upward enough to realize she was speeding along on the water.

The man looked over his shoulder, his face contorted. *Sid!* He dropped next to her, his hands rough as he grabbed her, pulling as though to lift her from her position. Desperation filled her as she tried to kick out but her sluggish movements seemed to do little to keep him away. The boat lurched, and he dropped her, pain searing along her back as she fell against something hard. The pain seemed to jolt her more awake, and she forced her body to sit up again, but the boat was bouncing over waves, making even coordinated movement difficult.

Glancing toward Sid again, she felt the wind and cold water whipping against her face, causing her to blink furiously.

"We'll both go, bitch," Sid called out over his shoulder.

Confusion hit again as she tried to make sense of his words. The rush of air increased as the boat bounced higher. Looking beyond him, she spied two large boats nearby. *He's too close!* Another slap of water along with the wind brought sudden clarity. *Oh, God! He's trying to crash us against one of the boats!*

She made it to her knees before a crack sounded out, reverberating over the water. Sid's hands jerked back from the wheel as his body fell backward, landing with a thud, knocking her over. Fighting to push him off, red covered her hands. Her gaze dropped from her hands to him, his open eyes and mouth giving him a surprised expression, and the red blossoming from his shoulder had her scrambling away. A scream from her lips was carried off with the wind.

"Pippa! Pippa!"

Hearing her name, she jerked her head upward, continuing to bounce as the boat sped forward. She half-crouched and half-crawled toward the helm, reaching up to grab the wheel. Terrified, her heart raced at the speed of the boat and her lack of control over its direction. Looking at the panels in front of her, she might as well have been in a spaceship. Dials, knobs, levers, computer screens.

"Pippa! Pippa!"

Looking over, she spied the two larger boats veering to either side, her name coming from the loudspeaker of one. Unable to discern who was there, the sight of a group of large men flashed by her eyes. *Keepers! Josh!*

Her heart leaped into her throat at the idea that help was nearby, but with Josh unable to maneuver her speeding vessel, she had no idea what to do. A large lever was just to the side of the wheel, and a flash of memory hit her of seeing the senator's pilot change the speed of the yacht during the rainstorm with a throttle. She grasped it but had no idea if she should push it or pull it. *Forward—go. Backward—slow. Right?*

She looked up again to see that one of the large boats had circled around and was just behind her and to the side. Her boat hit another wave and bounced up, then landed hard. Crying out, she looked over her shoulder and spied Josh standing on the side of his boat, his knees bent as though he was ready to leap. *Oh, God... he's going to try to jump! No!*

Swiping the water from her eyes, she grabbed the lever and pulled it backward, feeling the boat immediately slow just a little but enough she knew she was doing something right. She tried to pull it back more, but her hand slipped off as another wave splashed over the bow, hitting her in the face.

Another bounce of the boat, and she landed on her knees, her fingers grasping toward the wheel. A noise to the side had her whip her head around just in time to see how close the other boat was. So close, she could see Josh's face as he leaped toward her. For a second, it seemed as though he was suspended in the air before he landed with a heavy thump behind her. Twisting more, she turned just in time to see him sliding on the floor-board, almost toppling over Sid, still moaning as he lay in the bottom of the boat. She cried out, unable to speak as he regained his balance. Stumbling forward, their bodies slammed together.

"Hang on," he said, banding one arm around her before leaning forward to grab the throttle with one hand. Somehow, he managed to do it all while holding her tight. He pulled back, and the boat slowed to a crawl. She looked over her shoulder as he switched off the engine, and the roar that had filled her ears suddenly ceased.

"Josh, thank God you're here!" she cried, her arms wrapped around him.

"Babe, you okay?"

She stared up at him, his assessing gaze roaming over her before stopping on her neck. His eyes darkened, his jaw tight.

"Fuck… you were drugged."

She scrunched her nose in pain as her fingers found the bruised welt on her neck. "He… he was at your house." She jerked her head to the side, staring at a now-unconscious Sid. Before she had a chance to react, Josh shifted her so that the only thing in her line of sight was him.

"Look at me, babe, only me," he ordered softly.

She nodded, blowing out a deep breath. "Yeah, okay." She held his gaze, asking, "How did you know where to find me?"

He lifted his forefinger and gently traced the chain around her neck, pressing softly against the lighthouse charm dangling at the end. "The tracer. So I'll always be able to find you."

Before she could speak, another thump landed on the boat, and they turned to see Cobb with a rope in his hand, pulling them alongside the larger vessel with Keepers all grinning down at her. Cobb bent over Sid, administering first aid until the Coast Guard boat arrived.

Cobb stepped closer, his assessing gaze also roaming over her. "You okay, Pippa?"

"Yeah, yeah, I'm good. Thank you."

He turned to Josh. "FBI is on their way. A Coast Guard vessel picked Thatcher up and will be here soon."

With the boat tethered to Keeper One, she clung to Josh's arms to steady her legs as they moved to the side where the Keepers tossed down a rope ladder. She clung to the rails as Josh stayed right behind her, almost cradling her with his body.

"Welcome aboard," Walker called out as he bent to take her arms.

By the time Josh had followed her onto the deck of Keeper One, another boat on the horizon appeared. He murmured, "Thatcher is here. FBI will take over the investigation. You'll have to be interviewed again, babe, but I want you checked out first."

"I'm fine, honestly."

"Not until we say you are," he said, bending to brush his lips against hers before leading her over to Bray. "Let him take a look at you."

She sat on one of the deck bench cushions as Bray medically assessed her. "I don't know what he gave me," she replied in answer to Bray's question. "He overpowered me, and then I felt a prick in my neck. Everything went into slow motion, and then I was unconscious. I have no idea how long I was out because when I came to, we were in the boat. But it couldn't have been that long because I think he was anxious to dump me overboard."

"You look good, but I want you checked out at the hospital for toxicology," Bray said, his gaze moving from her to Josh's.

As the weight of the events pressed on her chest, she dragged in a heavy breath, her fingers reaching out to grasp Josh's hand.

"It's all good, now, Pippa."

"Thanks to you all. If it wasn't for you—"

"Us? Damn, babe, you're the one who slowed down the boat so we could jump over. If you hadn't done that, you might have had to jump into the water, and that would have been way more dangerous."

She pressed her lips together, knowing he was trying to make her feel better. *But if they hadn't been in the water at the same time... If I didn't have the necklace on... If Sid had tossed me before I woke up... If he hadn't been shot...*

"Sweetheart, I can hear the wheels turning in your mind. Remember, no *what-ifs*. You're here in my arms, right where I want you to be."

She melted against him, his arms sure and secure as he banded about her. He lowered his head, and she lifted on her toes, their kiss saying everything.

That night, lying in bed, arms and legs tangled together, Josh held her tightly, almost afraid to let her go, needing to prove to himself that she was truly safe.

She'd talked to Agent Thatcher before returning to Josh's house, and Josh had been on the phone with Mace during the evening as the case heated up. It seemed Sid's capture had sent Mark into talkative mode, confessing to assisting Sid in disposing of Hank's body. He maintained he knew nothing about money laundering, saying that the Sidorovs were simply political donors that Sid wanted him to court.

The Feds would interview Demetri, but Josh knew the Russians would slip through their fingers considering they weren't present for Hank's murder, and if Thatcher couldn't get his hands on the crushed automobiles, there would be no evidence linking them to anything more than an outing with the senator. Just thinking of the case had his arms tighten.

"If you don't quit squishing me, I'll never get to sleep," Pippa laughed.

"Sorry," he mumbled, loosening his arms slightly, his lips against her forehead.

They were silent for a moment, her fingers tracing over his tattoos. "Have we really only known each other for six days?" she asked.

He leaned back slightly so he could see her peering up at him. "Yeah… just six days."

She fell quiet, and he gave that to her even though it made him nervous, knowing her mind was churning.

"Is it possible to fall in love that quickly?" she whispered with her cheek still on his chest.

He lifted her chin to stare into her beautiful blue eyes, seeing the same hopes and fears he knew were in his own. "I know the answer to that question for me. It's yes. Hell, yes. Abso-fuckin'-lutely, yes."

Laughter slipped out, and her face brightened with her smile. "You sound definite."

He brushed her hair from her face, loving the silky feel of the tresses between his fingers. "I am definite. I don't care how we met. Or the extreme circumstances that brought us together. Or the fact that you're living in my house and haven't mentioned once that you're planning to go back to your apartment."

"Well, I do have to get some clean underwear at some time," she joked, her eyes full of light.

"Underwear is overrated. Especially since I plan on us staying in this bed for at least two days."

"Just two days?"

He tightened his grip, grinning. "Well, two days in bed sounds like a good start. Then we'll make it in the shower… and downstairs… and in the bunker…"

She laughed again, keeping her head on his shoulder so her gaze held his. He loved the feel of her fingers trailing over his skin and pulled her closer.

"I'm not a man given to fast decisions, quick choices, or easy answers. But some things don't require a lot of time to know what is right. What feels right. What works." He dipped his head to touch his lips to hers. Pulling back, he said, "I'm in love with you, Pippa."

If he could have bottled her smile to bring out on any future cloudy days, he would have. It speared through his chest making his heart ache with joy, and he swallowed deeply, waiting for her response.

She didn't make him wait long. "Same here, Josh. I don't care that you first found me bedraggled and a mess. I don't care that you had to take care of me and I had nothing to offer you but a pretend name. I don't care that you were placed in the position of providing for my safety as we got to know each other. I don't care that it was only six days ago. I'm in love with you, too." Her sweet smile took on an impish grin. "But I'm still going to make you take me on a first date."

His thumb swept over her soft cheek. "I can't wait. We can do it tomorrow."

"I'll need to go by my apartment to get something appropriate to wear."

At that, he sucked in a quick breath, the idea of her leaving and moving back to her apartment disappointing even if he knew it probably made sense. "Sure," he managed to get out.

She bit her bottom lip, thoughts moving behind her eyes. "But I could always bring some more things here… if that works for you—"

"Yes," he agreed instantly. "If that's what you want."

She sucked in her lips. "Well, not permanently. Not now." She traced his lighthouse tattoo. "We may be in love, but I have several things in my life that I need to get straight. Pick up my diploma. Say goodbye to my professor mentor and Lisa. Check on my job applications. Date this amazing man I just met."

He barked out a laugh. "Well, I definitely want you to date the amazing man you just met as long as it's me."

Her mirth slowed as her hand cupped his jaw. "It's you, Josh. It's only you."

"Then the rest of everything will work out," he assured, leaning down, eager to taste her lips again.

28

TWO WEEKS LATER

The sun was setting behind the trees, sending sparkling diamonds of color over the water. It wasn't that the party-goers didn't appreciate the wonders of nature, but with the tables groaning with food, the drinks flowing, and the laughter ringing out, the sunset was taking a backseat to the fun.

Knox was leaving for the cruise assignment two days later, and several others had shorter assignments taking them out of town as well. The timing was perfect for a party.

Pippa moved amongst the Keepers and their women, playing hostess with ease. No matter where Josh was or who he was conversing with, he managed to keep an eye on her, still stunned that this woman was in his life. Each day, he discovered more about her that he loved. More that made him sure he'd found his soul mate.

She'd accepted her diploma earlier that day, and even though she'd shunned the graduation, he'd surprised her by making what she thought was just a party to say goodbye to Carson into a happy graduation celebration for her, as well.

The past two weeks had been a whirlwind, but considering the way they'd met, he wondered if everything for them would be a whirlwind. And he had no complaints.

When they'd made a trip back to her apartment, she exclaimed at how dark it seemed after being in his light-filled house. It hadn't taken much convincing to have her move in with him, both knowing and accepting that they were ready. His dining room now held her dining table, the large piece of furniture he'd seen in her apartment and now knew had belonged to her parents. His living room also provided a home for the two wingback chairs that she'd saved from the sale of her parents' house and held beloved memories of them reading in the evenings.

They'd gone to visit his parents last weekend. She'd been nervous, having never met the family of someone she was dating. He'd assured her that he'd never introduced a woman to his parents either. Then she'd worried they would think everything was too rushed, but he'd laughed. "Babe," he'd said. "My parents know I never make snap decisions. One day, one week, one year... they won't care how long we've known each other. They'll love you." And they did.

She'd said goodbye to Lisa at The Maine Event and to her professors. He wondered if she would miss her study group and friends as they all left for job offers all over the country, but she'd simply shrugged, saying that since most of them were about five years younger, she felt like her life was at a different place. Mace had talked to her about a position with LSI, but she deferred after talking to Josh. She wanted to work outside LSI for at least a year so that she and Josh could build their relationship without the pressures of working together. And she felt that she would be a more valuable employee for LSI if she came with more experience first. She and Mace agreed to revisit the arrangement when she felt ready.

And, as far as her social life, the LSI women had certainly slid right into her life, offering her friendship and a sisterhood that she seemed to crave.

Now, seeing her smiling face as she moved around the deck, it struck him that while she appeared happy, she was in full-service mode. Excusing himself from his conversation with Tate and Clay, he made his way over to her. Catching up with her as she refilled one of the platters, he captured her around the waist, bending to nuzzle the side of her neck. "Babe, you don't have to play hostess. We all just serve ourselves here. I want you to enjoy yourself."

Her hands held his shoulders, her smile beaming toward him. "Sorry, I guess it's a habit. But honestly, I love to make sure everyone has what they need. Especially now."

Tilting his head to the side, he questioned, "Now?"

"Yeah. This is so different. I'm not ignoring what's going on around me. I'm listening to conversations and joining them. I'm not just filling trays and glasses but happy to make sure our friends have what they need. I'm a participant, not just a server." She lifted on her toes and met his lips. "And I love that you did this for my graduation along with saying goodbye to Carson."

"You don't have to be grateful for this, you know," he assured.

"Oh, but you'll want me to be grateful."

"Yeah?"

"When I show you my gratitude in bed tonight."

His eyes widened and he was glad the lengthening shadows over their backyard would help conceal his erection. Kissing her again, he stepped back, working to gain control over his cock and now hoping the party would end soon so he could appreciate the gratitude.

As though she knew his thoughts, she laughed. "Don't worry, Josh. I plan on a lifetime of showing you my gratitude."

"Right back at you, babe," he vowed, kissing her again. "A lifetime of love."

The top of the Lighthouse

The party at Josh and Pippa's house was over and all the Keepers had gone to their homes. All except Mace and Carson, who had driven back to the LSI compound. The two iconic men had climbed the lighthouse steps, both with their whiskey tumblers in their hands. At the top, they walked past the prisms and out onto the railed deck overlooking the glorious expanse of the Atlantic Ocean at night.

They were silent for a few minutes, each lost to their own thoughts. Memories of his grandparents who lived nearby when Mace was a little boy moved through his mind, growing up thinking that the lighthouse and the keepers who kept the lights burning were heroes. Taking another sip, he turned toward Carson as the other man spoke.

"Owe you, man." Carson sighed as he nodded. "Said it then. I'll say it now. Owe you."

Mace knew what Carson was referring to. A time in the desert. An IED explosion. Twisted, hot metal. Several men dead and one trapped underneath with enemy fire approaching. Mace's team took out the threat while Mace lifted the weight of vehicle parts from Carson, allowing him to crawl out. Injured but not severely, they both managed to get back to Mace's men. But that's what they did, and no thanks were needed because the brotherhood was everything.

Mace growled. "That shit goes without saying. Don't insult me by saying it again."

Carson snorted, taking a sip of the amber liquid that offered an easy burn. Nodding, he said, "Maybe I mean about taking me on as a partner."

Clicking his glass against Carson's, Mace nodded. "That was an easy decision. We'll do well together."

"Do you ever think that there could be more like us out there? More who would join the LSI organization?"

Barking out a laugh, Mace twisted his head to look

at Carson. "You're just getting started and thinking of expanding?"

Carson grinned. "Nah. Just thinking that we can't be the only ones crazy enough to want to keep fighting battles for a common good."

"There are lots of others doing the same thing. But we can always keep an ear to the ground in case we hear of someone with our goals. For now, though, we focus on you and LSI West Coast. You've got good people. You've got the training and the skills. With our backing and contacts, you'll step into a world that will need you."

"What about Rick? He wants to come with me, but his brother is here. His new niece is here. I didn't come to take any of your Keepers."

Mace nodded. "I've talked to Rick, as well. We both have. He's every bit as good as Rank, and with family here, we'll see him a lot. But sometimes, siblings have to have some separation. They'll both be Keepers, but Rick needs to expand his boundaries outside the shadow of his older brother. I think he'll make a damn good LSI WC Keeper, and he's got my blessing to go."

Nodding, Carson said nothing as the two men finished their drinks while staring out over the moonlight reflecting off the churning water below.

"Well, I've got an early flight. Appreciate everything, Mace, especially your hospitality. Can't wait for your family and any of the Keepers who want to visit California to come see us."

The two men shook hands, holding tightly for a moment, their eyes never wavering, years of friendship and camaraderie passing between them. After descending the steps, they set the glasses in the sink on the way out to their vehicles. Just before Carson climbed into his rental, Mace called out, "Hey, Carson." Gaining the other man's attention, he grinned. "I'll make sure to come out for your wedding."

Carson shook his head, rolling his eyes. "Fraid you'll need an earlier reason to come to California. Me getting hitched just might be a long wait!"

Mace waved toward the retreating vehicle, watching the taillights disappear. He turned and looked up toward the lighthouse, a wry grin on his face. He'd thought the lighthouse only provided light to those in need, never realizing it seemed to provide a light toward love at the same time. Chuckling, he knew there was a time when that thought would have never crossed his mind.

Climbing into his SUV, he couldn't wait to get home to Sylvie and David, proving he was right about the lighthouse's power. *Oh, yeah... Carson will find out.*

Don't miss Carson's book!
Carson
And the next Lighthouse Security Investigations!
Knox

ALSO BY MARYANN JORDAN

Don't miss other Maryann Jordan books!

Lots more Baytown stories to enjoy and more to come!

Baytown Boys (small town, military romantic suspense)

Coming Home

Just One More Chance

Clues of the Heart

Finding Peace

Picking Up the Pieces

Sunset Flames

Waiting for Sunrise

Hear My Heart

Guarding Your Heart

Sweet Rose

Our Time

Count On Me

Shielding You

To Love Someone

Sea Glass Hearts

Protecting Her Heart

Baytown Heroes - A Baytown Boys subseries

A Hero's Chance

For all of Miss Ethel's boys:

Heroes at Heart (Military Romance)

Zander

Rafe

Cael

Jaxon

Jayden

Asher

Zeke

Cas

Lighthouse Security Investigations

Mace

Rank

Walker

Drew

Blake

Tate

Levi

Clay

Cobb

Bray

Josh

Knox

Lighthouse Security Investigations West Coast

Carson

Leo

Hope City (romantic suspense series co-developed
with Kris Michaels

Brock book 1

Sean book 2

Carter book 3

Brody book 4

Kyle book 5

Ryker book 6

Rory book 7

Killian book 8

Torin book 9

Blayze book 10

Griffin book 11

Saints Protection & Investigations

(an elite group, assigned to the cases no one else wants…or
can solve)

Serial Love

Healing Love

Revealing Love

Seeing Love

Honor Love

Sacrifice Love

Protecting Love

Remember Love

Discover Love

Surviving Love

Celebrating Love

Searching Love

Follow the exciting spin-off series:

Alvarez Security (military romantic suspense)

Gabe

Tony

Vinny

Jobe

SEALs

Thin Ice (Sleeper SEAL)

SEAL Together (Silver SEAL)

Undercover Groom (Hot SEAL)

Also for a Hope City Crossover Novel / Hot SEAL...

A Forever Dad

Long Road Home

Military Romantic Suspense

Home to Stay (a Lighthouse Security Investigation crossover novel)

Letters From Home (military romance)

Class of Love

Freedom of Love

Bond of Love

The Love's Series (detectives)

Love's Taming

Love's Tempting

Love's Trusting

The Fairfield Series (small town detectives)

Emma's Home

Laurie's Time

Carol's Image

Fireworks Over Fairfield

Please take the time to leave a review of this book. Feel free to contact me, especially if you enjoyed my book. I love to hear from readers!

Facebook

Email

Website

ABOUT THE AUTHOR

I am an avid reader of romance novels, often joking that I cut my teeth on the historical romances. I have been reading and reviewing for years. In 2013, I finally gave into the characters in my head, screaming for their story to be told. From these musings, my first novel, Emma's Home, The Fairfield Series was born.

I was a high school counselor having worked in education for thirty years. I live in Virginia, having also lived in four states and two foreign countries. I have been married to a wonderfully patient man for forty years. When writing, my dog or one of my four cats can generally be found in the same room if not on my lap.

Please take the time to leave a review of this book. Feel free to contact me, especially if you enjoyed my book. I love to hear from readers!

Facebook
Email
Website

f

Made in United States
North Haven, CT
17 February 2023

32747612R00183